The Ritual

"It is time, sister," Rifa said firmly. "You know how it must be done. Come Ki. It's time. Let the grieving be over!"

"No." Ki breathed the word. "I am not ready to bid them farewell!"

The Romni were sad that Ki insisted on clinging to her grief, linking her life to the death of her family and not going through with the ceremony. Ki would be like a ghost among them. They would have nothing to do with her.

Ki must choose between the living and the dead . . .

Other fantasy titles available from
Ace Science Fiction & Fantasy:

and much more!

HARPY'S
FLIGHT

MEGAN LINDHOLM

FANTASY
ACE BOOKS, NEW YORK

An Ace Book

Published by arrangement with the author

ISBN: 0-441-31746-4

First Ace Printing: February 1983
Published simultaneously in Canada

Manufactured in the United States of America

Ace Books, 200 Madison Avenue, New York, New York 10016

ONE

THE woman was an improbable speck on the vertical cliff face. Without skills or tools to aid her, she moved awkwardly up the exposed shale layering. Her close-fitting leather jerkin and coarsely woven trousers were impregnated with gray rock dust. Like an insect, she had taken on the color of the cliff she scaled. Sweat had plastered her brown hair to the top of her skull. Intricate knots and weavings confined the length of her hair, but the wind had picked loose a few strands of it, to spiderweb it across her eyes. She rubbed her narrow face against the gray rock. Her hands were occupied.

Some long-ago cataclysm had riven this mountain, sending its green face sliding down into a heap of stone and earth at its base. Far above the woman the mountain still wore a cap of earth and greenery. But the woman climbed over bare shale. This morning she had stood in the tangled brush and young trees that sprouted from that long-ago landslide. She had peered up the slick black rock to a certain ledge more than three-quarters of the way up the mountain. She had measured herself against the task of reaching that ledge and found that it was hopeless. Then she had begun her climb.

Now her left hand clung to a tiny ledge in the shale. She cautiously took some weight on it. The ledge cracked free, clean as if chiseled, and slid down the mountain face. Ki frantically scrabbled her hand into a second crack and clung, panting, to the cliff face. She knew she was close. The ledge, little more than a dent in the cliff's face, called to her like bloody water to a shark. She could glance narrowly over one shoulder to see the valley floor. She had left it in the predawn light. She had to be near her goal. She was pressed too tightly to the rock to turn her eyes up to see. The sun shone down on the top of her head. It had climbed the skies faster than Ki had scaled the cliff. Time was slipping away from her, crumbling under her like the rotten stone she climbed.

She had climbed recklessly at first, kicking free of ledges and scrabbling for handholds she might never find. Her hatred had burned hot in her. But as the rock face became steeper and more slippery, the holds more precarious, her anger had subsided to a dull, aching emptiness. Now she clung flat to the mountain, her face pressed against its sun-warmed stone. Only death was inside her now. She could remain still for a moment, but she could not rest. With her arms raised to cling, she dared not draw a full deep breath. Every clenched muscle in her body cried out to loosen. Ki ignored them.

She scraped her left foot up the smooth shale, her softly shod toes feeling for any indentation they might cling in. They found a tiny ledge. Ki placed her toes gently on it, cautiously added the weight of her leg. It held. She pressed more weight on it, sliding her body up. Her chest and belly scraped shale, the cramp in her fingers becoming well-nigh unendurable. Her whole weight hung now on her left fingers and the toes of her left leg. Her right hand was free to crawl up the smooth shale, seeking a place to cling.

Ki blinked her eyes, trying to clear them of rock dust, stinging sweat, and a strand of hair that clung to her eyelashes. Her forehead pressed hard against the rock. The muscles in her left hand were clamped so tight she could not feel her fingers. Then her creeping hand found a ledge. Her fingers rested on it, then her whole hand. It was a good, deep hold. Ki sucked in another hissing breath. Her right hand had reached high over her head for that hold.

She put more weight on her left foot and took some of the burden on her right hand. Now her left was free to scuttle up the rock face, seeking a grip.

Her left fingers fumbled their aching way onto a ledge level with the one her right hand had found. Ki pressed down on her straining left toes to drive her body higher.

Abruptly her ankle scraped fiercely against the rock as her foot found no support. The stone had crumbled away. Ki heard the tiny splinters and shards rattle down the cliff face. Her body was falling, to bounce its way down the rocks, blood splattering from her at each impact. A sob caught in her throat as she realized that she still clung to the cliff. Both hands gripped the ledge high over her head. Her right toes still clung in their crack. Her left foot sought blindly for support, found a tiny projection to rest on.

It took all her courage to turn her head a tiny bit to see past her shoulder. There was nothing to see. There were no notches she could shift a hand to, no safer position to crab her body over to. Smooth, gray-black shale. She was pressed flat against the cliff, hands high, body stretched. There was only up and down. She tilted her eyes to peer downward. Her guts tightened inside her. That left only up. She did not stop and debate her next action. She took the deepest breath her position would allow her, sagged slightly from her handholds, and bounced her body up as she kicked free from her toeholds.

Her left hand slapped rock. Her hands jerked as they took her full body weight. She had made a gain. Her left hand was flat on the ledge top. Her right hand, wrist, and forearm rested beside it. Stinging sweat rubbed into her scraped belly and chest. Her legs and feet dangled limply.

Ki pulled. Her spread hands found no place to grip on the flat shale ledge. They began to slip back toward her. The scanty layer of rock dust, twigs, and small shale chips they displaced showered into her face. Twigs clung to her hair, dust coated her eyes. Ki choked, fought the cough that rose in her. When the spasm passed, she drew several short breaths into her laboring lungs. Her muscles screamed as she dangled, her spine twisted in her uneven reach. She imagined tendons snapping free, bones popping from their sockets. Don't think of that. Force the aching, sweating body to stiffen and straighten. Down she pressed on her hands, refusing to let them slide any closer to the edge. Her weight hung in space, suspended by the puny leverage of her hands. It was impossible. Even if she had been rested and fresh, she could not have lifted her own weight this way. She forced her muscles to try.

Her face scraped the rock as she lifted her chin. Now her eyes pointed up instead of at smooth gray rock. She tightened her screaming belly muscles so that her bent legs and feet pressed lightly against the rock face. She clung like a spider. When her legs had the most purchase she could find, she took one short nervous breath. She frog-jerked her legs straight. The slight impetus pushed her up. She got both forearms flat on the ledge.

She heaved with her arms. A spasm of pain leaped up in her

left wrist and shot to her shoulder. That was the wrist that had suddenly taken her full body weight when her right handhold had crumbled away earlier. At this new abuse, it roared a protest into her spine. Ki fought to ignore it.

Her body rose. Her eyes came up above the level of her elbows. Through sweat-stung eyes she saw the ledge. Rain had washed dust and debris onto the ledge. The wind had littered it with tiny sticks and twigs torn from the brush higher on the mountain. It was strewn with shards of black shale worn away to black sand. At first, all Ki realized was that the ledge was large enough for her whole body to rest on. Then her eyes took in its full extent. Back in one corner was a sheltered area, heaped high with sticks and branches. Behind it a heavy woven hanging stirred slightly in the breeze. The lee of the mountain protected it from the ever-present wind. Old bones and gobbets of rotting meat littered the ledge near the hanging. Ki smelled the death stench of it.

Suddenly, strength was hers. Shoulders cracking, she heaved herself up, hooked her chin, then levered her body up, catching her weight on her rib cage. She panted, then scraped more of her body over the edge. For a ghastly moment her body caught and she could pull it no further. She knew what held her back. Sven's knife in its tooled-leather sheath was tied to her belt. The sheath had caught on the edge of the ledge. Ki strained, but the mass of her body weight was still dangling. Her flat-spread hands found no grips. Panic powered her. She jerked her body with a seallike flop, bruising her thighs as they landed on the cliff edge. She scooted forward, knees and feet coming at last to rest on the ledge. She was up.

Ki rolled onto her back and lay still. Her muscles quivered in relief. The blue sky loomed over her, the fierce white eye of the sun staring down at her. But the sun was alone in the sky. She still had time.

She rolled onto her belly, drew her protesting body into a crouch, and then stood. She glanced about herself, but quickly focused her eyes on the ground before her. To be this high sickened her stomach and whirled her head. Only an icy sense of triumph held her calm. She drew her forearm across her wet forehead, trading sweat for abrasive shale dust. Her heartbeat steadied.

The woven hanging made small popping sounds as it rippled in the wind. Ki stared at it, letting her anger rise inside her. She waited for it to possess her, to give her purpose and drive. "As I found mine, so you shall find yours," she promised. She strode toward the hanging. A hard stick rolled beneath her foot. Ki glanced down. A bone, brownish-gray, with tatters of sinew still attached to it. Ki set her teeth. She moved past the ceremonial nest by the entrance, a tradition with Harpy folk. That much of their custom was well known. But beyond the hanging, Ki would be venturing into territory no living Human had ever reemerged from. Her hand crept down to check the knife that swung at her waist. Sven's knife, not Ki's. His blood still stained the sheath. She snorted the carrion odor of the ledge from her nostrils. Stealthily she pushed the hanging aside. The interior of the aerie den was in semi-darkness. Ki felt her heart hammering in her throat, a pulse pounding in her ears. She stepped within, letting the hanging fall behind her.

The den had been hewn into the cliff. The marks of tools still scarred the stone. A dish lamp, its tiny flame aflicker with the wind of Ki's entrance, rested in a niche in the wall. Other niches and carved ledges held various possessions: a set of brass chiming gongs; a wooden carving of a diving Harpy, talons outstretched before her; a jumble of silver and ivory ornaments; stone working tools; and various other objects, too foreign to Ki's experience for her to identify. Ki drifted past them. In a near corner of the room a shallow indentation in the shale held a bed of straw covered over with thick weavings and luxurious furs. Empty. Ki turned her eyes from it. She did not seek plunder or a place to rest. She took the small lamp from its niche and nudged the wick longer out of the oil so that the flame burned higher and cast a better light. She moved forward across the uneven stone floor. It was meticulously clean; no bones or scraps of meat were scattered here. It was the lair of civilized, sentient creatures. Ki set her teeth and clutched her grim purpose as tightly as she clutched the haft of Sven's knife. She passed a loom with a half-worked tapestry upon it; when finished, it would show a scene of Harpies mating in flight. Beyond the loom was a screen, painted a deep blue with the summer stars white upon it. Beyond the screen was that which Ki sought.

The second indentation in the shale floor was larger than the first. The straw that filled it was yellow, smelling of freshly mown fields. The weavings that covered the straw were dyed in various shades of blue. A single fur of some great white beast was spread over the weavings. Ki lifted the corner, feeling the weight of the thick hide, the softness of the white fur. A thought crawled across her mind—what creature had once worn this skin? She dismissed it. She was here on her own quest. Her fist closed tightly on the corner of the fur. With a shoulder-wrenching jerk, she ripped the hide from the bed. She hissed in satisfaction.

Three eggs. Any one of them would have filled Ki's arms and been a burden to carry. The shells of the eggs were a dark mottled brown. Individual blue weavings nestled about each one, sheltering it from contact with the others. Their shells had become leathery with their nearness to hatching. They would probably part with a splatter at a blow from Ki's fist. But she slowly drew from its sheath Sven's knife. She came close to the eggs, put one knee upon their mattress of weavings and straw. It gave softly with her weight. One egg rolled a quarter turn toward her.

Something brushed Ki's head. She sprang back from the contact. She looked up, lifting the lamp for more light. Bobbing and floating from her movement, the brightly painted wooden shapes swung on fine strings from their wooden support. Tiny Harpies, painstakingly carved and painted, whirled in a miniature flock over Ki's head. They circled round and round, like birds coming down to feed. Their bright wings were spread, their dull, turtle-beak mouths were carved open as if they were shrieking and whistling for joy. Their eyes had been touched with gilt to give them the gold color characteristic of a Harpy's liquid eyes. Ki watched them bob and circle. They were a child's toy.

The impact of the thought set her shaking. A child's toy, like a string puppet or a little wooden horse with wheels upon its feet. A toy for a thinking, growing being. Ki looked at Sven's knife in her hand and at the eggs on their bedding. The egg nearest her gave a sudden pulse of life, then was still again. Like a baby's kick.

Her hatred deserted her in a dizzying rush. She tried vainly to recapture the logic of her vengeance, the anger that had sustained her. The knife fell to the floor. A sudden disgust at what she had planned to do rose in her, splattering from her gaping mouth upon the floor. The bitterness of the bile in her mouth was the bitterness of her hatred for the Harpies. She could empty her body of neither. Nor could she complete the vengeance she had come to wreak. Another gush of stinging liquid shot from her nose and mouth as the spirit of the vengeance inside her ripped at the spirit of justice that dwelt there too. Ki stood panting, her whole body quivering with the conflict inside her. Her mercy was despicable weakness; her vengeance a cowardly injustice. The eggs were before her, the knife upon the floor. It would be the work of an instant to part the shells like the rinds of sun-rotted fruit. The unborn Harpies would gush from their amnions. The translucent little wings would never stretch leathery-pinioned and wide. The silent, closed faces would never become aware, greedy, and mocking. The birdlike talons would never rend flesh, the tiny forearms would remain forever curled to the undeveloped chests.

She stooped for the knife. She would see those prebirth faces, the turtle beaks that held the lines of an idiot smile. She would look into the eyes covered with nictating membrane, evil eyes masked with cloudy innocence. Innocents. The uplifted blade fell slowly to Ki's side again. She shook her head, tears of rage stinging her eyes. This last month she had lived a dream of vengeance, tasted it in her food, pillowed her head on its comfort. It was here before her, the act that would culminate her grief and outrage. She could not do it.

A rectangle of light fell into the den, dimming Ki's lamp to nothing. Ki looked up dully at the silhouette in the door. It was the male. His turquoise plumage glinted in the sunlight behind him. His tall frame filled the entrance, dwarfing Ki to a half-grown child by comparison. His whirling golden eyes fixed on her as she stood before his brood, knife in hand. Ki's own green eyes lit with an unholy joy. Here, at last, was a fulfillment she could take. The knife turned to point at the Harpy. He was beast, man-killer, child-taker, an animal to be slain, not the sentient being this den would have her believe him to be. She did not move toward him, but stood still, waiting.

From the sky he could have hurtled down upon her, talons outstretched to rend, to slam her rabbit body against the earth and eat his fill of her flesh. But they were both on the ground now, within a den that roofed them over with tons of rock. He was not a creature designed to charge across land at an enemy—but he did. His long bird legs worked like plungers as he rushed at her, his whistle of outrage filling the cave. His forearms, no bigger than Ki's own arms, reached grasping toward her. But it was a beat of his great leathery wings that stung the knife from her hand and drove her to her knees. The lamp, with its burning wick and burden of oil, flew from her grasp.

The whip of plumage across her eyes blinded Ki. She scrabbled across the floor, seeking by touch for the weapon he had struck from her hand. The floor was hard and cold to her fingers, empty of the blade she sought. She heard his laughter burst out high above her—the evil laughter that had laced her nightmares for too long. She screamed herself, a sound that burst from her born of agony and hatred. The deeper, piercing scream of an enraged male Harpy echoed hers. Ki sobbed, and rose weaponless from the floor, determined to at least be standing when she met him.

She was knocked to the floor again by his headlong rush as he shot past her. She lit on her shoulder and hip with a painful slam. A jab of pain leapt up in her hip, sharper than the shock to her shoulder. Her hip had slammed against the haft of the knife. She rolled, her hand closing on it, and came to her feet to meet his next rush.

It did not come. As her stinging eyes focused, Ki saw a blaze of yellow flame that illumined the whole back of the cave. The falling lamp had scattered its oil across the straw and weavings of the eggs' nest. The lit wick had ignited it all. It roared with fire, the dry straw flaming readily. A flame licked out to catch the starry screen, to leap to the unfinished tapestry on its frame. In the midst of the burning nest the male Harpy stood like some nightmare demon rising out of hell. His tiny forearms clutched one of his eggs to his chest. The flames were roaring about him, making the leathery pinions of his wings curl and blacken with a terrible stench. He roared in hatred and agony, but the sound of his pain could not cover the dull poppings as the other two eggs burst at his feet. There was a shushing noise as the amnions temporarily quenched the flames about them; then a terrible smoke arose as the flames boiled away the liquid. Ki backed away from the scene, arms raised to blot the image from her eyes, the stench from her nose. She stumbled over the uneven floor, then was abruptly seized from behind, engulfed in plumage that became merely the door hanging as she fought her way clear of it. It fell about her as she stumbled, blinking, in the day-brightness on the ledge. She looked about her, uncomprehending. Never had she stopped to wonder how she would escape from that height when she had completed her vengeance. Now the fates had seized her revenge from her and left her with a problem: She had not died.

A screamed whistle betrayed the speck that plummeted from the sky. Ki ducked instinctively, crouching against the oncoming fury. The speck became a hawk, an eagle, and finally the unmistakable outline of a diving Harpy. Blue-green plumage and hide glinted against the paler blue sky. The cilia, like hair, blew long and turquoise behind her. She fell on Ki like an arrow from the sun.

The ledge offered Ki no shelter, no place of concealment, not even a niche to defend. She grasped her knife in both hands, raised it high and straight above her head. She did not doubt that the plunging talons would kill her with the first blow. Ki only hoped that she would feel the metal of her knife in the Harpy's meat before she died.

The Harpy veered. Her whistle of outrage changed to a heartrending scream, so human that Ki echoed it. The Harpy opened wide her blue wings, flapping them frantically to break the speed of her dive. Ki was forgotten. The Harpy's small bony forearms were outstretched instead to the gaunt figure that staggered from the den mouth on stalky legs. He spread wide his wings, showing the seared plumage that dropped from them to smoke on the bare ledge. His dull turtle beak was opened wide, gasping for clean air. His eyes were clouded over with a protective white membrane. As Ki gaped in horror, he dropped to his knees and rolled over, the leathery egg still clutched to his high bird chest. Even as Ki watched, his forearms jerked spasmodically and the egg fell, to split open on the ledge. The ruined infant rode the wave that should have been its birth. Before Ki's eyes the tiny body jerked, splashed in the egg liquids, and was still.

The female Harpy landed on the ledge, fanning Ki with the wake of her outstretched wings. Her golden eyes darted from the ruined egg to the still, smoking body of her mate. Dark, foul-smelling smoke poured from the gaping aerie den.

Her leathery wings were still half spread as she whirled on Ki. "Gone! All gone!" A world of loss was in the words she cried.

"As are mine!" Ki shrieked back. Her own grief and agony burst out afresh inside her, like an infected wound that covers itself over only to split and gush anew. The Harpy started for her; Ki rushed to meet her.

Ki was inside the range of the wide wings before she could be stunned by a blow from them. The top of Ki's head was not as high as the top of the Harpy's breastbone. Ki thanked whatever nameless fates had allowed her to meet the creature on the ledge instead of receiving the weight of that body in the ripping force of its talons.

The Harpy's bony forearms and clenching hands shot out to close in Ki's hair and jerk Ki close to her. The wide turtle beak gaped over her skull, the gust of her fetid breath enveloping Ki. Ki saw the single great taloned foot begin to rise, to claw her entrails from her. Ki did not resist the Harpy's jerk that snatched her toward the plumaged chest. Instead, she butted her head into it with a will of her own. Ki's left hand gripped the Harpy's right wrist desperately. She sprang to wrap her legs suddenly about the Harpy's high waist, curling her body up out of reach of the questing talons. Ki's right hand, with the bare knife in it, rose and fell. The Harpy staggered under the double impact of Ki's weight and the knife blow. The blade skittered across the Harpy's ribs, to finally sink into her tough abdomen. Ki clung to the knife haft, tucking her chin into her chest to avoid the Harpy's snapping beak. Ki dragged down on the knife blade with all the strength of her hatred. It bit slowly through the Harpy's thick skin and chewed down. The great wings beat angrily against her, but Ki remained curled on the Harpy's long belly, hugging her as tightly as a lover.

The wide wings beat wider. Ki was jerked up. She squeezed her legs tightly about the Harpy's body, refusing to be shaken off, to have her life dashed out on the rocks below—for now the ledge was gone. They were rising, then suddenly wheeling down. The hands locked in Ki's hair rattled her head. She lost her orientation; there was no up or down. The sky rushed past her, revealed and then hidden by the beating wings. Ki buried her face against the Harpy's body, trying to avoid the fingers that sought her eyes. Ki could not tell if they climbed or swooped. Ki dug her own nails into the leather and bone wrist of the Harpy. The Harpy drew her free hand clawing down Ki's face.

Ki loosened the grip of one leg, drove the knee in a short jolt to the Harpy's hard belly. The rhythm of the wings paused. Ki quickly locked her leg about the Harpy again. She pulled her knife clear of the creature, reached high, and sank the blade to its hilt in the Harpy's chest.

A too-Human scream. The control of the flight faltered. The great wings flapped and battered the sky erratically, not checking the speed of their sudden fall. Ki and the Harpy tumbled together, locked in disaster. Ki shrieked out her final triumph and terror. The Harpy was silent, perhaps dead already, her wings beating only in after-death spasms. Sky and cliff wheeled endlessly about them. One wing tip brushed the cliff face, swinging them about and checking, for an instant, their fall. Ki tasted the Harpy's warm blood as it spattered against her face. She clutched tightly to the tumbling body.

Suddenly, rough tree branches reached up and seized them, ripping them apart from one another.

Ki opened her eyes to evening. Idly she observed her feet and legs where they rested, higher than her head, in a tangled bush. Snapped branches above told the passage of her fall and let in the last of the day's light. Ki lay still, looking at the moon that was beginning its nightly stroll. The Romni said the moon saw everything there was to be seen, and remembered it all. She grinned up at it foolishly. It need watch her no more. She was finished. The moon had seen all that Ki would ever do. She could think of nothing left in her life that had to be done. She closed her eyes.

When she opened them again, the moon was higher, looking curiously down at her through the snapped branches. Her body wanted water. Ki herself felt immune to such needs, apart from them. But her body would not go away. She listened for a long time to the nagging of her dry mouth and throat. Finally she began to stir herself. She pulled her legs free of the bush so that they fell to the ground. Her left arm seemed to be gone. Ki looked for it, found it still attached to her body. She reached over and picked up its hand and set it gently down between her breasts. She cradled it there. Slowly she rolled to her right shoulder. She waited for a jab of pain from her disjointed arm, but it was silent and numb. The Harpy's dead eyes stared into Ki's.

She was not an armspan away. In death she was a broken thing, a kite of paper and sticks crushed in a gust of wind. Ki looked deep into the ruined golden eyes that had gone rotten brown in death. It was a cold look. She was glad that they had fought, glad that she had had the chance to rend that flesh and scatter its blood. She wondered if the Harpy could remember her death throes in hell. A grim smile set on Ki's face. She rolled up onto her knees, forced her shaken body to stand. For the moment, she had decided to live.

Ki read the stars that sprinkled the night sky. They had fallen far from where Ki had begun her climb, and farther still from where Ki had left her wagon and team concealed. She took her bearings, brushed hair and dried blood from her eyes, and limped off through the forest.

Gray daylight had begun to stain the sky and return color to the leaves when Ki heard the welcoming snorts of her team. They had scented her. She wanted to call out to them, but her throat was too dry. She limped toward the sounds.

The wagon stood in a small clearing. The unhobbled team raised their heads to gaze at her curiously. Sigurd snorted suspiciously at the smell of Harpy and moved beyond the range of Ki's touch. Docile Sigmund watched her limping approach calmly. Ki stumbled past him, watching him shy suddenly as he caught the smell of blood on her. She went to the water cask strapped to the side of her wagon. She let the spigot of the cask run wastefully as she wet her hands, her face, and head, then drank in greedy gasps. The coolness of the water awoke her shoulder, and it began to beat in throbs of hot red. Ki forced herself to reach up and turn the spigot off. She sat limply in the muddy place it had made beside the wagon.

Her shoulder had begun to swell; her jerkin was tight against it. She would have to find help while she was still capable. She climbed painfully up the tall yellow wheel of the wagon onto the plank seat. Behind the seat rose the small enclosed cuddy that made up the wagon's living quarters. She tugged loose a little wooden peg from its leather loop and slid the small door open. She clambered in, careful not to let her shoulder brush against the narrow door frame. She could not muster the energy to hop up onto the high sleeping platform. The folded blankets stacked on the straw stuffed mattress beckoned to her, but she could not rest yet. The walls of the cramped cuddy were dominated by cupboards and shelves, hooks and pegs. Ki tugged open a drawer and drew out the ragged remains of an old skirt. With her good hand and her teeth she ripped loose a piece and fastened a support for her arm. Then she snagged a sausage from a string that swung from a hook on the low ceiling. Her teeth sank into the tough, spicy meat. Her stomach awoke, growling, to remind her that a full day and night had passed since last she ate. Her jaws and bruised face ached as she chewed. She remembered again the Harpy's claws down the side of her face. Ki swallowed, and took another bite.

A small window in the cuddy let in the gray morning light, but Ki did not need the light to see. She knew the details of the wagon by heart. Sven's extra tunic still dangled from its peg. The painted wooden puppet, strings tangled by Lars's awkward young fingers, sprawled upon a shelf. A toy horse, only half-emerged from the coarse block of wood, rested on another shelf, Sven's carving tools beside it. He would never shape legs for it now. Unbidden, Ki's mind went to Sven by the fire, his large hands working delicately to bring the horse out of the wood. Little Rissa would be crouched beside him, her blond curly head pressing against his side, her small nose almost under the cautiously moving knife blade.

Ki climbed out of the cuddy, grunting as she lowered her body to the ground. She picked up the thick harness in one hand, jangling it lightly. The huge gray horses came obediently, puzzled at her croaking voice, and she moved them into their places with soft pushes and begging commands. She arranged each strap and buckle awkwardly with one hand and her teeth. No one worked the other side of the team; she had to move around it to tighten the straps herself.

She climbed to the seat and gathered up the reins. One foot kicked the brake free. No one scrambled up the wheel to hastily settle beside her. The morning air touched her coldly where a small body might have pressed against her. Ki gave a final weary glance at the sky. Clear and blue. She had freed the sky of wings. She shrugged and shook the reins. Muscles tensed, the grays leaned into the harness. Ki rode alone.

Two

THE wind carried to Ki's ears the sounds of laughter, a snatch of one of the old songs. She grinned in spite of herself. Her horses pricked up their ears, moved their ponderous hooves a little faster. Ahead, they knew, would be bright firelight, cool water, and fresh green grass. There would be other wagons, children with small lightly patting hands, and other horses freed of their harnesses for the night. Ki marked their sudden freshening and felt rebuked by it. She would not pull Sigurd and Sigmund into a ring of Romni wagons tonight. She did not know when, if ever again, she would rejoin their crowded campsites and noisy convivial evenings. Perhaps never. The ghosts that rode in her wagon seemed to crowd forward, to peer with her through the trees at the flickering camp fires that dotted the area.

Ki neared the turnoff where a narrow wagon trail left the main road to seek out a stump-dotted clearing. There Romni might camp unmolested for a night. The grays slowed, tried to turn. Ki tugged their heads back to her chosen path, tried not to hear the welcoming nickers of the camped horses calling to her team. She heard a rise in the tide of Romni voices by the fires. They would know she had passed. Some would be wondering who it was, and others would be telling in hushed voices. If she kept to her solitary ways, she might become a legend for them. Ki, the lone rider with her wagon full of ghosts. She smiled sourly. Ki, who had chosen to be alone over the customs of her adopted people.

The year had turned twice since Ki made her choice. Children were learning to speak that had been but belly bulges the night she had ridden swaying, into a bright circle of firelight and wagons . . . .

Big Oscar came at a run to catch her as she sagged off the

wagon seat. Rifa took Ki's light body from his arms and put her on soft skins by a small fire. With a jerk and a twist, Rifa brought Ki's arm back to painful life; she adjusted the crude sling and gave Ki a hot spicy tea to drink, with herbs of healing steeped into it. Limp on the skins by the fire, Ki watched the big burly Romni men unharness and lead off her team. Children ran to do what they knew was needed: to refill the drained water casks, to bring out onto the grassy sward Ki's own sleeping-skins and weavings. They let her sleep a full night. She spent the next day watching the large women in their bright flowing skirts and loose blouses, the dark, bird-eyed children in their bits and rags of clothing as they ran and shrieked at play. Among all the peoples of the world, here Ki felt most at home.

There were seven wagons at this encampment, a large group of Romni. The women were large, dark, heavy-breasted creatures. The beauty of their size and strength reminded Ki of their teams—tall, heavy horses with thick falling manes and bobbed tails. The men were thick, age making them burly as old tree stumps. The children played the ageless games of childhood, rolling and tumbling on the moss under the trees. People moved among the wagons, spreading bedding to air on the clean moss, putting flat slabs of dough to rise and bake on hot stones by the fire embers. A young couple entered the clearing from the trees, a brace of fat rabbits swinging from the woman's belt, the basket of wild plums they had gathered filling the man's arms. Oscar's hands were black with the gooey mix he was spreading on a beast's split hoof. Rifa was ever busy, oiling harness, nursing her latest baby, patching a worn coverlet, but somehow never far from Ki. She brought Ki tea and food before she could think to ask for it, smoothed a cool salve into the ragged gashes on Ki's face. No questions were asked of her. To the Romni, it was an old story. The man and the children missing, the woman battered and bruised. The Romni were not a people that shared and savored their hurts. They were a folk that lived their lives around the bad times, cauterizing their wounds with silence.

Night fell softly around them, the fires blossoming higher in the darkness. The dark of the trees became soft black walls enclosing an airy room roofed by the star-sprinkled sky. There was a coziness to children curling up on blankets by fires. A peace as palpable as the warm night air pressed down on the gathering. Slowly the adults began to gather at Oscar and Rifa's fire, drifting over to it after children were settled in sleepy rows on bedding by their own fires. The adults all brought firewood, piling it up on Rifa's fire until it became a blaze too hot to be enjoyed. Ki sat slightly apart from them all, one of her own sleeping furs slung across her shoulders. Her arm ached with a dull, unceasing pain. She could not blink an eye or move her mouth without the scabs on her face pulling at her skin. But the physical pains were only the shadow of the emptiness inside her and the knowledge that tonight her disjointed life would take another turn for the worse.

They spoke no word to her. She knew the custom they waited for her to follow. They expected her to go to her wagon, to bring out from it every thing that had belonged to Sven and the children. The possessions of the dead must not be kept by the mourner. They must be gifted out among friends so that the spirits of the dead could be free of them. Things too personal for Ki to give away she would place on the blaze for the fire to consume. And when the wagon was empty of all save Ki's own possessions, the women would help her unbind her hair from the knots and weavings that proclaimed her mourning. The time of grief would be over. Little mention of the dead would ever be made again, lest it trouble their spirits in the world they had passed on to.

Ki watched the tall flames of the fire reaching. The tips of the flames seemed to rip free of the fire, to blink into nothingness in the dark above the flames. Ki did not move. The Romni waited.

Rifa it was who took her courage in her hands and approached Ki. "It is time, sister," she said firmly. "You know how it must be done. When Aethan, your father, went on before you, you did not shrink from what you had to do. Come, Ki. It is time. Let the grieving be over."

"No." Ki breathed the word. Then she rose, to stand beside Rifa, facing the other Romni who stood waiting by the fire. She let the fur drop from her shoulders. The cool of the night prodded her injured shoulder, making it leap to fresh complaints. As she spoke, she felt the drag and pull of the dried cuts on her face.

"No." She said it clearly, loud enough to carry to all ears. "I am not yet ready to do this thing, my friends. My grieving is *not* yet over. I respect your ways. I have made them my own since I was a tiny child, playmate to many of you. But I must respect my heart's counsel as well. And I am not ready, yet, to bid them farewell. I am not ready."

The dark eyes stared at her, returning her look steadily. She knew there would be no rebuke, no anger, no raised voices. There was among them only regret for her. They would speak of it quietly among themselves, sad that she insisted on clinging to her grief, on linking her life to the deaths of her family. To Ki they would say nothing. They would speak no words to her, make no sign. She would be as a ghost among them, a person who had set herself apart. They could not have anything more to do with her, lest they and their families should also become contaminated with her longings for things dead. Ki knew the words they would say: "With one butt you cannot sit on two horses." She must choose between the living and the dead.

Ki watched them disperse from the fire, drifting away like swirls of smoke back to their own small campfires, their sleeping children, and their gaudy wagons. Theirs were the full wagons of the Romni, who live on the road by their wits and their love of the lands. Ki looked at her own wagon. Two thirds of it was empty and flat, left bare to carry cargo or items she would buy in one place to sell in another. She had never surrendered herself to trusting the road to support her. She had never fully given herself over to the Romni way.

"I am not a Romni." She said it aloud to herself, to hear the way the words sounded in her ears.

"Then what are you?" Ki's body jerked in surprise. She had not noticed that Rifa still stood in the shadows beside her, had not drifted off with the others. Ki's green eyes met Rifa's. The woman's broad face was in shadow, only her eyes speaking her feelings to Ki. Ki pondered the question. Her mind ranged over the lists of all the peoples she had ever seen, past all the settlements and towns she had ever trundled through on a wagon. No culture came to her mind, no set of customs to claim as her own. She thought of Sven's people, tall blond farming folk far to the north. She would have to seek them out soon with the news of his death. Were they her people now, whose customs she should share? Her heart shied away from the prospect. No, she had not taken on Sven's ways when they came to their agreement. Rather Sven had built a wagon, chosen a team, and taken on her own ways. He had lived like

Romni, and now he was dead, and his children with him. But Ki did not mourn him as a Romni woman would mourn her man. Because she was not Romni. The question came back to her. Then what was she?

"I am Ki," she said. The words came out clearly, with a certainty Ki had not known she possessed. Rifa received her words in the darkness. Her black eyes shone brighter for a moment, and then she cast them down.

"So you are. Return to us when you can, Ki. You will be missed among us."

Ki had left the campsite early the next day, before morning had even begun to gray the sky. No one had bid her farewell. No one had watched her leave or seemed to hear the creak and rattle of her wagon as it moved off. Now as she moved down this road in darkness, leaving another camp of the Romni farther and farther behind her, she wondered if there had been any there that knew her. With a wry smile, she revised the question. Were there any Romni anywhere that would know her anymore?

The night was too dark to travel further. The team was plodding on listlessly, their hearts not in their pulling. Ki chose a place where the road widened. Off to one side was a trampled area, muddy in the rainy season, no doubt, but dried now into hard ridges. Beyond, the ground fell away to a dried-up marsh of coarse, hummocky grass and Harp tree scrub. There was no fresh water for the team, but Ki had let them pause to drink from a stream earlier in the day and the dew these nights was heavy on the grass. They would manage.

She climbed down from the seat to free them of their harness. She ran a cursory rag over their hides, talking low to them as she did so, rubbing hard where the harness had rested on their sweating bodies. She did not hobble or picket them, but turned them free to get what grass they could. Their huge bodies demanded a tremendous amount of fodder. Ki worried almost constantly about it. She listened to them rip and chew the rough grasses as she searched around the base of the Harp trees for dead wood. The breeze strummed them lightly.

Ki made her small fire in the shelter of the wagon, away from the road. She drew water into a kettle from her water cask and put it on to boil. From the cuddy, she brought brewing herbs for tea, strips of dried meat and shriveled roots, chunks of hard hearth bread, and three withered apples. She poured off some of the hot water into a pot, adding the brewing herbs. To the rest of the water in the kettle she added the dried meat and roots, chopped into chunks. She hunkered down to wait for her tea to brew, her back against the knobby support of one wagon wheel, and bit into one of the withered apples. Each huge horse drifted over, shuffling and nudging, to claim an apple. "Spoiled ones," Ki chided them, watching the immense muzzles lip the apple from her hand. They chomped them wetly, then returned to their grass. Ki wiped her hands down her trousers and rose to get a mug from her dish chest.

The chest was strapped to the side of the wagon beside the water cask. Sven had decided to mount it there to save himself the trouble of ducking in and out of the cramped cuddy. He had hated to eat inside the closed cuddy, preferring the roadside as a setting for meals. Ki had not cared. She opened the carved lid of the chest. From it she took a single mug, one shallow wooden bowl, and a single wooden spoon. The lid fell over the rest of the dishes.

She drank her dark tea silently, considering her path tomorrow as the stew simmered the meat to tenderness. She did not like what she had gotten into this time. She did not like her cargo, her client, or the prospect of taking the wagon over an unfamiliar trail at a bad time of year. Here summer was failing, but Ki's trail would take her up the hills to where it was already fall and into the mountains where winter never totally surrendered to the other seasons. She frowned, wishing that she had not by chance encountered Rhesus, that he had offered her less money, wishing even that he had been unwilling to grant her as much time as she wanted. A week's travel to the south would bring her to gentler Carrier's Pass. Ki believed that, even with the greater distance involved, it would be the swifter way to go. But Rhesus insisted that such an obvious route would be watched. He wanted her to use the Pass of the Sisters. He had paid her well for his whim. So well that Ki had let her own common sense be bypassed. Tomorrow she would be among the foothills. By evening, she hoped to be on the doorstep of the pass. She sighed as she raised her eyes to the range that loomed ahead of them. It was a dark shadow that blocked out the stars.

She ate the stew rapidly before it could cool in her bowl.

Bowl and kettle she wiped clean with bread and devoured that
also. She finished her tea and dashed the dregs onto the fire.
With a neatness born of long habit, she stowed all her belong-
ings. She walked once around her wagon, checking wheels and
gear. The back of the wagon was filled with coarse sacks of
salt. A little of the pink stuff leaked from a battered top sack.
A brief check of the team and then she climbed up the wagon
and into her cuddy. The candle she carried drove the shadows
in the cuddy under the bed. She slid the small door closed behind her. The single window faced away from the road, fram-
ing a patch of night sky. Ki sat on the floor. Wearily, she
tugged off her scratched leather boots. She rubbed her hands
over her eyes, scratching the back of her neck under her
mourner's knots. She pushed her finger into an unobtrusive
crack in the cuddy wall and coaxed out a small peg. Its catch
released, a small concealed door swung open. Ki took out her
cargo.

The little leather sack weighed light on her hand. The contents rattled within as she hefted it lovingly. She tugged the
throat of the bag open, shook its contents out upon her palm.
Bits of fire—three blue, a red, and two large white ones rolled
into her hand. These were what Rhesus had paid so dearly
for. . . .

"Too many know of my purchases here!" Rhesus confided
to Ki. His eyes danced over the walls of his small inn room. His
shaking hand slopped her wineglass overfull. "I know I am
watched. I hear them outside my door at night. I push the table against the door, and still I do not sleep. They will cut my
throat! They will rob me! What will be thought of me if I return home with no goods to show from my travels and trad-
ings? I should never have bought those cursed jewels! But the
price was too good, the gems too fair to turn them down! Never have I possessed such perfect stones—and the prices I can
demand for them in Diblun!"

"Only if you get the stones there first," Ki observed. She
was not interested in his flutterings. She wished he would talk
business or let her go seek a commission elsewhere. But Rhesus had been so pathetically glad to see a familiar face in the
Vermintown street.

"I have devised a plan!" He smiled proudly and leaned
across the small table, lowering his voice to a whisper. "From
here to Diblun I shall send three swift couriers, youngsters on

fast horses, traveling light and armed. And you. But you shall not leave until they have been gone several days, and you will leave only after we have quarreled loudly at dinner below. . . . Ah, you see how my plan goes?"

Ki nodded slowly, her brows gathering over her wary green eyes. "And these young riders of yours? Have you warned them that they may pay with their lives for this little ruse of yours?"

"Why even divulge my ruse to them?" Rhesus shrugged eloquently. "They shall be given lesser goods to carry. And if a man is careful he can find riders to whom such danger would be a spice. I shall have no problems with that, and they will be paid for their hazard. But you, Ki, shall be the real courier that takes my prizes across the pass. Who would look for such a tiny cargo in such an immense vehicle—especially when you are loaded with sacks of salt to trade on the other side of the mountains?"

Ki sat looking into his small, closely set blue eyes. Round like a pig's, she thought to herself, and buried above an expanse of pale cheek. All the man's weight was in his tub of a body, supported by implausibly skinny legs. Yet he persisted in emulating the foppish and elaborate dress of the young men of this town. His short, scarlet cloak matched his tight leggings. His straining doublet was richly striped in gaudy colors. Ki turned her eyes down to the scarred table between them. Could she trust a man that dressed like that to have good judgment in his business affairs? A smile twisted her lips. Had she not been carrying freight for Rhesus for as many years as she had had a wagon, and Aethan before her? He was not her favorite client. He dealt too often in contraband and was grudging of paying what was due. He often cursed her when she insisted he fulfill his contract. But when he needed a trusted carrier again, he forgot their differences. It was a little late to fret about his good sense, or lack of it.

She took half of a generous payment, the rest to be paid on delivery of the goods. Had she been another teamster he might have worried about his jewels' safety. But he had dealt with Ki too long to doubt her honesty.

She remained in Vermintown for some few days, seeing Rhesus intermittently and restocking her wagon a little at a time. She and Rhesus appeared to be the best of friends, and the host and customers of the inn were shocked one evening when a quiet conversation between the two slowly began to rise in volume, and then became vitriolic. Ki climaxed the quarrel by calling him a pig in rooster feathers. Rhesus responded by slinging in her face the contents of his glass: the palate-stinging brandy of Vermintown. Then Ki left abruptly, upsetting the table and costly dinner over Rhesus as she did so.

Ki grinned hard as she returned the jewels to their hiding place. She was sure he would have words for her about that when she rejoined him in Diblun. She might call him whatever names she liked, but the wasting of good food was a sin he would not easily forgive.

She blew out her candle. In the dark she stripped off her dusty trousers and tunic and burrowed under the blankets on her sleeping platform. She spread her limbs wide on the empty bed, and tumbled into sleep.

THREE

THE Inn of the Sisters was on a small plateau at a place where the foothills began to seriously consider becoming mountains. Trees grew about it, but they had the stunted, wind-twisted look of trees that have survived constant hardships. The inn itself, of gray weathered wood, also gave the impression of tenacious survival. All its windows were tightly shuttered. Long and low, the building crouched beneath the lash of the ever shifting wind. The faded inn sign leaned as the wind pushed it on its chains. It was a picture of two Human women locked in a fierce embrace. Ki eyed it critically. The artist had demonstrated his lack of knowledge of Human body structure. Ki wondered what race owned the inn. The yard was no clue. Two open wagons and three riding beasts were pulled up to hitching rails. Ki glimpsed what might be a stable to the rear of the inn.

Ki let the grays come to a stop. The team was grateful. Since they began this morning, the wagon trail had become a combination of hard-packed earth and mountain gravel. The climb was not a steep one to this point, but the uphill grade was constant. Ki wrapped the reins loosely about the brake handle and hopped down from the wagon. She had heard nothing of this inn, either good or bad. She had spent her coppers already. Would she be wise to show a minted silver in such a place as this? As she considered, she ran her hands gently under the horses' collars and harness, lifting and resettling the leather. Sigmund rubbed his massive head against her. The wind tugged at her hood.

Ki turned to the creak and slam of the wooden door. The innmaster. He leaned toward Ki, seeming to take in her slender figure, booted and clad in brown leather shirt and leggings. She stared back at him, widening her green eyes. He quailed before her look, as Ki had expected him to. Few could abide the stare of shiny, wet Human eyes.

The Dene slid slowly down the porch ramp and across the inn yard to Ki's side.

"One Human alone?" he asked her, slurring his Common.

Ki nodded gravely, then remembered the gesture had no meaning for the Dene. "One alone, and a team of two horses." It was worth a try.

"We've quarters for Humans," acknowledged the Dene. "Provided they adhere to our customs and can pay the rates before they enter. Half-copper for the night for a Human. That includes a meal. One copper per night per horse as large as that."

The Dene had moved in close, as if admiring Sigmund. Ki's hopes fell. Its grayish top swayed as it tried to inspect the team without being rudely obvious. Its plump, limbless body pulsed. Ki knew the bare smooth hide was impervious to cold or heat. The eternal cool wind off the mountains would never trouble this innmaster. Knowing what would come next, Ki silently climbed back onto her wagon box.

"Your team is gelded!" the Dene announced. Despite the slurred Common, its tone of dismay and outrage was clear. A rippling pink flush, mark of deep emotion for a Dene, spread over its body.

"Gelding a team is the custom of my people," Ki replied. She gathered up the reins hastily.

"You will find no shelter here with us!" the Dene thundered at her self-righteously. "Denes do not associate with sentient beings that mutilate other beings for convenience!"

Ki nodded wearily, then translated the motion for the Dene. "I know. I know. You Denes might be a little more understanding if someone stabled a team of stallions with you for the winter. No, don't raise a fuss. I'm on my way already."

Ki shook the reins, and the team reluctantly leaned into the harness. The tall yellow wheels began to turn.

"The Pass of the Sisters is closed!" the Dene shouted triumphantly behind them. "You will have to go back down the hills. If you wish to cross the range this time of year you must go south, to Carrier's Pass."

"I've heard I can cross here if I am determined."

"If you are a fool! It has snowed much already. You must go back! You cannot go on. You will only have to come back this way, and we will not give you shelter!"

"I won't be back!" Ki promised over her shoulder. The creaking of the tall wheels over the rutted roadway drowned out what ever other warnings the Dene shouted after her. Ki drove on, trying to put the inn from her mind. At the sight of it she had felt a surge of hunger for a meal of fresh red meat. She had imagined a soft feather bed in a well-lit, warm, dry room. Well, she had heard of Dene inns, she comforted herself sourly, and of what they considered fit lodgings for Humans. Denes preferred a damp environment. Ki would have found no meat, no feather bed, no animal product there, but a damp bed of musty straw and a bowl of warm porridge. Such was the hospitality that a Dene provided for Humans.

Just as well, just as well. Nonetheless, the wind seemed more chill on her face and hands than it had before she had sighted the inn. Without checking the grays, she slid open the cuddy door and leaned back into the wagon. She snagged a small skin of sour wine off its hook. She wet her mouth with it and drank a mouthful. Habit made her sparing of all her stores when she had an unfamiliar trail before her. She had replenished her food in Vermintown before she left, but her caution was the habit of a lifetime.

The wagon seat rocked gently beneath her to the music of the eight steady hooves. She smiled down on the wide gray backs and sent a little shiver of encouragement down the traces. Sigmund tossed his head in acknowledgment and skeptical Sigurd snorted. They would carry her through. They had been through much together and had never failed one another.

It was late autumn in the country they now passed. The grasses were dry on the sides of the trail, and the spruce trees darkest green in preparation for winter. By the time she camped tonight she would be in a country that faced early winter. Sometimes, through gaps in the trees when the trail twisted, she could see the road further along where it snaked across the face of the mountain. The sun there shone on whites and grays and palest blues. Ki frowned at the unlikely circuit the trail followed. It was as if the makers of it had sought the longest path between the inn and the pass itself. The trail dipped into every shallow dale, went around every small rise of land between it and the pass.

She had driven away from the inn at midmorning. At noon she chewed dried strips of meat but did not stop for a meal.

Time enough for that when it became too dark for travel. A light breeze was blowing the chill of the mountain down to her. She shivered in anticipation of the deep cold to come.

Ki's wagon passed into the shelter of a rise of land, and the wind eased. The swaying of the wagon, the creaks like small creatures talking to one another, began to lull Ki's senses. On a familiar road she would have yielded to the temptation to drowse as her team picked its slow way over the trail. But she straightened her spine and pushed her hood back so that the cool air could touch her cheeks. A mountain trail like this could at any time turn into a runnel of washed-away gravel or a slush of standing water and mud. Then was no time to be awakened from a nap, as your wheels stuck with a jerk or your axle smacked against a standing rock.

And, she admitted to herself as she ran a hand across the back of her neck, the value of her cargo weighed on her mind. It was not the first time she had hauled such a shipment. The hidden cupboard had held jewels before, papers that recognized a bastard daughter as heir, and once a forbidden book sealed shut against curious eyes with green wax imprinted with a wizard's ring. Valuable cargo was nothing new. But the very elaborateness of Rhesus's precautions disturbed her. Suppose Rhesus was not the paranoid little man Ki had always supposed him to be? Suppose someone *was* watching him? Would not they have noticed the number of couriers that he sent out, and wondered? And there was the man's pompous ego to consider, and his fondness for brandy. It would be a great temptation to a man like Rhesus to boast of his own cleverness. Even if he resisted that temptation for days after Ki had left, what was the speed of a loaded wagon compared to a rider on a swift horse? Ki teased her wits with such questions as the day wore on. The very generosity of Rhesus's payment made her mission all the more suspect.

Night had not yet fallen when the grays waded across a shallow river that had spread across the road. It was not a bad crossing, for it was small, sound gravel under the wheels. But it offered Ki fresh water, the shelter of some small trees, and a level place for the wagon to rest. On the other side of the water, she had the grays pull the wagon off onto level ground beside a stand of spruce.

She cared for her team first, wiping their coats down and covering them with matching blankets. The blankets were a bit worn; she had received them at the same time she had been given Sigmund and Sigurd. For a moment she saw once more Sven's blue eyes dancing with joy at her surprise, felt the brushing touch of his wide, callused hands as he put into her fingers the stiff new leads that held the wide-eyed three-year-olds. She blocked the image from her mind. The blankets had been too big for them then. Now they were almost worn. She would replace them soon, she promised herself, knowing that she lied.

Ki shifted the leaky bag of salt at the back of the wagon. She lifted the bag below it, opened it, and shook from it a generous measure of grain. The team came to it eagerly, whiffling and snorting as they lipped it from the dry grass. Ki replaced the bogus salt sack, covering it again with the leaky one. That was one concession Rhesus had made to her: if she must haul a load of mock merchandise, at least let it be one that was useful to her. The team would not suffer in this crossing.

The horses moved off, cropping the dry grasses that sprouted sparse on the gentle slope. Ki settled into the rhythm of her solitary evenings, kindling a small fire in the wind-shelter of her wagon, putting on her blackened kettle to boil, parceling out food from her supplies. She brewed her tea, letting it steam itself to blackness before she drank. It coursed scalding down her throat until she could almost feel it splashing into the deep pit of her empty stomach. It made her conscious of the hollow hunger inside her. She set down the earthen mug, reached to stir the stewing soup with the meat knife.

Sigmund stamped and shied. Sigurd snorted and struck out with his front hooves. Ki leaped up as the horses jigged nervously away from the wagon. Her tea overturned as she spun about. She went down swiftly as the shadow from the dark struck her full-force.

The back of her head bounced off the hard earth, scattering sparks of light before her eyes. She fought back blindly, wildly, against the shape of a man she could hardly see. She kicked up from her position, keeping him from pinning her against the earth. She rolled up onto her knees, but even as she rose a rough shove on her shoulder flung her to the ground again. She tucked her shoulder as she hit, rolled nearly into her fire, and came up staggering on her feet. The man rushed at her. At the last possible moment Ki sidestepped the shape that hurtled

down on her, flinging out a clenched fist and stiff arm at throat
level. He gave a surprised croak of pain. His own momentum
betrayed him when Ki's flying body struck him from behind.
He rebounded from the tail of her wagon, sending them both
sprawling into the dirt. Ki rolled free of his clutching hands.
Heedless of burns, she seized her steaming kettle from the fire
and swung it in a splashing arc. The scalding liquid fell on his
chest, and the kettle itself connected with his jaw with a satisfying smack. The man went down, hissing in pain. Ki dropped
the kettle to snatch up the meat knife. One of her knees hit the
center of his chest as she leapt to straddle him, placing the bare
blade against the soft base of his throat. He gave one jerk,
then lay back quietly when the keen edge sliced shallowly into
his skin. He let his arms drop back to the dirt, hands open.

There was a moment when they held their positions, both
gasping in raw, cold air. The horses had halted their flight. The
light of the fire made shadows and planes of the unkempt face of
the man Ki held. With her boots on, they had been of a height,
but if the man had been fleshed out he would have had a full
stone's weight over her. He was not. He was thin as an or-
phaned calf. He had eyes dark as a beast's and dark, curling
hair in which leaves and bits of moss were tangled. It gave
him a wild and predatory look. His open mouth, gasping for
air, revealed even white teeth. He stared up at Ki, and his eyes
were those of a trapped animal, pools of anger and fear. For a
moment, as Ki straddled him, she almost wished he had been
able to overcome her—a quick and simple way to end it. The
stray thought shocked and disquieted her. She made more
sure her hold upon him, settling her weight heavily on his
chest. Her free hand patted about his waist. He flinched at the
touch, then went limp and still under her again. If he carried a
knife it was not there. He lay quietly beneath her weight, his
eyes alert but his body suddenly docile. His hands splayed upward on the ground, in token of surrender. She stared down
at him fiercely, green eyes narrow. He returned her searching
look. His bearded lips parted suddenly in a grin. He laughed
up at her.

"Well?" she demanded of him angrily.

"Well, yourself." He grinned feebly and visibly relaxed.
"You have yourself in a fine fix. If you were going to kill me
you would have done it by now. And if you aren't going to kill
me, just what are you going to do?" He chuckled, but it

changed abruptly into a racking cough. Ki felt a twinge of pity for him, but she did not let it show.

She leaned her face a little closer to his. "I would not be so sure, were I in your position, that it was too late for me to kill you. The knife and the throat are still convenient to one another."

He was silent beneath her again, striving to get his breath. When finally his lungs had stopped heaving he spoke calmly.

"I only wanted one of your horses. I meant no harm to your person. When you set your cup down I knew that you had seen me and that I would not get one without a fight. So I attacked, knowing that my chance lay in a quick victory over you. But things did not go as I planned."

He coughed again, and Ki became aware of the painful thinness of the man and the fever-brightness that lit the dark eyes. But she hardened herself, saying, "To take one horse from me in this place is to take my life. It's like saying you intended to cut off only one of my legs. What great need can you have that forces you to thievery?"

He seemed to consider his reply. "A man on foot cannot get through the pass. It is too far to walk in wind and snow; I have not the proper gear. I have tried it three times, and failed. But on horse, I could get through."

"So your first thought, naturally, was to steal a horse," Ki coldly concluded. "Sometimes one in need asks first, instead of taking action. If you had come peacefully into the circle of my fire and asked me for help in getting over the pass, do you think I would have refused you?"

"Twice I have tried that way. And twice folk with wagons have given me aid to the foot of the deep snows, only to turn back their wagons and return to the Inn of the Sisters. A wagon cannot get through. I have begged, each time, for the use of a horse, but it was always refused me. Theft is all that is left to me."

"You could return to the Inn, wait out the winter. Or go farther south to Carrier's Pass and cross there." Ki did not like the tone of this conversation. She felt ridiculous talking to someone while she perched on his chest. And his strange attitude was contagious. Ki, too, had begun to regard his attack as impersonal, a thing to be excused, like a stranger's jostle in a crowd.

"The Denes do not welcome me. They say I paid them in

bad coin. How was I to know? Think you that if I had any money left, good or bad, I would be living off small rabbits and wild greens? You must know how Denes are. Their love of dumb beasts is great; their tolerance for sentient creatures who do not conform to their way is small. My life would pay for my small debts. I can not go back."

"You still have not said why you must cross," Ki persisted stubbornly.

A shadow passed over his face. The trapped beast peered from his eyes. He glared as if her question were of the greatest impertinence. Ki stared back at him. She did, after all, have the upper hand. She wished to know all the facts before she decided what to do with him. His scowl deepened with her continued silence. Then slowly it faded from his face. He made a gesture that might have been a shrug. "What does it matter who knows, then? I need money. My family lives over the mountains. I have relatives that have helped me in these small matters before. And so, I go to them again."

Ki scowled. It seemed an implausible tale to her. To take such a risk just to . . . then the man beneath her coughed again, and she found that she had involuntarily moved the blade to keep from cutting him. She tightened her lips, frowning in disgust at herself. Slowly she rose. Even more slowly, she made a show of sheathing her knife. He watched her closely. He made no move to rise but remained as still as if her weight still pinned him.

Ki deliberately turned her back to him but kept her ears tuned to any sudden movement. She picked up the spilled kettle, frowned at the food that remained in it, and set it back on the fire. He still did not move as she drew water from her cask and added it to the kettle. She glanced over at him in annoyance. His ridiculous posture, flat on his back, hands spread upwards on the ground, disarmed her completely. She wanted nothing to do with this man. She would banish him from her campfire, eliminate him from her worries. She watched the slow rise and fall of the ragged tunic over his bony chest.

"You will ride with me," she instructed him at last. "Like yourself, I must get over the pass. As we both must cross, we may as well do so together. Now, get up and take some food. You are no more than a bundle of sticks."

"And broken sticks at that," he readily agreed. With a

grunt and a sigh, he drew his body together and rose to his feet. He ran his hands over his ribs. "Or at least cracked sticks. Your weight is no joke to a man who has been fasting as I have." He grinned at her and scratched his scraggly locks. He shook his head, then combed his fingers through his dark hair, removing the leaves and scraps of moss it had gathered during their struggle.

Ki frowned at him. She could not comprehend the jesting tone he took. It had been long since anyone had dared to joke with her. She could not be comfortable with his good humor. She had just thwarted his thieving attempts, beaten him down, and held a knife to his throat. And now he smiled at her, a crooked smile. What did she expect him to do? Anything but that.

She took more food from her supplies, never quite taking her eyes off him. She recreated the stew in the kettle. He watched her. She looked at him, and his grin grew wider.

"You have no intentions of trying to bind me? Have you no fear that I will somehow overpower you and make off with one of your horses?"

Ki shrugged, shaking a scanty measure of tea into the pot and returning it to the hot stones by the fire's edge. "The horses are already quite spooked tonight. As you see, I do not picket them. Should you wish to steal one, you must first catch him. Overpower me, kill me—that task is still before you. With my blood-smell on your hands it would be nigh to impossible to catch one of them. No, you have no interest in stealing now. Your only hope of getting over the pass lies in your doing as I say."

Ki glanced down at her mug of hot tea. She had just poured it. Regretfully, she handed it to him across the fire and rummaged in the dish chest for a second mug. He was silent as she filled it, silent as she sipped. He held his mug in both palms, letting the hot tea within it warm his thin hands. Ki sipped, watching the stranger over the rim of her mug. She smiled behind her tea. So, now she put him at a loss, feeling as if he did not know how to behave. Childish! She sneered at herself as a bubble of triumph rose in her.

The stew came to a bubble, and Ki filled two bowls with it. She passed him a bowl, letting him juggle the hot tea and hot stew as he tried to find a place to settle himself. She seated herself back against a wheel and began to eat. For a time, he re-

mained standing, holding mug and bowl as if they were strange
artifacts of an unknown use. His eyes on her, he sank finally to
the ground. When she looked up, he was setting down his mug
and taking up his spoon. He ate with an attitude of great thor-
oughness, as if he wished to be sure of every morsel. When he
had finished, he set the plate aside. He moved to her fire,
picked up the teapot slowly, looking at Ki uncertainly. She
pretended not to notice his stare. He refilled his mug.

They sipped tea, eyeing one another, not speaking. There
was nothing to say. But there was everything to say, Ki reflected, uneasy and tinged with anger within. Exasperation crept
over her. Damn him, this was her fire and her wagon. How
could he make her feel uneasy at it, as if she had no right here,
not even the right to question the ridiculous and offensive way
he had intruded himself into her life?

"I'm Ki." It came out almost as an accusation.

"I'm Vandien," he rejoined. He smiled and sipped his tea.
The shadows of the fire on his face showed Ki how he might
have looked were he washed and fed and dressed decently. It
was not a bad way for a man to look. Muscle clung compactly
to bone on his body. He was scarcely taller than Ki and only a
bit wider through the shoulders. A much-worn leather tunic
covered the chest and torso that narrowed down to his hips.
His leggings were leather also, worn thin and patched.

He had a straight nose that seemed to begin right between
his dark, well-formed eyebrows. His mouth looked small beneath the uneven growth of beard and moustache. No doubt
he usually shaved his face. His hands were neat and well-
formed around his mug. They were small and callused, as if
they had grown used to hard work only in adulthood. He
smiled as her eyes rose again to his, as if he could read her
thoughts.

"What takes you over the mountains, Ki? You have the advantage of me. I told you a bit more under the courtesy of the
knife than most strangers divulge to one another."

He drank tea, watching her coolly over the rim. Ki shrugged
casually.

"My business. I've a load of salt to deliver, promised some
time ago and soon to be late. And I've thought lately of shifting my trails. I know this side of the mountains too well. I've
heard there's better work for a teamster on the other side."

"Not much different from this side. You must be a most

dedicated trader of salt, to be so determined to cross this pass in winter." He was not calling her a liar. Not quite.

"So I must be," she conceded drily. "At least it keeps me from turning to thievery."

"Ah!" he cried and mockingly seized at his heart as if he had been pierced by a rapier. "I am rebuked!" He let his hands fall and laughed aloud. Ki unwillingly smiled in return. The man was insane. She sipped tea.

"Tomorrow we shall be in snow. The day demands an early start."

Vandien raised his mug in a strangely formal gesture. "Drink with me to an early start," he intoned in a mystic voice. Then he downed the cooling tea that remained in the mug.

Ki did not drink with him. She remained frozen, mug in hand. She felt as if he had moved a rock in her mind and the toad beneath it had winked one yellow eye. The warmth in her body drained down into the cold pit of her stomach. She watched him narrowly.

But when Vandien lowered his mug he did not stare at her knowingly as she had feared. Instead, he gathered a handful of dry grasses, polished clean his bowl, and shook the last few drops of tea from the mug. He held up the cleansed items for Ki to note, then set them again by the fire. He stretched. Then he dropped to all fours and crawled under the wagon.

Ki watched him, mystified. He curled up like a dog and closed his eyes.

Ki cleaned her own bowl and mug slowly and rose stiffly to put them away. She banked up the fire and moved about her wagon, putting it to rights for the night. The horses had drawn close again. She went to them, reassuring them with small tongue-clicks and gentle scratchings on their throats. Then she sought out her cuddy.

She did not kindle a light tonight. Enough starshine and firelight came through the small window. She hopped down into the cuddy and stepped to her bed. It was no more than a flat wooden platform elevated off the floor for the sake of storage beneath it. It was large enough to hold two bodies close and comfortable. It was not a sumptuous place to sleep. There was a mattress-bag stuffed full of clean straw to soften the boards beneath. For coverings, Ki had two worn woven blankets, one a dusky blue, the other a brown-gold. In a moment of abandon in Vermintown, she had spent part of Rhesus's advance on a bed covering of shagdeer hides stitched together. The shagdeer hides were an unwarranted luxury, lush and new in their softness. Ki could strip naked and slip beneath the old woven blankets, pull the shagdeer hide over them, and be as warm as if she slept by a fire on a summer night. After the continual chill of the day, it was a tempting prospect.

But beneath the wagon was a man in a tunic gone threadbare, who huddled and shivered like a beast. Ki sat slowly on the bed. The shagdeer hide was rich and warm. The worn blankets had little to recommend them. Their colors had faded, their nap grown worn and thin since the day she had first seen them spread smooth on a mattress of fresh hay inside a new wagon that smelled still of tree sap. When she and Sven had slept beneath these blankets, there had never been a need for a shagdeer covering. The soft touch of them as she raised them to her face was like the gentle movement of a large hand against her cheek.

Ki roughly folded the shagdeer hides. Then she crawled out of the cuddy onto the seat. She leaned over the edge of the seat and threw the bundled hides at Vandien's shivering form. She did not wait to see his startled look or hear any words of thanks. She went back to her cuddy, sliding the small door to and fastening its seldom-used hook.

She did not shed her dusty clothing, but crawled up on the platform and spread the worn blankets over her lap. Her hands rose in the darkness to loosen for the night her widow's knots. The touch of them on her fingers brought to mind the echo of Vandien's strange words. She sat still in the darkness, her hair loose upon her shoulders, remembering. . . .

Ki had been long on her road to Harper's Ford. She had sent word ahead of her coming and of the sad tidings she must bring them. She would be expected. Yet, as she caught her first glimpse of the long meadows and apple trees that fronted the familiar road, her heart quailed within her. Could she not go on past quietly, her team clopping softly in the night, raising small puffs of dust with every step of their feathered hooves? She had sent them word of their loss. There was really nothing further she could offer them. How could she comfort them, who could not comfort herself? She was tired of her own emotions. Since Sven had passed she had been strung like the strings of a Harp tree, and every breeze had seemed to play upon her. There was nothing left in her of anger or pride or gladness. Her quick laugh and sudden tongue had been stilled. Her wits had grown dull with no Sven to whet them. Every emotion in her was stilled, forgotten, like a city when the sea takes it back.

Or so she thought as she raised her eyes for one look at the twisted apple tree that had been a trysting place for them. Her eyes froze. A young man stood there, his hair pale in the evening light. A farmer's smock hung nearly to his knees. His light hair hung long and loose to his shoulders, as befitted a man unspoken for. Ki's tongue clove to the roof of her mouth as he lifted one arm in greeting. In a dream, she stopped the horses. Sven came across the meadow to her, silently, moving through the tall grasses in the graceful stride she knew so well. She dared not speak, lest she break the spell. She did not care how this could be. Just let him keep coming closer. As he drew near, the trueness of his features did not alter. He did not fade nor float as a ghost should; she heard the brush of the grasses against his striding legs.

"Ki!"

Her heart fell. That tenor voice was not Sven's but that of Lars. Lars, the youngest brother, as like to Sven as ever.

She sagged back against the cuddy door. Her shaking heart fell to her stomach. Neither spoke as Lars mounted the wheel and seated himself on the seat beside her.

"Shall I drive?" he offered softly.

Ki shook her head. She stirred the reins, and the team pulled. She could think of no words to say to him. Once more a desert possessed her heart. The pain would be new to Lars. Yet the months of bearing the pain alone had taught Ki no ways to quell it.

"Poor sister Ki. I had cold words ready for you for not letting us know sooner. I forget them now. If a time of healing has still left you looking thus . . ." Lars let the thought trail off. The wagon creaked beneath them. The horses' hooves went on clopping in the dust. Lars leaned back heavily against the cuddy door. Ki felt his body sway with the wagon. Irritably, he hunched forward to gather and lift his long hair from the back of his neck. He wiped the sweat away with his sleeve. Ki smiled at the gesture. He was the image of Sven before he was a man.

"I remember how he hated having his hair down on his neck. He used to tease and say that was the only reason he had come to an agreement with me: so that I would bind his hair back with a thong as befitted a taken man."

Lars nodded sourly. "It's a foolish custom, but one mother will not hear of parting with. I almost wish I were a boy again, with my hair cropped short. It's to my shoulders already, and keeps on growing."

"It will soon stop, by itself," Ki said comfortingly. "But if it is such an irritation to you, you could always find a woman to take you and bind it back."

Lars's shoulders thumped against the cuddy door as he threw himself back in disgust. "You, too, eh? I feel like a yearling at a stock fair. Rufus reminds me of my 'duty.' Mother must have Katya over to help wind the wool, to put shingles on the barn, to aid with the spring calving. Strange. Up to last year, I was help enough for her when such things needed doing. Now she must have the two of us—and no more, mind you."

Ki chuckled. She knew they were both keeping their minds from a darker subject. She knew it, and worked at it.

"So your mother plots against you, with the aid of older brother. What of this Katya? Can she be so distasteful that you must resist?"

"Katya." Lars rolled his eyes up. "Katya is plump and pretty, and as exciting as corn bread. Already she has the look of a farming woman. Hips that could birth a nation, shoulders that could take an ox's yoke, hands to steer a plow, breasts to nurse a brood."

"Sounds daunting," Ki murmured.

"Daunting. That's the word for her. We grew up as friends, you know, liking one another well enough. She has grown to be a solid, pleasant woman—a woman to go fishing with, or hoe with in the fields. But not a woman I would choose as a mate and partner. I have never desired her that way."

"Then keep your hair loose upon your shoulders, Lars. It becomes you so. Soon enough a woman will find you and come to bind it back for you."

"I hope she begins looking soon," Lars grumbled softly.

Evening was cooling the world. Night scents were beginning to rise. Through the trees on either side of the road Ki could make out the dim lights of small houses. Those were the homes of Sven's kinspeople, those related by blood or tied by their oaths to the family. These were the people who would demand of Ki their Rite of Loosening. Landholders all, they would come with their farmers' eyes and earth-worker hands to ask of Ki what had become of their Sven. A cold feeling twisted inside her. She did not want to lie.

Ki turned tired eyes to the night sky. She tortured herself. If she narrowed her eyes and did not look at Lars too directly, she could pretend. Many evenings Sven would tie his horse to the tail of the wagon, to trail along. He would clamber up on the box beside her. The children would be drowsing in the cuddy as they talked in low voices and watched for a good stopping place. Some evenings they didn't speak at all. The sound of slow hooves and the wagon's creaking was all the conversation they required. Those were long, companionable evenings, with Sven's shoulder gently bumping against Ki's as she drove.

"How did it happen?" Again, Lars broke Ki's spell.

She hesitated. She tried to find words for it. It must be a tale he would believe. It must be a tale they would all accept. A thousand times Ki had imagined herself at this moment, when one of Sven's people would ask that question. She did not want to lie. She did not think she could.

The words came to her brokenly, sounding strangely distant to her own ears. She might have been speaking of a famine in a far-off country, or blighted fields on the other side of the mountains. "They . . . Sven took the children. Young Lars was big enough to sit behind him and cling to his shirt. His little legs stuck out. He couldn't wrap them around that big horse. Little Rissa he put before him. She thought it great fun to be up so high on that big black horse. You never saw that beast of Sven's, Lars. A full stallion, and given to sudden, unpredictable tempers. I had advised him against such a horse, but you know how he was. He loved its spirit and the chance to measure his will and spirit against that of the horse. Usually it was not a fight between them; it was a trying, a challenge between two high-spirited animals. But sometimes . . . stubborn, stubborn man."

True, every word of it. As far as she had taken the tale. Ki let the silence lengthen. She had pointed Lars onto a false trail. She hoped his mind would take it up. Silently she begged Sven to forgive her for laying their deaths on his judgment in horses. When Lars did not speak, Ki knew he was trying to spare her. He thought he knew the way of it. Good. She broke the silence for him.

"I would warn you, Lars. I know nothing of this Rite of yours. I fear I shall bring shame on myself before the family."

Lars snorted. In happier times it would have been the beginning of his forgiving laugh. "You have always worried overmuch about offending us, Ki. We know you are not of us. Cora, my mother, will guide you through. And Rufus, too, will be at your side to help you if needed. Do not be offended. It is not often done this way, but it can be, especially in cases where the sole survivor of a family is a small child. The Rite Master has approved it."

"To your Rites I am myself a child. I take no offense."

"Did Sven never speak to you of our customs?" Lars ventured.

"Sometimes. But we spoke little of death customs. Sven involved himself with life. He did say . . . Lars, you may think me crude to ask this in such a way, at such a time. Your mother worships Harpies?"

Ki's words had sounded steady and calm. Only her heart shook in her body. She longed for Lars to deny it, to laugh at her for believing Sven's tall tales. Then she could relax, could share with them the truth of Sven's death.

Lars spread his large hands upon his knees. "It must sound strange to you. And Sven would make it more so, with his jibes and mocking ways. It is not worship we give them, Ki. We know they are not gods. They are mortal beings like ourselves but, unlike us, they have a closer link to, well, to the Ultimate. Fate works more directly upon them. They hold the keys to the doors between the worlds. They have a knowledge denied to us, and abilities . . ."

". . . abilities born of those other worlds. I know the phrases, Lars. Sven told me that your mother sacrificed a bullock to the Harpies on the eve of our formal agreement, and a yearling each time I gave birth. You are right—it seems outlandish to me. To me they are carrion-eaters, preying on herds and flocks, taking savagely, mocking, cruel. . ."

Ki ran out of words and sputtered into silence. Lars shook his head tolerantly. "Myths, Ki. The common myths about the Harpies that so many believe. I do not blame you. If I had seen only what the Harpies do and not been educated about their customs, I would believe it also. But a Harpy kills only in need. Only when it must feed. It is not like a Human, who may kill for sport or sheer idleness. Harpies have learned the balancing points between the worlds, between death and life itself. They could show us the paths of peace our own kind have forgotten."

"Religious bunk!" Ki did not realize she had voiced her bitterness aloud until she saw the rebuke in Lars's eyes.

"I am sorry," she said with true contrition. Lars had just lost his brother. He did not need to have his beliefs mocked. "I judge them, as you say, by what I have seen. I come from a different people, Lars, and I have been raised on the old tales around the Romni fire. When I was small, I believed that the moon was the mother of us all. She had birthed every race: Human, Harpies, Dene, Tcheria, Alouea, Windsingers, Calouin, and all the others. To each she gave a different gift, and she placed us all on this world. She gave us a law: Live in peace together. And she watches over us eternally from the skies to see how well we will obey. It is a simple tale, Lars, and perhaps I do not believe it now as I once did. But I do not believe that any one of the sentient races is superior to any other. I do not believe that Humans owe an atonement to any people, least of all to the Harpies." Ki slapped the reins angrily against the dappled backs before her. She had let her words carry her away. The horses stepped up the pace willingly. They had been this way before and knew this turning led to clean stables, to a feed of grain, and a thorough rubbing and cleaning of their hides. These were the pastures where they had been birthed and where they had galloped as ridiculous colts until the day Sven put their lead ropes into the unbelieving hands of young Ki. Of their own accord the team quickened its pace once again. Sigurd raised his huge head in a whinny of greeting. An answer rose from the stables.

A lantern appeared at the door of the long, low stone building. Ki heard the murmur of voices, saw Rufus direct his sons to open the stable doors and be ready to care for Ki's team. Lars sighed.

"They sent me ahead, you know. I was supposed to prepare you for this Rite, and I have not. But I doubt that anyone could. Let it be a healing to you, Ki, a sharing of your sorrow. Let the pain spread out to be carried by all of us, and you will find your own burden less. That is how it is intended. You say Sven spoke to you of some of our customs. Of them all, this is the one I think is the most powerful, in uniting a family and dividing its woes."

Ki nodded grimly. She dreaded it all. She had no idea what this Rite of Loosening would be. Among strangers, she would have to do her best to fulfill this Rite for them. Her final sacrifice to the memory of Sven. A last debt to pay before she went on her own way. She would think of Sven and do it well.

Rufus was bringing the lantern to the wagon seat. Ki climbed down quickly before he could offer help. Lars leapt down from the other side. Already the boys were loosening the harnesses from the horses to lead them away to cool water and clean straw. Sigurd and Sigmund went wearily.

"You've been a long time making your way to us, Ki," Rufus greeted her. Straight lips, cold eyes. He put his hand under her elbow, irritating Ki immensely. Was she blind, that she needed to be guided to the door? Lame, that she could not walk along? Sven, she rebuked herself sternly. She bowed her head.

"I needed a time alone, Rufus. I fear that you may not understand. But I meant no offense or neglect to you. It was too great a tragedy, too sudden a rip in my life."

"Leave the girl alone!" Cora barked from the doorway. "If she wants to explain, she'll do it once and for all to everyone when we are all gathered. She needn't undergo a private rebuke from every one in the household. I am sure she had her reasons, and we shall all hear them. But at the proper time, Rufus. Now let her go. Ki, you look like a beaten dog, and that's the truth. No slight meant to you, as you well know. Hard it is to lose one, let alone three. When Sven's father took the bloody cough and died . . . I won't talk of it now, but I know the pain behind such looks. You know the way, Ki. Same room as always. Lars, fetch her a light down the hall. The beasts have been seen to, have they? Of course they need grain, you young idiot! If I don't see to it all myself . . ."

Ki felt swept along by a river into a bright common room of the house, cut free from Rufus's grip by Cora's tongue, to be washed down a hallway to a bedroom by Lars. She had not greeted any of the people clustered in the common room to receive her. And Cora was chattering on like a magpie to cover her grief and shock. Speeding up life to get past the bad parts,

Sven had called it. Talking to everyone at once, seeing to every tiny detail as if they were all helpless babes. Ki wished that such a defense could work for her.

"I'll leave the candle here, Ki. Refresh yourself and rest a bit. It will be a long evening, and you have already been through much. Take your time. They have waited this long; it will do them no harm to wait a little more." Lars shut the heavy wooden door behind himself with a solid thunk.

Ki sank onto the bed. It was thick with Cora's best weavings and new sleeping furs. A white bowl rested on a stand by the draped window. Ki knew that the cool water in the graceful ewer beside it would be scented with fresh herbs. This was a room for ceremonious occasions. Cora had insisted that Ki and Sven spend their first night here after they made their agreement formal. They also slept here when they returned twice to present their children to the family. Sven told her that his father's body had been laid out upon this bed. The room had seemed a colder place to Ki after that. She could take no comfort in the thickly padded bed or scented water or rich shagdeer hide on the floor. So she would take a note from Cora and hurry herself through this bad part.

She washed her hands and face in the cool, scented water. She took down her hair and carefully redid the knots and weavings smoothly. She had no clean clothing to put on. She had left her things in the wagon. It would be too awkward to walk out past all those people to find clean things and return to change again. Ki was paralyzed by indecision. At any other time it would have been a minor dilemma. But now it brought a blackness crashing down on her, a depression no logic could lift. To go before them in this dusty skirt and blouse seemed an insult to their ceremony. To make a stir by going for clean garments seemed a vanity and an insult to Sven's memory. She sank onto the bed and put her forehead in her hands. It was all too much. They wanted too much of her. She had nothing left to draw out of herself and give to their rite. She was empty, and her being here was an empty act. She could not decide what to do. She was tired of it all. She pressed her hands to her temples. Weariness, hatred, and anger—would she ever feel any other emotions?

A tap at the door, and Cora was entering before Ki had even raised her head.

"You look a little better, dear. Now, I've taken liberties,

and I hope you won't mind them. As soon as word came. Well, you know me. I try to think of everything. It helps sometimes, to think of everything at once. There's a robe here, in this chest. I wove it for Lydia as a gift, you know, a surprise, but I had not reckoned on what birthing that second huge boy of hers would do to her belly. So, naturally I never gave it to her, nor even showed it to her, for I didn't want her to think I thought she had let herself go a bit. No one has seen it and I had set it aside for you even before . . . ah . . . word came. Weeks ago, in fact. It's clean and fresh and new. I know you Romni don't usually wear green, but tonight is a night for our own customs, and I didn't think you would mind. Something new and fresh, sometimes it gives you an extra bit of strength to go on, you understand. So I'll just lay it out here for you."

Cora paused expectantly as she smoothed the robe out across the foot of the bed. Their eyes met. Cora's eyes had always been dark and deeply shining. Ki had once hoped her children would inherit those compelling eyes. But now they were dull, as if her bright spirit had congealed there. Ki saw the mirror of her own anguish and despair. But there was no relief in finding that her suffering was shared. They were two fish, trapped in separate pools in a drying riverbed. Their tragedy separated them, and their courtesy was a sham between strangers.

"It's lovely, Cora. I've never felt much bound by the Romni traditions about green. Thank you. It *is* exactly what I needed right now." Ki hoped she sounded warm. All she felt was tired, and shamed by her dusty dress.

"I'll just go out, then, and let you make yourself ready. Not that you need to hurry. Lars told us all how tired you are. We'll wait for you." Cora hurried out, fleeing from herself.

Ki shut her eyes tightly, sat still for a moment. Then she rose. She stripped off her dusty clothes. She dampened a cloth in the scented water and smoothed it over her body. The robe slipped on coolly. Tiny yellow flowers had been worked at the throat and cuffs. It was a bit long for Ki, but surely no one would notice that tonight. She smoothed it over her hips and forced her spine to straighten.

The common room was a long, narrow room with a low ceiling. It had no windows, but was dominated by a huge fireplace that blazed at one end of the room. The floor was of flat mortared stone, the walls of thick gray river rock and clay. They kept out the heat and cold alike. A long table stretched down the room. Folk crowded benches on both sides of it. The table was laden with platters of meat freshly taken from the huge fireplace, with fruit piled high in bowls, with steaming pots of vegetables, and with pastries stuffed with berries. Conversation was muted among the people gathered there, humming like a hive of bees at nightfall: A gathering of the family.

Ki stood framed in the dark hallway, afraid to enter and afraid not to. How could she cross that open space alone, to where an empty chair at the head of the table awaited her? But Lars had been watching for her. He was suddenly at her side, escorting her across the room without touching her. She made her way up the table, past murmured greetings from relatives she had met only once or twice before. She could not even put names to all of them. Lydia, of course; and Kurt and Edward, sons of Rufus; Haftor; and beside him, looking so like him, must be the sister she had never met. The faces merged as Ki nodded acknowledgment of their greetings. Lars took his place, waving her on to hers. She passed three old women she did not know; Holland, wife to Rufus; an old man; and Rufus himself. At last the empty chair gaped at her. Ki seated herself and looked up. At the far end of the table, incredibly distant, sat Cora. How could Cora guide her from there? Everyone sat expectantly. Ki waited. There was food on the table before them, and drink. Was she supposed to make some signal for them to begin? Was the Rite of Loosening a family meal, a coming together to share food and sorrow? Ki's eyes sought Lars, but he was too far down the table to help her.

At her right elbow, Rufus suddenly whispered, "I bring you sad tidings."

Ki jerked her head to stare at him. What tidings could he possibly bring her worse than what she had for them? But Rufus was nodding and making small encouraging hand signs. Ki surmised his intent. She cleared her throat.

"I bring you sad tidings." She said it clearly. She paused, wondering how to word her phrases for such a mixed group. From the old man fumbling with his fingers at the edge of the table to the little girl scarcely able to see over the top of it— how make it comprehensible to all? But from Ki's gulf of silence their response thundered at her:

"What tidings do you bring us, sister?"

Ki took a deep breath. At her elbow, Rufus hissed, "There are three ye shall see no more. Drink with me to this sorrow."

Ki shot Lars a venomous glance. No doubt he was supposed to have versed her in her lines before she arrived here. Lars shook his head apologetically at her. Rufus tapped his fingertips impatiently on the tabletop beside her.

"There are three ye shall see no more," Ki intoned. "Drink with me to this sorrow."

"There are three we shall see no more. We drink with you," came the murmured reply.

Rufus's lips were folded flat and tight when Ki looked to him for instruction. Damn it, he could be as angry as he wanted. She was going through this for their sake, not for any satisfaction of her own. The least he could do was help her to do it as correctly as possible. She caught the tiny movement of his finger. For the first time, she noticed the strangeness of the table setting. Above her plate, in a precise row, stood seven tiny cups. They were handleless, with a shiny gray finish. She raised the first one and brought it to her lips. The entire table followed her motion. Peering over the rim, she saw that each consumed the entire contents of a cup in a quick swallow. Ki copied them. It was not the wine she had expected. The stuff in the cup was warm and viscous, with a faint taste, like the smell of clover. She set the empty cup before her.

"Sven, Lars, and Rissa: they are gone from us. Drink with me to this sorrow." Rufus muttered the words. He seemed resigned now to this role as prompter. So much the better. It would go swifter that way for them all.

"Sven, Lars and Rissa: they are gone from us. Drink with me to this sorrow." Ki spoke the words soberly. She would put on their tragic puppet show for them.

"Sven, Lars and Rissa: they are gone from us. We drink with you," they responded.

Again a cup was raised and emptied. Ki waited for her cue.

"You're on your own now," mumbled Rufus, staring at the tabletop. "Tell us how it happened, in your own way. Follow the pattern we've set. Save a cup to end on."

Ki glared at Lars, and he ducked his head. Could she tell the tale as she had told it to Lars and be convincing? Ki looked at the remaining cups to gauge how best to tell it.

"They rode together on a great black horse. Drink with me to this sorrow." Ki hoped to Keeva she was doing this right.

She would have Lars's head for this later.

"They rode together on a great black horse. We drink with you," repeated the chorus. The gathering at the table seemed satisfied with her beginning. Ki raised the third tiny cup and drained it. Suddenly; the room quavered, became a dream. She sat tall on her wagon seat. A slight wind stirred her hair. A smile was on her face. There was a presence on the seat beside her, warm and encouraging. Ki knew it but, oddly, she paid no mind to it. All was as it should be. 'Round the wagon galloped Sven and Lars and Rissa. "Snail Woman, Snail Woman!" Sven roared in a mock taunting. Rissa's tiny voice echoed him, full of laughter. "Sna-o Wo-man, Sna-o Wo-man!" Lars was too convulsed with laughter to speak, too occupied with hanging on to Sven's shirt tail. Rom's black coat shone in the sunlight. The light ran along his muscles, clenching and unclenching beneath his satiny coat. Lars's blue shirt was still too long for him; it flapped behind him, snapping in the wind they created.

For a moment, Sven pulled Rom up. "Shall we show her how a horse ought to move?" he asked rhetorically. The children shrieked their encouragement. Rom was off like the wind. The grays snorted in disgust.

"Their pale hair blew behind them," Ki was moved to say. "Drink with me to this sorrow." Someone mumbled a response to this. In another place, another Ki raised a tiny cup and tossed it off. It tasted like nothing now. She watched them go, Sven and Rissa laughing, Lars bouncing on the shining black haunches of the horse. Rom's hooves threw bits of road up behind him. The grays plodded on. The wagon swayed and squeaked.

"Over the hill the three rode," sighed Ki. "Drink with me to this sorrow." A far wind sighed in the trees. A dampness in Ki's throat. The presence watched with Ki as Rom disappeared over the long rise of hill. The blue sky rested on the hill top, empty. They were gone. "I came behind, too slow," grieved someone. "Drink with me to this sorrow." The wind stirred the tall grasses by the road and they rustled dismally. But the day was bright, and Ki on the wagon smiled and swallowed. There was a warm patch of air beside her, warning her that this was enough. Time to come back now. Time to stop. Ki ignored it. There was something she had to do. A task, a chore not to be neglected. Suddenly she was seized by a com-

pulsion to see the other side of the hill. She wanted to whip up
the team, shake them into a trot, a ponderous gallop, to crest
that rise. But she did not. On they plodded, the wagon
creaking cheerfully. Ki could not understand why she smiled,
why she did not stand and lash the team into action. Someone
was tugging at her, dragging at her arm. There was no one
there. The wagon creaked on, inexorably. Hurry, hurry, hurry. Clop, clop, clop, slowly on the rocky road. She crested the
rise.

Ki screamed, wordlessly, endlessly. She could not draw a
breath for words. The howl óf her grief rushed out of her. She
heard that howl bounce back to her, an echo careening back
from nowhere.

Suddenly another Ki was aware and fighting. This was hers,
hers alone to bear. They must not see, she must not see. She
must not think of what she saw. Harpies take the softest meat.
Cheeks of face and round child bellies, buttocks of man, soft
visceral tissue, haunch of horse. Don't see, don't hear, she
begged. Harpies, two blue-green, flashing. Laughing, screaming, tumbling in the air above Ki. Beauty keen as a knife, cold
as a river. Whistling their mockery at her loss. Ki could not
comprehend her own pain. Not again, not again, someone
screamed. The closer she moved to the bodies, the fiercer
came the pain, like a heat radiated by a fire. To scream was not
enough. She could not cry. She howled like a beast. She must
not let them see the Harpies, see how they circled above her,
screaming with laughter as she howled.

The presence engulfed Ki, pulled her down. She fought it.
It could not take her. She would not let it wander and look
where it wanted. But the presence was strong. It dragged her
back, taking her back to the world where Sven was already yellow bones. Ki struggled fiercely, and suddenly they both fell
into a deep. Down they went in a swirl of red and black. Then
the presence was gone and Ki was alone. She floated, she
swirled with the warm and sleepy waters. Her ears hummed
and buzzed. The waters were deep and Ki was deep within
them, moving through them, though she did not swim. She slid
through their warm, liquid touch without effort. Ki watched
with lazy eyes as a flaming Harpy swirled past her in the current. His smoking plumage trailed behind him. She saw the
unborn Harpy slide past her, twirling with the momentum of
his smashed egg. She watched a Harpy and a woman fall slow-

ly, beautifully, down the face of a rocky cliff. The Harpy body
hit the trees first, went spinning gracefully down, to land and
crumple gently, artistically. It was all most interesting and
amusing. And the waters were deep and very warm.

A table. A long table. Many faces. Someone was holding
her in her chair. What had happened to Cora? Why was Rufus
helping her away from the table? So pale she was, stumbling as
she walked. Who had felled that oak of a woman?

Ki felt her teeth chattering on the rim of an earthenware
mug. Milk. They poured milk into her, laced with some fiery
stuff. Haftor's homely face leered close to hers. She jerked her
head back. It slammed into someone's chest. Groggily, she
tilted her head back. Lars. She grimaced apologetically. His
stern face did not change.

Ki swept the common room with confused eyes. What was
everyone so excited about? They were all talking over a loud
hum, milling about, and eating vast quantities of food very
rapidly. "Eat, eat, eat." It was Lars, speaking behind her.
Why did he nag her so?

The clamor of voices began to be distinguished into separate
speakers, into words and sentences with meaning. Lars stood
behind her, his hands on her shoulders, keeping her from sagging from the chair. Haftor—shaggy-haired, ugly Haftor—was
holding a cup for her. She could not see what made the loud
humming.

"It will dissipate the effect. Please, Ki, eat. It will help
Cora break the link if you do. Please, Ki." Lars's voice came
clear suddenly through the babble about her. The cup came
back, and Ki drank deeply in long, shuddering gulps. When it
was empty, Haftor set it back on the table. The humming faded to a secret singing like a gnat in her ear. She looked into
Haftor's stormy face. His dark blue eyes were hard, cold.

Reality snapped back into focus for Ki. Abruptly she shook
herself free of the supporting hands. She would have sprung
up from her chair, but her legs would not obey her. Lars
stepped away from her.

"Haftor, get her to eat. Let me see what I can do to settle
things. Gods, Ki." Lars stood looking down at her, shaking
his head. He gave a small sigh, as if words were not sufficient.
Then he moved off, circling the table, touching a shoulder
here, patting a child reassuringly as he passed. Many of the
faces that turned to him were marked by recent tears. As Lars

moved about, the jabber of disturbed voices dropped to an ag-
itated mutter, scarcely louder than the hum in Ki's ears. But
the guests sitting closest to Ki were silent, their faces averted
from her. All were eating hastily, as if possessed of a great impartial hunger. No one was savoring the carefully prepared
dishes. They could have been eating cold congealed porridge,
with each one assigned to consume a certain amount. Haftor
had taken Rufus's chair, beside Ki, and was eating in the same
bizarre manner. He seemed to feel her eyes on him. He looked
up at her. Fascination warred with disgust. Watching her face,
he chewed rapidly and swallowed. His dark eyes were deep
glacial blue.

"What happened?" Even as she spoke, Ki was aware of
how inane she sounded. She felt as if she had been abruptly
awakened from a deep and dream-filled sleep, to be plunged
into the middle of this strange activity.

Haftor ran his tongue around inside his mouth and decided
to speak. "What happened, Ki, is that my aunt and cousins
were disturbed by how long it took for news of Sven's death to
reach them. In their haste, they called the Rite immediately.
They put someone in a position to do a lot of people a lot of
harm . . . and she did. Some are saying from malice toward
us. Some, like Lars, are pleading it was ignorance."

Haftor savagely forked up a piece of meat. Ki remained
staring at him, chilled by the wrath of his words, cut by the
coldness of his manner. He paused, the mouthful suspended
on his fork.

"Eat!" he commanded her, jabbing his own loaded fork in
the direction of her plate. Ki looked down. She found with surprise that someone had heaped high the plate before her.
"The more and the faster you eat, the better. It will melt
away the effects of the liquor, break all the links between us."
Haftor looked about the table, at the people gobbling large
mouthfuls of food. "This is parody," he growled. "Sven was a
man among us, a good man. To see people at his Rite eat this
way, to chase away the moment of sharing, rather than to
savor it." He shook his head, baffled, and turned his attention
back to his plate.

Ki ate methodically, moving food as if she were forking hay.
She tried to fit the pieces into her head so that they made a sen-
sible pattern. She knew better than to try to ask questions of
Haftor at this juncture.

This was to have been a sharing, this Rite of Loosening. A dim understanding came to her. She had gone back to Sven's death time, and they had come with her. This was their lessening of grief. She would have to answer no endless, awkward questions, speak no details best forgotten. They had seen it all, as she had, and shared it. And had she let them? She did not know. She had tried not to, that she remembered. She had tried to spare them the grim and grisly details, the scene that would reveal their Harpy godlings as carrion crows. And had she, or hadn't she? Did they hate her because she had revealed the Harpy's nature to them? Or were they angry because she had refused to share Sven's moment of death with them?

The dining dragged on interminably. There was no conversation near her, and the tone of that farther down the table made Ki glad she could not pick out the words. But Lars could hear them. She watched the apologetic way he moved his hands, the many times he bowed his head to a rebuke. Rufus reappeared. He was stonily silent as he heaped two plates high with food and stalked back to his mother's room with them. What could have happened to Cora to make her leave her table when guests were present? Too many questions.

Ki looked about the table. Slices of dripping fresh meat heaped on platters; colorful chopped and spiced fruits; bright vegetables in wide bowls. Sawdust and ashes in her mouth, gravel in her throat.

Guests began to stand, to step away from the table. People were leaving in groups of twos and threes. An exhausted Lars was accepting their farewells. His face was gray. No one bade goodbye to Ki. Lars would have been grateful for a similar silence. It was a disturbed, disgruntled group of people that were leaving. Heedless of manners, Ki rested her elbows on the table and cradled her face in her hands.

A touch on her shoulder. She looked up quickly. Haftor's dark eyes were haunted now, an uneven flush on his face. He looked almost drunk to Ki but did not smell of wine. He looked down into the face she turned up to his. When he spoke, it seemed he formed the words with difficulty.

"You did not merit the harshness of my words. I realize it now, and in a few days the others will as well. Few of them know you at all; that makes it harder. Ignorance, not malice. A will stronger than any of us, even Cora. It doesn't undo the damage to know that, but it makes the wound throb a little less

hot. If any are to be called to fault, it should be Rufus and
Cora. They should not have permitted you to lead us, even
with Cora as guide. They should not have been so anxious to
have the Rite so soon. They should have versed you better in
our customs. But I think you know how Cora is. To know
they had died months ago made her all the more anxious to
loose them properly as soon as she could. I'll try not to hold it
against you, Ki. But people here tonight were frightened badly
and feel cheated of their Rite. Some will wish you had never
returned to Harper's Ford."

Ki bowed her head. This was probably as close as she would
get to kind words from anyone tonight. Like a child, she
wanted to shriek out to the departing guests that it was not her
fault, that she didn't mean to do it. Haftor seemed to read her
thoughts, for he patted her shoulder awkwardly before he
moved away from her.

Ki remained motionless, caring little what anyone thought
of her behavior now. The mutter of voices was less. She heard
the door close firmly. Silence fell. Ki sat listening to it and
waiting for the humming in her ears to cease as well. A log fell
suddenly in the fireplace. Footsteps, and the chink of gathered
crockery. Lars was stacking the plates on the table. Ki rose
disspiritedly to help him.

She picked up two plates, eyed the food remaining on them,
and set them down uncertainly. She pushed her seven small
cups into a cluster and gathered the ones from the next place
setting. She paused, and set them down. She did not know
how to do this, and she could not make her mind go logically.
If only the humming would stop. She felt overwhelmed by
even this simple task. She did not know how to clean up after a
meal of twenty-some people. She longed to be crouched by
her night fire, wiping out her single cup, polishing clean her
wooden bowl with a bit of hard bread. She wanted to be alone
again with her grief.

Her head began to throb with a dull pounding. Her eyes
were sandy and dry, her mouth thick. Weariness fell on her
like a dark, heavy blanket. She raised her cold hands to her hot
face. Footsteps came behind her.

"If you don't mind, Lars, I shall go to my wagon and
sleep. Leave the mess. I'll help you clear it in the morning."

"I think we must have words first, you and I, about what
you did here tonight."

Ki jerked about to face Rufus. His voice had been cold, his face was stern. But even he recoiled from the emptiness in Ki's eyes. He composed himself quickly. "It's a little late for remorse, Ki. You did your damage very completely."

Ki stood looking into his short, wide face. He had his mother's dark hair. Only his eyes had a look like Sven's, but Sven's had never been so cold. Ki did not try to speak. To this man she could never explain anything.

"Let her go, Rufus. Can't you see she's completely exhausted? Your words had better wait for tomorrow when your head is cooler and Mother is better. This night has rattled our family to the core. Let's not complete it with a rift." As Rufus glared at his youngest brother's impertinence, Lars turned to Ki.

"Go to bed. Not in your wagon, like a stranger, but under our roof, as is right. There is a lot of healing for all of us to do. Let us begin it tonight."

Ki went as if reprieved, forgetting even to take a candle. In the darkness of the room, she let her body drop onto the bed. She willed herself to the blackness of sleep. But when it came, it plunged her back into the deep, warm waters. The same images drifted past her slowly, and the humming became the far-off whistle of an endlessly hunting Harpy.

Ki's fingers tucked up the last strands of hair into the mourner's knots she still wore. She wondered if Vandien was already asleep beneath the wagon, rolled up in her shagdeer cover. The echo of his words still disturbed her. She shook her head slowly, feeling her knotted hair brush against the back of her neck. She thought she had put those memories aside, buried them deep. Sven's family and its customs were no longer any concern of hers. The damage she had done them had been inadvertent. She had never meant them harm, but had only wanted to shelter them from the grisliness of the truth. She pushed her guilt back down in her mind, refusing to dwell on it. It was done. She rode alone. Through the swirled glass of her tiny window she picked up the tiny, bright points of a few stars. She must sleep now if she were to make her early start.

She curled up under the worn blankets, nestling her body into the straw mattress. She forced her mind back beyond the painful memories. She took out her memories of Sven and fondled them. Almost she could touch again that long, pale body of his, the almost hairless chest drawn smooth against hers. His beard, when he had begun to have one, had been reddish, a little darker than the blond hair of his head. It had been softly rough against her face. He had been a head taller than she when first they made their agreement formal, and after he had grown even taller and filled out with manhood. His hands had been large upon her, but ever gentle. Ki closed her eyes tightly cradling herself in her memories. She slept.

FOUR

MORNING poked gray fingers in the cuddy window, to stir Ki within the homey shelter of Sven's blankets. Without, the sounds of early morning and the tiniest vapors of chill slipping in through the crack under the window. Within, semi-darkness and body warmth and immense comfort. Ki could hear his footsteps moving about, stirring up the embers of last night's fire. Now he would be putting the kettle on. There was the chink of mugs, then the creak and list of the wagon as a man's weight was put upon it. He would be moving silently so that the children would not wake. He fumbled at the door. It slid, then caught harshly on the hook Ki had latched the night before.

Ki was jerked out of fantasy to wakefulness. She rolled off the edge of the bed and landed on her feet. She saw his fingers in the crack of the door, tugging, trying to open it quietly.

"I'm awake." She spoke flatly, without fear, warning him.

There was a motionless silence outside the door. Then she heard him jump lightly down from the wagon. Ki hastily refolded her blankets and pulled her boots on. She closed the door, unhooked it, and slid it open. As she climbed out onto the seat, she nearly upset a steaming mug of tea that rested there. The chill of morning hit Ki in the face. Vandien was unsuccessfully trying to coax Sigurd to the harness. The gray bared his big teeth snidely and put back his ears.

"What do you want, man?" Ki demanded of him as she climbed down off the wagon.

The tone of Ki's voice froze Vandien. When he turned slowly to face her, his eyes were hooded, his mouth humorless.

"An early start, as promised. I've been over this pass before in kinder weather. I tell you that in this weather we shall need every scrap of daylight we can muster for traveling if we are to reach a safe stopping place tonight. The Sisters do not let any pass easily. The longer we take, the longer we shall be in their shadows. Now I shall ask you a question. Why do you snarl at me in such a suspicious voice?"

Ki's head was cocked, her smile thin. "Suspicious? Of someone who wanted to steal only one of my horses? I dislike being awakened by someone trying to enter my wagon."

"I was bringing you a mug of hot tea. That was all."

Vandien's voice had become soft and very low. His arms hung loose at his sides. Everything about his posture spoke of offended innocence. Ki would not be taken in so easily.

"What would stir your heart to such consideration for me?" she asked acidly.

Ki spun to keep her eyes on Vandien as he strode rapidly past her. He stooped suddenly and threw her the carefully folded shagdeer cover. It thudded solidly against Ki's chest as she caught it. He had not tossed it gently.

"I can't imagine what would provoke me into relapsing into civilized behavior."

He moved to the fire, began to kick it apart with more energy than the task called for. Ki looked about. He had stored most of her gear already, incorrectly. The shagdeer cover was still clasped to her chest. Slowly she took it to the wagon and put it inside on the sleeping platform. As she came out of the cuddy again she looked down at the mug of tea on the seat. She sat down on the seat, and sipped at the tea thoughtfully. It was already lukewarm in the chilly air. She looked down into the mug as she spoke.

"You didn't want anything to eat?"

Vandien stopped trampling the ashes. "I hadn't thought about it," he admitted, a bit stiffly. "I've become accustomed to eating rather infrequently lately." He glanced up at the sky. "Sun's already climbing."

"We'll eat as we travel, then," Ki replied briskly. She hopped down from the seat, stowed her mug. She chirruped to the team. Sigmund and Sigurd raised their heads. Sigurd snorted in disgust, but they both came ponderously to take their places. Ki moved between them surely, fastening straps become stiff with cold, warming the icy bits in her palms before slipping them into place. Vandien stood apart, watching. His one move to help had been met with a warning stamp from Sigurd.

Ki clambéred onto the wagon and picked up the reins. There was a moment of awkwardness; Vandien stood on the frozen ground beside the wagon, looking up. Ki looked down into his dog-brown eyes. His curly hair hung low over his forehead and stirred slightly in the chill wind. By daylight, he was a lithe, narrow man, hardly larger than Ki herself. He did not fit her experience. In time, she might grow to like his mocking ways and unpretentious stance. But she did not want to take the time. She would take him over the pass, as she had promised last night. But no more than that. She was sick to death of having others involved in her day-to-day living. Never again would she let anyone depend on her for anything. If his knowledge of the pass could help her through it, she would consider it an even bargain.

Slowly Ki moved over on the wide plank seat. She motioned him to get up. He was scarcely settled before she released the brake and shook the reins. The wooden wheels jerked out of their frosty emplacements. The creak and sway of the wagon began.

Ki slid the door of the cuddy open behind them. "There's food in the cupboard under the window. Apples, cheese, and I think a slab of salt fish."

He moved to fetch it, touching nothing in the cuddy other than the cupboard she had indicated. He emerged from the cuddy and set the food on the seat between them. Ki waited, guiding the team, and then glanced over at him impatiently.

"I haven't a knife," he reminded her.

The wheels creaked, the wagon swayed. Ki kept her eyes on the trail ahead as she drew the short knife from her belt and passed it to him. A moment later she felt a nudge and took from him a slab of cheese on a slice of dried fish. They ate slowly. The withered apples could not completely clear the salt of the fish from their mouths. Ki reached back, snagged the wine skin, drank, and passed it to Vandien. He accepted it, drank briefly as she had, and passed it back. Ki rehooked it and shut the cuddy door. Vandien leaned back on it, stretching his booted legs before him.

"I had almost forgotten how pleasant it could be to ride instead of walk. I shall hate to see the deep snow. You will know then, as I do, that it makes the way impassable for a wagon. You will decide to turn back then."

"I am going through," Ki asserted quietly. "And the wagon goes under me." Vandien gave a snort of what might have been amusement. Ki did not deign to reply.

The wagon-trail ground upward, twisting and dodging among stands of spruce and snaggles of alder that grew in the shelter of rocky outcroppings. Where the bare outcroppings of rock thrust tall, the trail detoured around them. Often it seemed to pass on the far side of hummocks of land instead of winding closer to the pass. Ki wondered who had made such a roundabout trail to go through the mountains. The grade was easier on the pulling team, true, but sometimes the detours of the path made little sense to her. Ki had used passes that followed the bed of a river, or sought the lowest place in a range of mountains to cross. This trail seemed to do nothing but sneak and slink across the face of the mountains. Sometimes the path seemed to run out entirely, and the team pulled the wagon over flat, lichened rocks and mossy places. Ki saw little sign of game, other than an occasional school of lichen mantas. They were only distinguishable from the gray-green lichen they consumed by their comic flutters as they moved hastily from the wagon path. In places, they coated the earth, hiding the trail.

Once, Ki thought she had lost the trail entirely. But just then Vandien raised a gaunt hand, jabbing a finger between a stand of trees and an outcropping of gray rock.

"There are the Sisters! First glimpse you get of them."

Ki followed the direction of his point. She had expected the Sisters to be the two tallest mountains in the range, or at least the two they would pass between. They were not. White snow shone on the mountain's face. Their trail ran clearly across it and around. They would have a drop-off on one side of the wagon and a sheer wall of rock on the other. The mountain rose straight up from the trail's edge, smooth and white. Where the mountain rose straightest and the drop-off on the other side was most extreme, the Sisters stood. Ki now understood the sign back at the inn.

The Sisters were a strange outcropping of black stone, jutting in relief from the smooth plane of the otherwise gray rock of the mountain. They shone smooth and dark, free of any traces of snow. They looked like the stylized, symmetrical silhouette of two long-haired Humans. The faces were patrician, royal in outline, the noses and lips of the two faces lightly touching: Sisters, greeting one another.

"Did you see them!" Vandien exclaimed as another stand of trees veiled them from Ki's eyes.

Ki nodded, strangely moved at the sight. Vandien seemed to understand the rise of emotions in her . "Devotion. To me, they always seem to sing of selfless love. This is the only place on the trail that gives you a full view of them. Up close, they lose the resemblance and turn into plain outcroppings of black rock. But from here it's a sight to make a minstrel weep. The first time I saw them I longed to be an artist, to capture them in some way. Then I realized they were already captured, for all time, in the best possible form. No mere Human could improve on that!"

His dark eyes snapped and glowed with intense pleasure. He flung himself back against the cuddy door. Ki could find no further words to add to his. But she had caught his spirit of admiration for the Sisters. He seemed pleased that she shared it.

By midmorning they were into shallow snow. It went from a wet layer that the horses' hooves churned up into mud to a deeper layer that made the wagon wheels stick and slide. The team heaved at the traces, sweat showing on their gray, dappled coats as steam rose from them. Their progress slowed. There was no broken trail ahead of them. Snow blanketed it smoothly. No encouraging footprints or wagon tracks led the way. When Ki stopped the team briefly at noon, Vandien shrugged knowingly and looked at her from the corner of his eyes. She ignored him. Climbing from the wagon, she waded forward through the calf-deep snow to the team. She dried their coats with firm strokes of a piece of sheepskin. Patient Sigmund nuzzled her thankfully, but Sigurd only rolled his eyes dolorously.

"Time to turn back?" Vandien asked lightly as she climbed back onto the seat.

"No. As we go higher, the snow should be drier. The wheels will stop their cursed slipping. The horses will not be working as hard. Though," she added, suddenly frank, "I will admit we are not making as good time as I had hoped for. I may not have figured correctly the amount of time we will need. The trail snakes about."

"Powder snow will not be as wet, but it will be deeper," Vandien commented sourly. "And, past the tree line, you will find the snow deeper than you might expect. Soil and brush give way to rock and lichen there. Nothing grows to break the drifts. But let us go on. We may as well ride in comfort as far as we can before we abandon the wagon."

Ki glared at him. Then she unfastened the cuddy door and slid it open. When she came out she passed Vandien several sticks of smoked meat. She settled beside him once more and took up the reins. With a shake, she started the team. The twisted tough sticks of meat filled their mouths and kept Vandien from any more speech.

The broken trail fell away behind them as they wound their way up the mountain. The tall trees they had traveled between in the morning grew shorter as the day progressed. The air became colder, making the skin of Ki's face feel stiff and strange to her. She gave the team their heads, shaking her own head at Vandien when he wanted to take the reins for her. She moved back into the cuddy. She returned shortly wearing a heavy wool cloak and fur-skinned gloves. She pulled the thick hood up about her face as she sat down. From under one arm she produced a thick shawl of undyed gray sheep's wool. Vandien wrapped it about himself gratefully, but without comment. His own garments were worn to thinness from his sojourn in the hills. Though he had not complained, Ki had noticed his shivering. She wondered what small demon in herself made her want him to admit to feeling cold. Grudgingly, she admired the way he handled himself. He made no demands, nor offered humble thanks. For Ki, it made her giving easier. Bad enough that he had dog eyes without him dog-fawning on her.

Only stunted and twisted spruce was left of the forest now. Scrubby brush poked up hopelessly from the snow and helped to show Ki, by its absence, where the trail was supposed to run. Above them the mountains glared down whitely upon the gaily painted wagon and straining gray horses. Ki looked in vain for another glimpse of the Sisters. The twisting trail had put another hummock of earth between the wagon and its goal. Ki's eyes watered from the brightness. When she bowed her head to rest her eyes, the cold froze the tears and stiffened her lashes. She wiped a gloved hand across them and shook the reins lightly.

Once, against the clear blue sky, she caught sight of the falling speck that was a distant hawk. She raised a furred glove to point at it. "I didn't think they would hunt this high," she commented.

"He seems to be an outcast," Vandien shrugged. "He's been seen before, by other folk crossing this way. They say he hunts the pass and higher hills. The moon alone knows what he finds to hunt. Poor bastard. I doubt if he's ever warm."

The horses toiled on steadily. The snow was growing deeper about the wheels, but still the wheels turned and the grays pulled. Except for an occasional sigh of wind, the creak of the wagon and the blowing of the horses were the only sound and movement on the trail. Ki saw no sign of game. She pitied the lone hawk. She moved her toes inside her driving boots. A tingle of warmth came back to them. Her lips were dry, but she knew that if she licked them they would crack and bleed. Vandien gestured at the trail ahead of them. "We'll have a pretty time getting your precious wagon over that!"

"That" was a ribbon of silver cutting across their path. The blue-shaded white of the snow was cut by its shining. It wove down from a rocky cleft to cut across their path and then twisted off until it was lost over a rise. Ki stood up on the seat, straining her eyes to see what it was. It was like a winding silver pathway that intersected their trail. She sat down again, brow wrinkled and mouth tight in puzzlement.

"Snow-serpent track," Vandien answered her unspoken question. "Surely you've seen one before."

"I've heard of them," Ki conceded. "But mostly around Romni fires at night, when one could discount one half of all one hears. I put them down as a fable, or a great rarity. What will it be like when we come up on it?"

"Like a wall of ice cutting our path. They may be a rarity elsewhere, but they are common enough in the Sisters' pass. That one was made by a small serpent, by the look of it. The big ones seldom come down this low. Sometimes they travel across the top of the snow, writhing along like a snake. Sometimes they travel beneath it, squirming along like a worm. The friction of their long bodies melts the snow, making a trough if they travel on top, or a ridge if they travel below. The snow receives the dampness of their passage and, as often as not, turns to ice. A big serpent can leave one as thick across as this wagon is long. But this one does not look that large. We'll see."

The creaking of the wagon filled in where their voices left off. Sigurd snorted once, and Sigmund echoed him. They had caught the scent of the serpent's passage. Stale as it was, it still disturbed them. They shook their heads and thick necks, making their long manes fly. Ki slapped the reins firmly on the wide, gray backs.

When they reached the serpent track, they found it only a stride wide. The team halted at Ki's command. Their nostrils blowing wide, the great heads tossed uneasily. Ki and Vandien both leaped lightly from the wagon and moved forward to investigate. Ki moved through the snow gingerly, with a catlike distaste for its cold and wetness. But Vandien went as one to whom its cold kiss was familiar and, if not relished, at least not to be disdained.

It was, as Vandien had described it, a low trough of solid ice that cut across the smooth snow before them. It could not be circumvented. To try to drive the wagon over it would be like taking the team and wagon over a log of equal size. Ki kicked at the low wall of ice, and a chunk flew off.

"Not as bad as it might be," commented Vandien. "We'll get through this one. The wagon will take us further than I had thought."

"It will take us down the other side of these mountains," Ki asserted quietly. She trudged back to the wagon. Vandien remained by the ice trough, blowing on his hands and trying in vain to keep the shawl from slipping down from the back of his neck. Ki returned with the firewood axe. She broke chunks of the serpent track away. Vandien tossed them to one side. Slivers and small hunks of ice flew whenever the axe bit, to sometimes sting the face or strike glancingly off their bodies. Vandien's ears peeked red from his dark hair. His hands, red at first, soon grew nearly white with cold. Ki found herself sweating inside her cloak, but knew the perils of loosening it to cool herself. They both worked rapidly, without pause, but Ki still cursed to herself at the time lost. The sun was beginning to slide from the winter skies. Already the tallest peaks of the range were casting their shadows down upon the incongruously gay wagon in the snow. The chill of night would drop soon. Vandien grinned to hear Ki curse. He made no comments himself.

When the way was finally clear, Ki found herself trembling from the exertion. The cold had sapped her energy more than she had realized. It seemed a heavy task to take a moment to stroke the frost from the muzzles of the horses, a burden to return the axe to its proper place. She scaled the wagon, sat down heavily on the seat. Vandien was already there waiting on her. They dusted the snow from their leggings before it could melt and chill them more. Ki took up the reins. A creak and a jolt, and the wagon lumbered through the gap they had cleared.

The grays' heads were drooping as they threw their weight steadily against the traces. The wagon moved more slowly than before. The wind here had been free to sculpt the snow into uneven drifts. The team faced them doggedly, already spent with the day's labors. The sweat dried on Ki's body. She began to shiver in spite of her woolen cloak. She chewed at her lower lip, then hastily wiped the moisture away on her glove. She looked across at Vandien. He had tucked his numbed hands between his thighs in an effort to warm them. His tired eyes were fixed bleakly on the trail before them. As far as Ki could tell, it led on endlessly into deeper snow.

"Where, damn it!" Ki surrendered suddenly. "Where is the shelter you hoped we would reach by nightfall? You said you knew a stopping place when you urged me to an early start this morning. At least give me a goal to make for. I need a marking point to measure our progress against."

Vandien's face was too cold to permit him a smile. It showed in his dark eyes instead. He lifted a pale hand made bloodless by the cold.

"Do you see that line, a sort of dark place like a crack in that ridge? There is a narrow, steep-sided little canyon there, as if long ago some god had riven the mountain at that spot. The canyon itself will be shallower in snow, and within is a place, not quite a cave, but a dent in the wall. Between that dent and the wagon, folk and horses could shelter for a night and not come out of it too badly. It has been used before. There is even a supply of wood there for one who knows where to look for it."

Ki folded her lips in vexation. In the morning turmoil she had forgotten to take firewood. No doubt, to Vandien it looked as if he rode with an utter fool. No firewood, unfamiliar with her trail, and not even aware of the beasts she might encounter. She was abashed, but to speak in her own defense would only make her appear a greater fool. She silently followed his pointing finger.

All day they had been wending their way across the mountain's tumbled and ridged skirts. Ki made out the dark area he pointed to. It was yet far away, and off the main trail, but they would make it. She looked up at the mountain peaks that rose before them in time to see the sun slip behind them. Ki had not reckoned that, within the reach of the range's outstretched arms, her daylight hours would be shortened. The silver of the mountains went to blackness, and the shadows reached out for the wagon with greedy hands. The colors went out of the landscape; they moved in a world of grays.

Ki cursed, then acted. She wrapped the reins loosely around the brake handle so that they would not be pulled off to drag. Then she leaped off the side of the wagon into the unbroken snow and ran up ahead of the straining beasts. At their present pace, it was only too easy. She fell in ahead of Sigmund and began to trudge along, breaking him a trail through the snow. It would be small help, she knew, but in the thickening darkness every minute would be a help. Besides, the motion warmed her and drove off the shivering she had been prey to since they chopped through the snow-serpent's path. She started when Vandien moved suddenly up beside her, breaking a way for Sigurd. Behind them, the horses' heads came up a notch, encouraged both by the company and the broken trail.

"Do your people never speak before they act?" asked Vandien sourly. "Sometimes a man feels a fool in your company."

Ki raised her eyebrows. "Do your people never act before they speak?" she asked acidly.

"But, of course. When we go to steal horses."

Ki glared across at him in the dimness. His face was solemn, but his eyes were laughing at her. Bested, Ki grinned back. It cracked her cold lower lip. She dabbed blood with the back of her glove.

A low hissing noise rose behind them, building to a crescendo and then slowly dying away. Ki pulled her hood closer about her face.

"The wind rises. We may be caught in it before we reach shelter."

"No wind that," Vandien replied calmly. "Snow serpent. A larger one than made our wall today, if my ears can still judge."

Ki quickened her pace. Her logic told her that to try to flee before such a beast in the deep snow would be purest foolishness. What chance would they have against a beast whose natural milieu was snow? Her mind raced through a catalog of her possessions, seeking an appropriate weapon. Vandien had lengthened his stride to match hers. He panted with the strain and glanced, annoyed, to see why Ki had increased their pace. Ki's eyes met his. The whites showed all around her eyes as she returned his gaze.

He laughed lightly, without malice. "No need for alarm, Ki. That serpent came upon us, caught our scent, and fled. They have no interest in us. They feed only on the snow itself, gathering the nutrients it offers before they return it to the earth as an icy wall to thwart travelers. Some say that in summer they burrow into the earth itself. They need be of no more concern to us than large earthworms would be to a gardener. Their only threat is in the trails they leave behind them."

Ki expelled a long, ragged sigh. Her pace slowed. Anger edged her voice. "You might have mentioned that when we were chopping through the trail back there. Or when the subject of snow serpents first arose. It would have saved me much worry."

"And you might have asked. It would have cost you only a small bit of pride. Of that abundance you carry, you can afford to part with a little. You have never been through this pass before, have you?"

Ki clamped her jaw, not trusting herself to reply. The sudden blaze of anger she felt for this arrogant little man warmed her. She resumed her swifter pace. Vandien matched her, refusing to show how it strained him.

"Fools. By the Hawk, I am under a plague of fools and cowards," Vandien said conversationally. "The cowards that turn their wagons back, and the fool that forces hers through. You know nothing, then, of the Sisters and their ways?"

"Don't teach me my trade, man. I am a teamster. What can you tell me? There is a path that goes, and I will follow it. I have been through worse passes, ones that make this trail look like a crack in a farmer's furrow. My team and I met them and surpassed them. We will conquer the Sisters as well."

Vandien marched on silently in the gathering darkness. Ki glanced at him but could make out nothing of his features except for his straight nose. He had pulled the shawl up so that it hooded his face and fell about his shoulders.

"No one 'conquers' the Sisters," he said quietly. "We may

elude them, or make ourselves unobtrusive. But we shall not 'conquer' them. There are tales of the Sisters. Beauty is not always kind." He spoke calmly, but there was a hard control in his voice. "But tales are best saved to be told about a fire, with hot food before one."

"And blankets to hide our heads under when the scary parts come," Ki scoffed shortly. His tone irritated her. Its mystery reminded her of a local guide who had taken her, for one minted coin, through the high temples in Kratan. He had told her horrendous tales of priestesses that mated with snakes, and the scaliness of their offspring. Afterwards, he had tried to sell her the mummified scaly finger of such an infant. Ki had been disgusted, as she was now. What did this Vandien take her for, a fool? Small wonder. What would Ki call a teamster who found herself in an unknown pass in winter snow without a supply of firewood?

They slogged on through the snow. It packed and caked on Ki's leggings and melted on her thighs. Once a trickle of melted snow found its way down inside her boot, sliding like a finger of ice down her leg. As she walked she flexed and unflexed her toes. They would slip to numbness, and then return to stinging pain as she moved them. But as long as they hurt, they were still hers. She breathed through a fold of her hood, trying not to pull the icy air directly into her lungs. A little frosty patch built up before her lips from the moisture of her breath. It was another irritation for her. As the last light fled, the cold seeped in deeper and deeper about them. It was a palpable thing, fingering their garments and slipping in wherever it found an opening. At the wrist, at the back of the neck, at the small of the back—it was like icy forefingers prodding nerves.

Vandien veered sharply left. Ki flanked him. Then she realized that for some time she had been simply following his lead, not even trying to make out the trail before them. It humiliated her; but she swallowed it, knowing there was no way she could make that out to be his fault. He did know this pass; that much he had proved. And if he found them shelter for the night from this beastly cold, then he would have earned any help she could give him to get across the pass.

It was full dark now. Sigurd was letting his displeasure be known with noisy snorts. It was time to stop for the night. No one could know where they were going in this blackness. But

Vandien moved on steadily, and Ki matched him. Her weary eyes, the lashes rimed with frost, could make out little of her surroundings. Gradually the walls of a little arroyo were closing in around them. The snow became shallower, as if they were wading out of a lake. It was only about their ankles when Vandien abruptly stopped.

"This is the place. Circle the wagon about so that it cuts off the wind from the mouth."

Ki nodded dumbly and obeyed. Weariness flowed through her more sluggishly than her own chilled blood. In darkness she halted the team. She had to bare her hands to the cold to unharness the drooping horses. The buckles clung to her bare fingers. Vandien had disappeared. Ki could spare no thought for him. She had her team to care for. In spite of cold and weariness, she meticulously rubbed down the horses, drying away sweat and damp from their hides. She blanketed them with their own blankets. A trip to her cuddy, and she reinforced their blankets with her two worn ones. It posed a problem for her, but they had earned the extra warmth.

She heard the mutter of Vandien's voice and the sounds of frozen wood-chunks hitting against one another. Sparks blossomed in the darkness in a shower. Ki's sandy eyes sought out that area as she shook out a generous measure of grain for the team. She heard a muffled curse from the spark place, and finally a tiny, ruddy glow lit the silhouette of a man's sheltering hands. Ki returned the sack of grain to the back of her wagon.

The flames of the fire were leaping now. Its spreading light marked out the new boundaries of the world; the edge of the wagon and the curving wall of stone and ice that closed it in. The team shed its natural fear of the fire to draw closer to its tiny warmth. Ki drew near herself, staring into its flickering depths. Vandien put on another ice-rimed log. It sizzled and smoked, and then caught. Resin began to pop and crackle. The sudden warmth made the chill mask of skin on Ki's face ache. She held out her hands, warming them without removing her gloves. The warmth did not penetrate to her feet. They remained remote parts of her body, her toes small chunks of ice in the ends of her boots.

"We cannot rest yet. If we stop moving now, we will freeze before we start again." It was Vandien's voice, unutterably weary and miserable. Ki shook her aching head. He was right.

"I know. There's no need to remind me. I've been this cold and tired before, and I'll likely be this cold and tired again," she informed him. She knew she was being unfair. There was a reason for it, but she was too tired to search her mind for what it was. At least her irritability warmed her a little. Vandien seemed to understand her frame of mind, for he ignored her words. Without replying, he began to open the dish chest, taking out the kettle and packing it with snow. He handled it with the palms of his hands, awkwardly, as if he were fingerless. The skin of his face was stretched yellow over his cheekbones and forehead. Frost spiked his beard.

A window seemed to open in Ki's mind. Her heart smote her for her thoughtlessness, for putting the privacy of her grief before a man's life. She moved swiftly, allowing herself no time for memories or regrets. She climbed stiffly up the wheel. The cuddy door moved stiffly in its tracks. She sought in the darkness. There was his smell again, and the familiar feel of garments washed and mended by her hands a thousand times. She turned off her memories, ignored the voice that whispered betrayal.

Vandien was tamping down snow into the kettle, taking no more care with his fingers than if they had been lifeless sticks. His hands were white in the firelight. The veins showed blue, sinew and bones outlined.

"Stand up," Ki ordered him gruffly.

He rocked slowly to his feet with motions that could have bespoken mere stiffness and fatigue, or been pure insolence. Perhaps both, Ki thought. She shook the folds of the heavy cloak out, pushed the shawl from his shoulders and settled the cloak around him. Hastily she bared her own fingers to lace and tighten the leather ties that his own stiff fingers could never manage. The cloak was hopelessly too big. When she jerked the hood up about his face, it fell far over his eyes. She bunched it about his face as best she could. Vandien stood strangely docile under her ministrations. She could feel his violent shivering, hear the chatter of his teeth. The heavy mittens were of wolf hide, lined with sheepskin. She pulled them up over his lifeless hands. They went nearly to his elbows.

"Somewhere in the wagon there would be his sheepskin leggings," Ki remembered aloud as she looked down at Vandien's thin leather ones.

"I walked frozen all day, while you had these in the wagon?" Vandien's voice was indignant and bewildered.

Ki nodded slowly and raised her eyes to his. The mittens, the heavy cloak, the pale face of a stranger within them. Dark eyes looked out of Sven's hood, flecks of anger glowing in them. The shock of the wrongness seized her, and she turned away from it. She tried to remember how Sven had looked in them. Larger, yes, but what else? The image wavered in her mind, would not come.

She spun away from Vandien to face the dark and cold. But Sven was not there either. She crouched, hunkering her body down, making herself small and separate from all things. She huddled, searching her mind for a clear image. But they all seemed blurred by time. She rummaged for emotions, for love and grief. She found only anger. Sven would have remembered the firewood. Sven would have asked ahead about safe stopping places. He should be here to do those things. But he wasn't, and she couldn't even see his face. She hunched forward, shivering with a cold not of snow. A heavy fur mitten was resting on her shoulder.

"Come, get up. You'll freeze there, and it won't change a thing. The water for tea will be hot soon. . . . Ki."

He did not ask for explanations. He did not try to help her rise or comfort her. She heard the squeak of his boots against the dry snow as he returned to the fire. Ki rose slowly, feeling as if her guts were dropping back into place inside her. Her mouth was full of bitterness. She went to the cuddy, lit the small candle briefly to take out the dried meat and withered roots for stew, to search coldly in the back of Sven's cupboard for his winter leggings.

Vandien had brewed the tea. He pushed a steaming mug of it into her hands, taking her burdens from her. He cut the meat and roots into smaller chunks than Ki did. He felt her eyes on him and made a show of returning the small knife to the dish chest. He grinned at her as he did it, a fey grin by firelight. Ki could not return it. She sipped her tea and felt the warmth slide into her body like sanity into her mind. She did not watch Vandien as he donned the leggings, but busied herself with stirring the soup. They ate hastily as soon as the meat had softened, sucking noisily at the burning liquid and scalding their tongues.

The broth burned the bitter taste from Ki's mouth. Her shivering calmed. She felt the heat of the fire begin to seep through her boots to her feet. Vandien stacked the rest of his firewood and spread the shawl over it, making a place to sit. Ki moved to his invitation, sinking onto the lumpy seat gratefully. She could look at Vandien only as long as she looked at his face and not his garments. He sat quietly beside her, at a comfortable but companionable distance. She found he was watching her quietly. The weariness in his eyes shamed her. She moved uneasily, going to the cuddy and returning with coarse, hard bread. She broke it into a chunk for him and one for herself. She watched the struggling fire, chewing the hard bread slowly. Damn the man! What did he want of her, watching her with those martyred eyes?

"The Sisters," Vandien began softly.

"Ah! You promised me tales tonight. I had nearly forgotten." Ki's tone was falsely light, bantering. He did not rise to it.

"Beauty is seldom kind." Vandien spoke it like a lesson learned. "And the greater the beauty is, the more unkind it may be. You have seen the awesome beauty of the Sisters. It is a beauty beyond any race's creating. Such a thing can only be natural. And yet they are remarkably regular, perfect in their symmetry. Hard they are, impossible to chip or mar, if any could find a desire to do so. They rise beside the trail that goes through the pass. In clear weather, in summer time, they are high above the path, so that a man on horseback may not touch them, even standing in the saddle. But in winter the snow rises, and with it the trail. When the trail is high, you may walk on top of the crusted snow and touch their beauty. But legend has it that they do not like to be touched by any other than themselves."

Vandien's eyes were masked and far away, as if walking the pass in memory. He stared into the fire, and Ki saw the outline of his face. He had pushed the hood back from it while he ate. He had a strong profile. Were he clean and shaven, and not so thin, he would not have been an ugly man. He turned his eyes from the fire to Ki, and they came alive, seeming to hold the fire he had gazed into. He seemed puzzled at her stare. He gave a slight shrug and continued.

"I have never touched the Sisters. I have heard men brag of such a reaching, but they were not men I desired to imitate. The kiss the Sisters share is only for each other. And I think they are a jealous pair. For, in winter, the pass is not safe.

There is no sign of violence, no evidence of a battle or treachery. But wagons and Humans and beasts are found crushed within the pass, beneath the shadow of the Sisters' kiss. One crosses the pass in springtime, only to find the poor crushed bodies as if ground by a mortar and pestle. The deeper the snow is, the greater the chance of mishap. The snow has not lain this deep within the pass in many a year. . . ."

"Avalanche," murmured Ki sleepily. The drone of Vandien's dreaming voice had lulled her to the edge of sleep. "Poor folk, crushed under chunks of ice and snow, to lie revealed when the snows melt. Ugly. But at least they all die together."

"Snow never clings to the Sisters' faces, nor to the steep rise above them. Year after year, that wall of the pass is as bare as a knife blade. No snow settles on the Sisters. The cliffs stand bare there, year after year, while their burden of snow settles in the trail beneath the Sisters. And the trail there can be treacherous with ruts and troughs from the snow serpents passing. Human and Dene are not the only ones to use this pass. We shall have a pretty time with it."

"At least they die together." Ki was seeing the fire as if it were at the end of a long, black hallway. The image stirred vague, unsettling memories. The air inside her nose was cold, but she herself was toasty warm. Warm feet, warm belly, warm face, warm fingers, warmth coasting lazily through her. Vandien's chin had nodded onto his chest, the floppy hood falling half across his face. Strange face, all dark eyes and bones. Strange man. . . .

The sap in one of the logs bubbled, then exploded with a loud pop. Ki jerked her head upright. "Vandien! Wake up! Fools we are to doze before a dying fire in this weather. To bed now, and travel in the morning."

Vandien straightened himself slowly, rubbing and pulling at his face. He moved to the fire, stacking on two more logs close over its dying flame to feed the embers during the night. "We'll load the rest of the wood and take it with us. Tomorrow."

"Tomorrow," agreed Ki. She rose stiffly and moved about the camp, stowing gear with a tidiness born of long habit.

The door to the cuddy complained as Ki jerked it along its groove. Inside, all was still and cold. She let her eyes become accustomed to the dark. A faint, ruddy glow from the fire came in through the small window. It was enough. On the straw-stuffed mattress was the shagdeer hide cover. She had given the other blankets to the horses. Ki leaned out the cuddy door. Vandien was crouched by the fire, arranging it to his satisfaction. His face was pinched with the cold and his days of privation. The labors of the last few hours had told on him cruelly, much more so than on Ki, who came to the snows fresh from warmer lands. She studied him for a silent moment, knowing he could see nothing of her face or eyes as she peered at him from the dark cuddy.

"Vandien!" He looked up at her, and she motioned to him to come. She moved back into the cuddy and shook out the shagdeer cover over the whole platform. She felt the creak and give of the wagon as he climbed up on the seat. She looked up to find him peering inquiringly in the door.

"Wipe your feet before you come in," she cautioned him. "The cuddy is tight and will hold most of our warmth. We don't want snow melting in here."

He hesitated awkwardly. He came down into the cuddy as cautiously as if he expected the floor to give way beneath him. He slammed his head against the ceiling, then crouched to clear it. He stood still, silently looking about. The man and the children had left their marks on the cuddy, and Ki had taken pains not to erase them. His face changed subtly as his eyes took in Lars's puppet, a tiny pair of soft leather shoes that dangled from a peg. He moved back slowly toward the cuddy door.

"I shall be fine sleeping under the wagon. I'd have the fire."

"Don't be a fool. Once you went to sleep there you would never wake up, to check the fire or anything else. Shake out the cloak and leggings and hang them on those pegs."

She did not watch to see if he obeyed her. She dusted the snow out of her outer clothing and hung them up. She moved around him to slide the cuddy door shut. Vandien eyed her as she cut off his retreat. The fading light from the fire made a tiny square on the ceiling of the cuddy. And still Vandien stood awkwardly in the center of the cramped cuddy.

"We may be crowded sharing the platform, but the body heat will be worth it." Actually, as Ki well knew, the platform could hold two very comfortably. She waited for Vandien to make one of his acid comments. But he did not.

"I could sleep on the floor here," he offered. "If I rolled up in the cloak, I would be fine."

Ki moved past him without a word to climb up on the platform and crawl under the shagdeer cover. She settled, feeling the cold mattress close about her body. It was colder than she had expected. "You'd better bring both cloaks with you," she said imperturbably. "We'll need them to be comfortable."

She watched him in the dark as he took both cloaks off the pegs. He shook them out and let them settle over Ki and the shagdeer cover. Moving gingerly, he edged himself up onto the bed and eased himself under the hides. He ended by lying on his back so he faced slightly away from her. The round of his shoulder was but half a hand-span from her own. The platform had not been designed for privacy. Ki could feel the heat of him seep across that small space to touch her familiarly. She was both repelled and unwillingly warmed by it. She heard the small sounds of his settling: the crack of knee joints, a clearing of throat, the crackling of the straw as he snuggled his body into it. His breathing steadied in the silence. She listened to it in the dark, holding herself still and silent.

"Sleep well." His voice startled her, coming from so close beside her and so unexpectedly. She jumped, and then tried to pretend that she had been settling herself.

"We'll make an early start." She was unwilling to let his remark hang in the silence.

"Yes." Ki lay staring up in the darkness as Vandien watched the wall of the cuddy. Each was unwilling to be the first one to sleep. Ki could hear faintly the crackling of the fire outside the wagon. One of the horses stamped and shifted. The bed began to warm her. Almost warm enough to sleep comfortably. She let her legs stretch and relax. The dark pressed on her eyes. She closed them to shut it out.

She only realized she had slept when she opened her eyes sometime later to darkness. She was not certain what had awakened her. She remained motionless, listening to the stillness, searching for some sound that might have disturbed her. As long as she lay still, she was warm. She knew that to shift might open some small crack in her covering, let the cold air seep in to touch her.

Gradually, Vandien came into her awareness. In sleep they had shifted, gravitating toward each other's warmth. Vandien had rolled over to face her, his body curling toward her. His head had lolled forward, to rest heavily against her shoulder. It was the tickling of his dark, dense curls against her face that had brought her to wakefulness. She smelled his smells, the acridness of his sweat and the fern-sweetness of his hair, like crushed herbs—so different from her own man's soft blondness and smell of leather and oil. But the leaning weight of Vandien against her brought him into reality for her, made Vandien a whole person, not one of those shadows with which she had consorted for so long. He pressed against her solidly, breaking into the sealed world she had defended. The world twisted about her, and Vandien, sleeping here beside her, breathing so slowly, was the reality—and Sven became the shadowy being beckoning to her from some other world. Her mind struggled with the tangling images.

In rebellion, she shut her eyes, closed out Vandien's nearness. Sven was hers. She would not forget Sven and her children. She would never let them go. She groped for their images in her mind, but it was Lars she summoned up. Lars, brother to Sven, looking up at Ki where she perched in the limbs of the twisted old apple tree. . . .

"I thought I might find you here," Lars said.

"Please go away," Ki pleaded softly.

Last night's ritual had drained her. When she had awakened at last, it had been late in the day. She had dressed in her own dusty garments, feeling angry and displaced. Here was no quiet privacy of washing herself in a stream, of making her solitary cup of tea and facing the day. Here she must dress in dirty clothing and face a room full of people before she could even cleanse herself. Her head ached abominably and her ears still hummed.

Armed with her anger, she had entered the common room. It was empty. Cora's wooden table, cleared of all traces of last night's appalling feast, was in its usual place against the wall. The fireplace stood cold and empty. Last night might never have happened.

Ki had been free to go to her wagon and change into her clean brown shift. She had checked her team only to find them grazing contentedly in the pasture. She had crossed the pasture and walked through a narrow belt of trees, to the apple trees and meadow that fronted on the road. She had been sitting in the tree, careful to keep her mind as empty as the road she watched. Now here was Lars, to bring it all up again.

"I can't just go away, Ki. I wish I could. It's time some of it was said, anyway."

"Some of what?" Ki asked angrily. "I don't even understand what happened last night, but somehow everyone holds me responsible for it. Maybe you should start there, by explaining that to me."

"Maybe I should," Lars conceded wearily. He stood, arms folded, as Ki dropped down from the tree. A little self-consciously, he seated himself on the grass. Ki reluctantly joined him.

"Last night was not your fault. In a sense, none of it was your fault. You are not one of us—I do not mean that unkindly. But you were not raised in our ways, and you have never chosen to learn them. The Rite of Loosening—did Sven never speak of it to you?"

Ki shook her head. "We had our minds upon living, not dying. It was obscene for Sven to die. Obscene!"

Lars nodded. "It was. And you showed that obscenity to us, in every detail."

"And what should I have showed you?" Ki asked bitterly. "You harped on me about sharing my sorrow. Having tasted the cup, do you turn your face from it?"

"You do not understand." Lars pressed the heels of his hands to his temples, then forced his hands to fold themselves and rest quietly in his lap. "A woman raised in our ways would have shown us her man and her children racing away on the horse. She would have shown us, as you did, their wild beauty as they went, hair streaming, voices trailing laughter behind them as they galloped up the hill. Then she would have told us that they never came back from their ride. This is our custom in the case of a violent death; not to reveal it in all its hideousness. And she would have saved for us a cup to end on—a healing, loosening cup. With the last cup she would have given us, as a gift, a memory of them she cherished. A moment, perhaps, of a child seen sleeping by firelight. When my father died, the gift my mother gave us was an image of him as a young man, muscles bared as he raised the first roof beams of our home. It is a gift I cherish still, the glimpse of my father as I would otherwise never have seen him. Thus, it is called the Rite of Loosening, Ki. We let them go. We set our dead free, and in place of mourning we offer to our friends a quiet moment of our happiness with the one who is gone."

Lars fell silent. Ki cast her eyes about, abashed. She spoke huskily. "I suppose that could make it a very beautiful thing, this Rite of yours. But it was never explained to me. All you told me was that I must share his death with you. Do you wonder that I waited so long before I came to you? I will be honest. But for my oath to Sven at our agreement, I would have let my road take me past here."

"I know," Lars replied gently. "If that was all there was to it, Ki, we could all forgive."

He pulled a long stem of grass up and rolled it thoughtfully between his fingers. The wind touched his hair with gentle fingers, pressed his shirt softly against his chest.

"Mother feels it most. She is the most devout in the family, the one closest to the old rituals. The ablutions and prayers the rest of us omit or forget, she still observes. The doctrines we have set aside as superstition, she clings to. That is why it was worst for her. You held a cruel mirror to her faith, Ki. You were strong of spirit, stronger than she. When she tried to turn you gently away, to bring your mind back from that long hill, you fought her and kept us there. Some felt last night that it was deliberate; that you wanted to force us to see Harpies as you see them. With hatred, disgust, fear. When we share the liquor of the Rite, we must feel what you feel. You showed it to us, hideously scrambled, now revealed, now hidden, all flavored with your emotions. It took all Cora's strength to drag us back. You drained her. She keeps her bed still, from weakness. And Rufus," he went on, his eyes fixed on the ground. "Rufus feels it, not as blasphemy, but as shame, a blot upon the family honor. Those two take it hardest. But none of us will ever recover fully from it."

Lars shifted uneasily and began to rise. Ki put out a hand to detain him. He looked at her, puzzled.

"I did not mean for you to see it at all. I let you think the horse had killed them last night when we talked on the wagon. I knew nothing of this drink of yours, this bizarre sharing, as you call it. I never meant for any of you to know the Harpies had done it."

"We, who know Harpies, could have faced that if you had told us of it. We would not have demanded to see, to poke our fingers in your sores. You walk too lightly among us, Ki, never leaning, never trusting us to understand. One would almost believe that you doubted our love for you."

Ki bowed her head to his rebuke. Should she deny the truth of his words? She had wanted Sven. She had gone after him with every means that seventeen years of life on a road wagon had given her. If Aethan, her father, had still been alive, perhaps she could have been dissuaded. But Ki had wanted Sven. To have him, she had to take on his family as well, with all the strange trappings of kinship. Doubly strange to Ki was his culture, for she had never known family other than Aethan or customs other than the Romni, which Aethan sporadically adhered to. And once she had Sven she had kept herself apart. She had taken Sven away, to her lifestyle. And now, because of her aloofness, in her ignorance, she had hurt them all.

Lars took her silence and downcast eyes as dismissal. Once more he began to rise. Ki wished she could let him go. Her head felt as if a bowstring had been stretched between her temples. It was tight, and getting tighter, humming all the while. She longed for silence and sleep. But she had to know it all. Ki caught his loose sleeve, pulling him back down beside her. She forced him to meet her eyes.

"Don't stop, Lars. If you think you have explained it to me, you haven't. You have told me how I bungled your Rite last night. I am shamed by the hurts I gave you all, however unintentional. But how have I blasphemed your religion? You say you all know what Harpies are. How they kill, how they feed. I did try not to show you that. The confusion in the images you speak—believe me, Lars, I was trying to turn us from the remembering. Do you believe I would willingly relive that, for any rite?"

After a moment, Lars began to shake his head slowly. "I suppose not. I can believe it when you plead ignorance. Sven was almost an outcast among us for the way he flouted our beliefs. I see he dismissed them completely when he went away with you. They meant little enough to him when he was here. He never once made tribute to the Harpies, not even after our father died. Mother felt that keenly."

Sparks flashed in Ki's green eyes at the mention of tribute. But still she shook her head at Lars. "You must go on. Begin it as if you were explaining your beliefs to a child. I begin to feel currents I had not imagined. I am heavy within with a foreboding that whatever I did last night was grievous beyond words. Speak to me as if I had never been told anything of your religion. You shall not be far wrong."

"It grows worse," Lars groaned. "What many saw as malice was total ignorance. If only it was to do over."

"It isn't," Ki replied impatiently. "It can never be undone. So, at least let me know the fullness of what I did."

Lars pulled at his face with a large hand. When he tipped his
chin up, the sun glinted on the downy hairs beginning on his
face. His beard would be like Sven's—late in coming and silky
against a woman's face. Lars met Ki's eyes and began
abruptly.

"In times gone by, this place was not called Harper's Ford.
Time has eroded its name to that. It was Harpy's Ford, the
only place to cross the river for many miles in either direction;
there were no bridges then. Harpies knew that as well as Humans. It made their hunting easier. You have seen the platforms raised on pilings in the river, near the crossing? People
wishing to cross the river undisturbed would leave offerings of
dead beasts there, to buy the Harpies off their children. They
and their families could cross in peace while the Harpies fed.
There would be no sudden rush of wings, no childish screams
above the sound of the rushing water. . . ." Lars's voice
trailed off. He rubbed at his eyes wearily. "There, Ki, see how
your visions have infected me? Before last night, never would
I have spoken that way of Harpies. But that was how it began.
Or so they say.

"But times pass, and simple customs become more ornate.
Harpies would sometimes be waiting on the platforms when
folk arrived there to leave tribute. They began to have words
with one another. My people began to discover the many peculiar talents of the Harpies. It became a religion. I know
you do not believe it, Ki, but they are higher beings than we.
You see their cruelty and believe it debases them. But it is not
cruel for a man to slaughter his heifer, nor for a Harpy to take
a man. It is the order of things."

Ki shot to her feet, but as quickly Lars shot up a hand to
seize her. He held her wrist, hard but not tight. With gentle in-
sistence he pulled her back down beside him. She could find
no words, but he read all in the quiver of her mouth and her
quickened breath.

"Do not be angry, Ki. You would like to strike me for my
words or, barring that, to run away from them. Bear this in
mind. Sven was my brother, not only your man. And still I

must say these things to you. We give the Harpies meat in tribute. In return, we get . . . many things. The drink last night was a secretion they provide. It makes a link between Humans, and strengthens that between Human and Harpy."

Ki turned her head away from him. Her belly churned in disgust. She twisted her wrist slightly, and Lars released it. But he spoke on stoically.

"After a death, especially after a good Rite of Loosening, they let us . . . this is so hard to explain unless one has experienced it. Let me make it more personal. If I took a lamb down to the platform and cut its throat, a Harpy would come. And while it fed I would spend time with my father. We would talk together, I could ask him advice, or speak of times we had together. The Harpy would open for me the door between the worlds. Or would have, until last night."

Ki felt a dim presentiment.

"You cut us off from the Harpies last night, Ki. Every person there, from that old man, a great-great-uncle, to that little girl, a cousin of several degrees. You gave us no useful memories of Sven or the children. We have no way to recall them when we go to the Harpies. They are gone to us, truly dead. My mother will never see her middle son again. I will never see my brother. . . . Dead. Now we know what other folk mean by that word. It is a knowledge we were happier without."

"And?" Ki insisted after a stretch of silence. Lars looked at her with anguish in his eyes.

"I hate the saying of these words to you. Rufus would have come, but I stopped him. For if you must be condemned in this way, I would be the one to do it. I try to make the words come gently, to lift from you the weight of them. But it was a grievous blow you dealt last night, and now you must see the wound.

"When I say you cut us off from the Harpies, I mean that we now must face a period of loneliness. None of us may see them at all, for a time, until meditation and atonement have purged from our souls the emotions you put there. For some of us it will take long. Others, such as the little girl, I hope, will soon forget and be healed. But until I can be sure I have cleansed my mind of your feelings I may not go to the Harpies to seek my father or my grandparents. Horror, disgust, hatred for what the Harpy does—those things would cut me off from that converse. I, perhaps, could live with that. As could Rufus and some of the others. But my mother is another matter. No one knows how often she goes to make a sacrifice and see again my father. It takes its toll on the sheep pens, and often I see the anger in Rufus's eyes when he finds the best ewe, the plumpest lamb, gone. But we say nothing. Mother is old, and the old cling more tightly to the rituals. You can surmise what you have done to her. For the first time since my father died, he is really dead to her. Gone. She can not summon him, can not lean on his strength. The emotions you have placed in us for Harpies have cut us off from this magic. Last night some said, in the heat of their anger, that you had re-slain for us all our dead. That because Sven and the children are dead to you, you made all our dead truly dead for us."

Ki raised her head wearily. There were no traces of tears on her face. All her sorrow was contained in her eyes. It seemed to Lars that no amount of tears could ever wash away the misery he saw there.

"Can you tell me that is all?" Ki asked dully. "Can there be more injury I have done to you, all unwittingly?"

"The Rite of Loosening," Lars said slowly, as if the words clung to his unwilling tongue, "Mother sets great store by it. By the Rite the souls of the dead are freed to enter a paradise, a world of a higher order. Unloosed souls must wander this world homeless and lonely, cold and crying. Last night she wept long for Sven and the little ones, condemned to such loneliness and fear."

"There can be no mending this," Ki said.

"The mending will be very slow," Lars conceded. "You've done us grievous ill." He took her hand, trying to take the ache from his words.

"No mending," Ki repeated. "A wound such as this leaves a scar long after it heals." Gently she drew her hand from his. "I think it best that I go. Think me not a coward, Lars. If staying to apologize would better the situation, I would. But staying here I shall be a shame to Rufus, a torment to your mother. I think I should be on my road, leaving you to heal yourselves."

Lars cast his eyes down quickly. He raised his hand to his mouth and then spoke softly. "I thought you might see it so. Rufus will not be pleased, nor my mother. They are very con-

cerned about appearances. For myself, I have a graver concern than that. My people, Ki—they are not used to abuse
from outsiders. They have been damaged. They will want revenge. They will look for a scapegoat, someone to center their
anger on, to bear the brunt of the Harpies' displeasure. And
the Harpies *will* be displeased. While we dare not go to them
with tribute they will not feed as well. We are one of the larger
families in the valley and by far the most generous with the
winged ones. They will miss our tribute. I wish you could
stay, Ki. I would like you to live here among us, in peace. But
who could promise that? My mind ignores the cries of my
heart. It tells me that you must go, tonight, in secret. Tell no
one of your plans. Travel swiftly, go to Carroin. The roads that
lead there are level and wide; you will make good time. Stop
for nothing. Leave the supplying of your wagon to me. I shall
do it today, in stealth. Too many eyes will be on you. Tell no
one: not Rufus, not Cora!"

Lars rose slowly from the ground. Ki remained sitting, her
heart beating slowly and painfully. Her mind whirled. She did
not wish to leave in stealth, to slink away like a shamed child.
She wanted to redeem herself in their eyes, to make them see
that she had wished them no harm.

"Tell no one!" Lars cautioned her once more. "Cora would
try to make you stay, unmindful of any danger to herself. She
would put her hospitality to her daughter by Sven above her
own safety. There were many that did not approve when Sven
joined you. Their tongues will wag long today." Then Lars left
her, striding away, leaving Ki surrounded by a cold premonition of danger.

FIVE

COLD nibbled at her spine, crept up around her to touch her, no matter how she shifted and burrowed deeper into the mattress. She opened her eyes grudgingly. Vandien was standing at the edge of the platform, rubbing his scruffy beard.

"Daylight's here," he said softly when she stirred. "We have to be on our way."

Ki stretched stiffly and moved gingerly from the shelter of the shagdeer cover. Even from within the cuddy she could tell that the cold had deepened. The freezing air pressed in on the wagon like a clenching fist. She struggled hastily into her cloak. Vandien moved past her to take his from the bed and don it again.

With the cold had come a wind that whooshed past the entrance to the canyon. Their tracks from the night before were almost completely erased. The grays were huddled together between the wagon and the cliff wall. Their heads were down and their cropped tails lifted slightly in the breeze. Vandien pulled the protection of the hood further past his face.

"Damn the luck!" he spat. "A wind like this is all we need to make things worse."

Ki looked at the sky with an expert eye. "The wind may be exactly what we do need to take the wagon through." She smiled a dry, cryptic smile at Vandien and jumped lightly from the wagon.

Sigurd whinnied shrilly at the sight of her. They were not pleased to be unblanketed. Ki gave them a small feed of grain to cheer them while she helped Vandien load the remaining firewood. It was not a large load. Vandien spent a single log to rejuvenate last night's fire and heat a kettle. The Humans broke their fast only with hot tea, sipping it from steaming mugs that cooled too swiftly. Camp was soon broken, Vandien gathering the equipment and Ki stowing it. The harness leather was stiff and hard to thread through buckles thickened with frost. Sigurd tossed his great head about when Ki approached him with the cold bit, then sulked when she finally succeeded in getting it between his jaws.

"We're off," Ki announced through lips already chilled and dried by the cold. With a creaking and snapping of wheels pulled free of ice, it was true.

Snow was shallow within the sheltering arms of the canyon. But when they emerged from the mouth it became deeper. As they turned out of the canyon, the horses' heads were pointed into the wind, and they pulled the wagon into a deepening drift of snow. The snow itself was a fine crystalline dust that swirled and lifted on the wind. The horses lowered their heads before it. It stung Ki's face with icy kisses. Vandien pulled his hood full forward and turned his head aside. Ki could permit herself no such luxury. Someone must use her eyes to guide the struggling team. Her face stiffened in the icy press of the wind. It blew up her sleeves, and inside her hood it circled to slide down the back of her neck. The reins grew stiff in her hands.

The grays plowed through the snow gamely. The tall wheels of the wagon sometimes stuck and slid without turning. Ki strained her eyes ahead, trying to pick out the trail in the swirling snow. All the mountainside looked amazingly alike. She nudged Vandien and shouted over the wind.

"Do you know this pass well enough to guide us through it in a storm like this?"

The hood nodded. He lifted a bundled arm to gesture that she should turn the team more to the right. Ki made the correction. The previous day they had traveled up winding canyons and between foothills, moving ever so gradually toward the Sisters where they overlooked the narrow trail. Now Ki found her path moving ever closer to the upthrusting of a mountain. As she followed Vandien's pointed directions, the team headed less and less into the wind.

The trail began to ascend again, at a steeper grade than before. It seemed to Ki that no sooner were they freed of fighting the wind than they were forced to battle an uphill grade. The wind itself did not cease, but battered the wagon broadside now. At least it was sweeping the snow across their rocky path in shallower drifts, rather than piling it up before them.

The mountain became larger, barer, and steeper on the right side of the trail, while on the left the ground began to drop away. From a gradual slope in the morning, it became by noon a gentle hillside that rolled away from them. On the right side of the wagon the mountain began to rear up in sheer walls of bare stone that climbed vertically before they became the rugged sides of the mountain above them. The grays' feathered hooves met bare, stony ground beneath the snow now. The wagon wheels no longer wallowed but rolled and crunched along. No sooner did the wind sweep a shallow drift of snow across their path than it eddied and swept it away again. Ki found she could follow the trail now without Vandien's help as it was first covered, then revealed by the shifting winds.

They traveled through a country of absolutes. If it was not snow or ice they saw, then it was rock. If it was not white or gray in color, then it was black. The wagon, obscenely gay in such a setting, creaked through a country in which nothing else moved except the wind-blown snow. The mountain moved closer to the trail's edge, until Ki knew that if she met another wagon or traveler coming from the other direction neither would have room to give way to the other. It was a possibility that she did not much fear.

It was hard to imagine spring in such a place, or anything other than snow. But here and there a patch of scabrous blue ice clung to the steep mountainside that reared above them, to show that thaws and running water were not unknown in the pass. The blue ice shimmered more brightly in the snow-paled sunlight than it should have. At last, they passed a chunk that was low enough for Ki to see plainly. The ice did not grow paler as they approached it, but bluer. Working within its depths she saw tiny, wriggling blue creatures.

"Ice maggots!" Vandien shouted over the wind as they passed narrowly under the shadow of the clinging ice. He shrugged casually as they passed, but to Ki they were new beings that both fascinated and repelled her. She did not realize the danger they presented until a great chunk of blue ice slid down the side of the mountain immediately behind them. It crashed on the path, sending rattling shards of ice bouncing off the back of the wagon. It obscured the way they had come with shattered chunks of blue ice. It would have smashed the wagon or killed the team, had they been in its path.

"Little squirmers chewed it loose," Vandien observed without rancor. "This pass would be a safer one to travel were it not for the maggots and the rotten ice they make. Keep the team moving. There's no sense in pausing, or even in looking up. If we saw a chunk coming down, there's no place to get away from it."

The wind was an ever-present shushing, a nosy cold creature that nudged its way into every opening garments might provide. Sometimes it shifted about to meet the wagon with a shout and smack of head wind. Vandien looked like a huddled pile of garments on the seat. "You could ride within the cuddy, you know!" Ki called to him. "There's no reason we both have to endure this. I don't need you to pick out the trail anymore."

Vandien shook his head, making no words. Ki was secretly glad of his company in the icy wind, but wondered why he chose to remain there. When the sun was overhead, the winds seemed to decrease in volume. The snow still swirled about the horses' hooves, but not as strongly. The trail, too, leveled out for a space and traveled horizontally across the mountain's face, as if taking pity on the weary team. Ki halted the wagon to let them breathe. She blanketed them as they stood in their traces. The trail was wide enough for her to walk past the team, to stroke the frost from their muzzles and share an apple between them. They managed it awkwardly around their bits, jangling as they chewed. The wind buffeted her as she climbed back onto the wagon and to its shushing sound added a whistle. Ki wondered if it were building up again. She wanted to rest the team for a while, but feared to let them stand long if the icy wind was chilling them. She entered the cuddy, closing the door behind her.

Vandien had thrown his hood back from his face in the still cold inside the cuddy. His dark hair was tousled about his face, and the wind had burned his cheeks red above his beard. The contrast made his dark eyes seem brighter, almost shiny black. They sparked at her, and Ki returned his smile as she pushed her own hood back. There was a certain triumph to having come so far in such bitter weather. It was a heady feeling, having prevailed against the winds of the world.

Ki hooked down a dangling sausage, used her belt knife to cut chunks of it against the small wall table. It was so cold, the meat made her teeth ache. They ate together, feeling the wind rock the wagon gently on its axles, hearing the faint whistle it made as it swept past the cuddy.

Vandien rose abruptly, opened the cuddy door to the wind and then pointed to a speck in the sky. "I thought that was too pure a note to be wind song. There he is again! Hardly ever see a Harpy aloft in this kind of weather, but then, that's a strange one. An outcast, did I tell you? Looks like he's caught in the wind."

Stomach quivering, Ki looked. He was so far away, she could not tell his colors; perhaps he was a brown, she told herself, or a deep purple. Or the ghost of a blue, whispered some sneering creature from a dark corner of her mind. The Harpy hovered, not overhead, but up the trail, and very high. His wings would dip, and he would circle high on the vicious winds to come again into position. His clear whistle cut the wind.

"Look how he fights that wind, Ki! Like he wants to stay over the trail. You'd think he'd realize that the wind against those cliffs is what's throwing him around."

Ki did not reply. She was listening to another voice in her head, to Haftor, standing dark and menacing in starlight, holding tight to her wrist: *Cora will not be able to contain such a secret. You killed those Harpies. That's a debt paid only with blood. Neither time nor distance will heal it. Harpies don't give up on blood debts. Neither do the men who serve them.*

Vandien glanced curiously over at Ki, wondering that she did not share his curiosity about the creature. Ki was crouched like a cat, looking out the door under Vandien's arm. Her eyes were glued to the speck that circled and whistled.

"Ki!" She jumped at her name. "We had best be on our way again. There is only one shelter spot between here and the bare faces of the Sisters. If we make it tonight, we may pass the Sisters tomorrow. Two days past that and we should be coming down out of the pass. Wagon and all, just as you said."

Ki turned haunted eyes on him. He would never know what courage it took for her to emerge from the cuddy, to bare herself to the sky and the death that hung there. She almost hoped the Harpy would try to dive on her, to be smashed by the winds against the cliff face. But he did not. He was too wise for that. He hung, rocking in the sky. His whistles grew louder and longer in the thin air. He cried his triumph to Ki.

Team unblanketed, Ki clambered woodenly back onto her wagon. She started her wagon rolling again. The grade was easier now; the snow and wind no longer had to be fought. The wind had suddenly switched to come from behind them. The team pulled with a will, undisturbed by the creature that whistled and cried over their heads. Had they not been foaled and grown to size in Harper's Ford, where the shadows of Harpies swept over the pastures? Ki wished the snow would mantle her from those eyes, the wind rise and dash it from the sky. But the sky only cleared and the wind became a shushing constant. The creak of the wagon could not mask the whistling that was not wind.

She hunched her shoulders, pulled her hood higher about her face. For one terrible instant she felt her face pucker and redden, and a part of her wondered if she would bawl in loud cries for the way destiny had caught up with her. She sobbed in a breath of the frigid air, and it braced her. Beside her, Vandien said loudly, inanely, "Have you ever heard the lay of the hunter Sidris, and how she went to slay the black stag with scarlet antlers?"

Even as Ki turned bewildered eyes upon him, he opened his throat and began to sing. He had a mellow voice that wandered willfully beside the familiar tune. He sang loudly, if not well, and she did not mind his missed notes, nor the places where he hummed to cover the words he had forgotten. He drowned the Harpy's whistle.

The song was a ballad, evidently of his own people, put to a Common tune. He began it with a long introduction of meaningless syllables, repeated at intervals through the song. The song was long and wrenchingly romantic as it told of the hunter who followed the mystic stag and died nobly in the slaying of it. Another time Ki would have mocked the sentimental words about the two futile deaths. Now she was caught up in them. When finally the song died away and Vandien subsided into a somewhat embarrassed silence (truly, he did not have a voice for singing), Ki was surprised to find that the whistling of the Harpy had stopped.

She turned her eyes up to the sky. He was gone. But she knew that he could find her again whenever he wished. There would be no turnoffs from this trail, no friendly forest to hide in. For a moment she considered warning Vandien. Might not he share the fate ordained for her? And then it seemed to her that the Harpy was like the blue ice that twitched with maggots and sometimes overhung the wagon on the narrow trail. No use to look up and worry. If it was going to fall on you, it would. It would find you. As Rufus had found Ki that day.

He had come to the apple tree in the afternoon, to find Ki still sitting there, considering the things she had done. . . .

"Cora would see you," he said stiffly. His eyes were deeply shadowed. Ki guessed that he had slept little. She rose with reluctance to follow him. This summoning boded no good for her. She trailed after him dispiritedly, ignoring the speculative looks she received from Lydia and Holland as she entered the common room. They passed down the narrow hallway.

Cora's eyes were closed. There was more gray in her hair than Ki remembered. Last night had been no time for noticing such things. Now Ki found herself remembering that when she and Sven were joined she had thought Cora sturdy as a tree. Her old cheeks still held a pitiful trace of that bloom, but they were no longer high and firm but wrinkled like apples stored away all winter. The single small window in the room let in little of the afternoon sunlight, and less air. Ki felt stifled. In the closeness her head throbbed and the buzz in her ears seemed louder.

Lydia, who had followed them into the room, plumped and smoothed the feather-stuffed coverlet that lay over the old woman. She sent Rufus and Ki a warning look. Rufus shooed Ki from the room and shut the door gently behind them.

"She cried out for you, but that was a while ago. She seemed awake. But she drifts in and out. Her body already fails under the burden you put upon her last night. Inadvertently," he added grudgingly as Ki knit her brows.

He beckoned again, and she followed him down the hall to another door. There were no windows in Rufus's room. His bed was narrow, pushed into a corner of the room and covered with a single brown woven blanket. Ki glanced about the room in vain for any sign of Holland's presence. There was no token of her, no garments of hers on the pegs, no weavings from her hands. So they couched separately.

Rufus went directly to a cluttered table in one corner. He drew up a small stool to it and sat, leaving Ki looking about the room, standing. For a moment his fingers played over some bits of paper and tally bars on the table. Then he turned his stool to face Ki again.

"I shall speak Cora's mind for her. I know what she would say. You are thinking of leaving," he accused her gravely. "Do not deny it. But I forbid you to do it, as head of the

household you have sworn yourself to. Ki, I will not pretend
to understand what went on last night. Lars has accepted the
blame for it, and I am prepared to listen to one of his lengthy
testimonials later. But it is you I must speak to about leaving.
Enough shame hovers over us now. Will you make the disgrace complete? Yes, there were words, hard words, spoken
against you last night. Lars seems to feel you are in danger. He
does not seem to remember that the people here last night are
your kinspeople. They may speak as they will to us, for they
are family. Families make wild words within themselves. They
mean nothing. But if Ki were to leave? Consider it. Consider it
from their pain. You came and you hurt them and you left,
with no indication of remorse. A harsh blow. And there are
things left unsettled by Sven's passing, things that your leaving
would put in jeopardy. There is the land that was Sven's, that
would have been your children's. You have a duty to it now."

"My duty is to my wagon and my road and my freight," Ki
said quietly. "I acknowledge no other."

Rufus sighed. He licked his lips and seemed to consider.
When he spoke, it was as if he felt the words were too basic to
need to be uttered. "My mother wanders in her mind, Ki. To
be fair, I will tell you that it began months ago, long before
your news or your singular performance last night. But this
may have been the final unhinging. The family knew that last
night. So, I take up the reins, as you might say. You speak of
duties, Ki. Of all that sat at that table last night, there is not
one whose well-being does not rest upon me. My brother Sven
was happy to wed you and to rattle off down the road with you,
to make his living as a common teamster. To let the lands
committed to his trust lie fallow, when they should have been
producing. Then I was the one who had to think of duty. I
kept the sheep and the kine, I tilled and planted his fields for
him, giving to each what they needed, asking of each what he
could give. Farming the land and feeding the family—this is
not a thing like the turning of a wagon wheel upon the road.
Rather, it is like the juggling at fair time, when one man keeps
the plates spinning on the table and the balls flying in the air at
the same time. It is a constant watching, a touch here, a flip
there, and never, never an unwary resting. Someone must
treat with the Windsingers for fair weather, must make the
trades with the Dene and Tcheria for that which we cannot
produce ourselves. Fields must be tilled and planted, buildings

repaired, cattle bred and slaughtered. That is what Sven left to Lars and me. Lars was too young to be more than a puppy at my heels. It has worn my mother out to carry it on, past the years when she should have been sitting before a tapestry, or rocking her youngest grandchild to sleep. It has driven Holland from my bed (yes, I saw your look) and made my sons but my apprentices. It has been heavy on me. I have not minded. But the time for it is past. You are a capable woman. Sven is gone, but Lars is here. This is an unseemly time to say this. But time is no longer waiting on my convenience. Heal the rift, Ki. Be one of us." Rufus paused, watching Ki gravely.

Ki fluttered her hands before her, indignation drowned in confusion and disbelief. She walked slowly to Rufus's narrow bed, seated herself upon it. "You ask the impossible of me, Rufus. I don't see what my staying here will solve. I cannot. I will not. I will not be hasty, or rude. I cannot even find anger at your assumption of authority. In truth, my temper has been drowned in grief. I am past anger such as that. I am tired of my own emotions. Since Sven passed I have been strung like the strings of a harp tree, and every breeze has played upon me. I have nothing left in me, of anger, or pride or gladness. So, I will simply tell you I can not. I can not drop my life strings and take up others, to weave a pattern not of my own choosing. Least of all will I live among people who despise me. Three days I will stay, for I do not wish to leave so sour. But that is all I can give." Ki rose and walked to the door.

"And what of the lands?" Rufus demanded. Ki turned at the panic in his voice. "A full sixth of the lands rests in your hands. Many are watching how they will fall. I do not have the money," Rufus gestured at his tally sticks, "to buy Sven's land from you. For, if I give you the money the family has, what will we use to buy good winds and fair weather from the Windsingers? What is the sense of land with harsh winds blowing across it, drying it out, and whirling the top soil away? And what is the sense of fair weather if the land that basks in it is no longer ours to plow? You must see the dilemma!"

"I am no farmer. I make no claim to your lands. I have no use for more ground than will fit under my wagon."

Rufus shook his head stubbornly. "It cannot be done that way. You cannot walk away from it. The land must be paid for. Such is our custom."

"Damn your customs!" Ki cried wildly. "Look what they have done to me! Look what they have done to us all!"

"Without customs, we are nothing. Not a people." Rufus and Ki both turned incredulous eyes to the door. Cora's eyes were weary but alert. She leaned on the doorframe, catching her breath. Her pale lips smiled at Rufus's look.

"I asked you to bring Ki to me. Not take her off and badger her until she gave way to your will." Slowly Cora shuffled across the flagged floor to seat herself heavily on the foot of Rufus's bed. Her breath came in harsh pants. No one spoke. Ki agonized over the effort she put into each inhalation.

"Boys never change, even when they are grown to be men." Cora managed a brief smile. "I remember a time when I gave each of my sons a switch and sent them out to bring the chickens in. Sven rattled his along the ground, spooking the birds along. Lars waved his in the air, forgetting his task entirely. But Rufus used his to knock the tail feathers off two of my best cockerels." She smiled again. "He bullies still."

Rufus opened his mouth angrily. Cora fluttered a hand at him. "Hush! I am too weary to be arguing with you. *I* sent for Ki. She shall help me back to my room. This rock you call a bed offers me small comfort here."

Abashed by her unexpected rescuer, Ki rose. Cora's hand on her shoulder was the weight of a bird. Slowly Ki guided her down the hall, back to her bedroom. An imperial wave of Cora's hand sent Holland scuttling from the room. Sighing heavily, the old woman seated herself upon the bed, then leaned back into her pillows.

The ensuing silence was difficult for Ki. Cora was occupied with breathing. Ki looked about the room at the heavy drapes and tapestries, at the bulky carved wooden furniture, and back at the heavy coverings Cora drew across her legs.

"You would be better outside, resting on a blanket over fresh hay, in a shady spot. The clean air would renew your strength."

Cora smiled mirthlessly. "The scandal of such a sight would renew the tongues wagging. Then they would all be even more convinced that my mind had begun to wander. You needn't look embarrassed, Ki. I know Rufus believes it is so. I spend too much time sitting silently, smiling to myself. And I take too much from the flocks and herds, so that I may visit the

Harpies and pretend that I am not a sagging old woman. At least the inroads I make on the animals will cease for a time. He will be happy of that small good from the ill winds that swept us last night." Cora paused, and subtly changed the subject. "Last night revealed one thing to me, Ki. You're a strong woman. Stronger than even I suspected. And I know how you sheltered Sven and the children. We have need of such strength here."

Ki bowed her head to the compliment even as she squirmed uneasily at what was coming. "My 'strength' did much harm last night, Cora. I would like you to know . . ."

Another wave of the hand. Veins and tendons stood out on the gaunt fingers. Age was nibbling the flesh from Cora. "I sensed your confusion and struggle last night. Two joined as we were in leading the Rite have few secrets from one another. I felt your fierce love for my son and your children. It is a great comfort to me to know he was so well loved. But I sensed much more than that. It was not your fault they died, Ki. Even if you had hurried your wagon up that hill, it would have changed nothing. Let go of your shame and frustration. And realize that nothing you can do now can change what happened then. Let go of your anger and hatred. I think that if you do so I can believe that the three have been loosed and moved on to a better life. It would be a great comfort to me."

Ki lowered her eyes. Unbidden, there floated to her mind a brief vision of the slain hatchlings, the crumpled mother. The humming in Ki's ears rose, until she felt it drowned the sight from her eyes. She willed the ugly image away. Was that the secret Cora had shared? Did she guess more than she was saying?

"These feelings you have found in me, Cora—I have tried to keep them private, to lessen the impact on you all. But it is not a thing I can let go of simply by saying I shall. Time, and the open road would be my best cure. So, you see, to do your will, I must do mine."

There. Ki felt she had sidestepped the noose neatly. She waited for Cora's next move. Old, Cora might be, but Ki doubted that her wits were slipping. Her hands and mind guided the family as surely as Ki's guided her team. She had been loath at first to release Sven to Ki. Ki had been a small thorn in her flesh, the one who came and went, free of Cora's control. Ki was the one who could not be predicted or maneuvered. Ki wanted their parting to go well. She did not desire this last battle of wills, with no Sven to buffer the tension.

"But why must you hasten away from us so soon? Did you not see the truth in Rufus's words? He is a bully, I know, but he did make his point. For you to leave now would be the final insult to a hurt and angry people. Why cannot you stay until we can honorably pay for the land Sven passed to you? Surely you can stay, at least until the Rite Master can come to us and help us make our peace with the Harpies. It would mean so much to me if you could stay that long. Rufus sees it as a matter of honor. Could you not stay?"

"Perhaps," Ki replied guardedly. Cora's words wove subtle webs around Ki of logic and guilt and dependence: We need you. You hurt us. How can you leave us? Cora had implied she did not approve of Rufus's heavy-handed ways. Was she going to show him how it might be done more subtly? Ki raised her green eyes to Cora's dark ones, trying to reach what might be behind them. Only two bright bird eyes in an old face that smiled at Ki, almost pleadingly. Ki looked down, confused.

"Why do you want me to stay?" she asked bluntly.

Cora sighed, shifted on her bed. "Must it all be spoken, perhaps too soon? I am old, Ki. You are strong but cushioned with wit and gentleness. Rufus is a bully, Lars a tenderheart. They need a wise hand on the reins. I dreamed that someday you and Sven would tire of the road, would come back to us. Now Sven is gone, forever. So I will ask of you what Rufus would have demanded. Ki, will you stay? You've a strong spirit. We have need of such strength, especially after such a trial as last night's."

Ki imagined she felt a two-edged blade. The invitation was made with flattery and a reminder of the harm she had done. A small bubble of anger perked up in her. Was she a child to be manipulated this way? She tried to formulate polite words, courteous words of farewell. Her mind struggled, suddenly began to flounder. Her head began to throb. She was being ungrateful to Cora. Had she not taken Cora's son away from her already? Her ears hummed until she could not hear anything else. Her vision seemed to darken in the sound.

Suddenly, to struggle through it seemed too great an effort. Ki had nowhere to go and nothing to do when she got there. She felt curiously empty as she said the words, the words she could barely hear through the humming in her ears.

"I will stay, Cora. I will stay until you have made your peace with the Harpies."

The snow whirled and swirled on the trail. Vandien had subsided to a heap of garments on the seat beside her, miserable with cold. The team plodded on stoically. Ki watched the snow whirl, baring and obscuring the trail, a shifting, never-repeating, white-on-white stirring. Eternally different, and ever the same. Like her days at Harper's Ford had been.

It was the rhythm of the days that had absorbed her, sapping her will away. She tried to look back, to pick out clear memories. There were few. For a moment her mind caught an image of herself kneeling on a floating dock on the mineral marshes at the far end of the family's holdings. . . .

The marsh smelled evil on hot summer days. The vapors stung Ki's eyes, made her nose run and her eyes water. It was one of the few places where her constant headache seemed to worsen. The buzzing of bright insects camouflaged the buzzing of her own ears. It was dismal, a smelly place, even on a bright summer day. No one chose to work here—no one except Ki. The others avoided the tasks of the marsh, but Ki went to them willingly. For here she could work alone.

She moved her heavy wooden bucket down the dock to the next wooden pin that jutted out over the water. She picked loose the knot in the thin cord tied around the pin and drew the cord up carefully. There was a beauty to the orange crystal that clung to the line. Ki let it dangle for a moment, watching the sunlight strike its facets. Then she deposited it gently into the bucket beside the others. Great care had to be taken with the fragile crystals. The Tcheria would not pay as dearly for broken ones. Ki took a fresh length of clean line from the pouch that hung from her shoulder. She lowered one end into the soupy water, then tied the other to the wooden pin that projected from the dock.

"She does not even dress as we do!"

Ki's eyes snapped to the unfamiliar voice. Katya stood over Lars where he knelt on a separate dock, retying a line on a pin. No doubt she thought herself a safe distance from Ki to speak about her, but voices carried strangely in the marsh. Ki kept her eyes averted, carried on with her work. Dead trees reared up from the marsh, their branches festooned with a slimy, pinkish moss. It partially hid the couple from Ki's eyes. But Ki saw the look of annoyance on Lars's face as he pushed back his long hair and squinted up at Katya.

"I didn't hear you come up," he greeted her.

"You don't seem to notice anything about me anymore, Lars. Look at her. Cannot she at least wear a smock and trousers like the rest of us?"

Lars looked as he was bidden. He saw Ki carefully pulling up a fresh crystal, eyes intent upon her work. A jerkin of brown leather trimmed her upper body above her coarse brown trousers. Lars and Katya were attired in the loose white farmer's smocks and trousers of the valley. Lars frowned.

"I doubt that she has ever given thought to what she wears," he replied. He deftly changed the subject with a courtesy. "You have not visited us for some days, Katya."

"At first I thought to give you time to recover from that hideous Rite," Katya explained. "But now, of late, when I stop by, you are always out working somewhere with Ki. You must know the story of the Rite has spread far and wide. Some say your own foolishness brought it upon you, but I do not see it so. I have only sympathy for your plight, Lars. I cannot imagine how it must be, outcast from the winged ones' society." Katya put a hand on his shoulder to make him pause so that she could admire the crystal he had just drawn from the water. He lowered it gently into his bucket and rose to move to the next pin. Katya stood squarely in front of him. Ki watched from the corner of her eye. Katya's thick, honey hair was braided up into a crown on her head. Folded arms framed her soft breasts. Lars rolled his eyes at the look of tenderness she gave him and edged around her.

She followed to kneel beside him at the next pin. "You look so worn, Lars. No one in the valley understands why you do not send Ki packing and get a little peace back into your lives. I think you should all try to forget what happened so that you may heal. You can scarcely forget, with her a constant reminder. I know it wears on your mother. Cora hasn't sent for me once since it happened. Does she believe I will think the less of her for her misfortune?

Lars slowly drew a crystal from the water. "She has much to do of late, Katya. Things she must see to alone. She has sent word to the Rite Master that we are in need of a special rite.

And she spends much time with Ki. I am sure that she misses your company. But she feels an obligation to Ki, to help her. Katya, if you had been present at the Loosening and had felt the tempest of emotion that Ki encloses, you would understand why my mother feels as she does. Ki must let go of those emotions or burst apart when they ripen."

Ki's ears reddened. Was it thus they saw her? She busied herself with tightening a knot already tied tight. She tried not to hear Katya's indulgent chuckle.

"That sounds like Cora. Anything little, anything hurt can find a home with her. She is not one to hold a grudge. Look at how she took in Haftor and Marna. Everyone else said she owed her brother's children nothing. Didn't he leave her to manage the family holdings alone?"

"My mother did not see it that way," Lars replied shortly. "They are her brother's children and as entitled to the family lands as her own."

Lars rose and walked rapidly to the next pin. He did not look to see if Katya followed him. Ki's head was down, her hands busy when Katya shot a glare in her direction. Katya hastened to where Lars bent over the pin.

"Sven's holdings," Katya's voice was abrupt, blunt, "will Ki keep them or sell them?"

Ki found her eyes glued to Lars's red face. Glints of anger showed in his pale eyes.

"She has never mentioned it to me, so we have never discussed it. There have been too many other painful topics to be considered. Lands and monies have never come up."

"It would be a substanital holding, would it not?" Katya pressed. "If half your grandparents' holdings came to Cora's children to be divided three ways by her offspring—that's a full sixth of the family's holdings that would have been Sven's, and are now in questionable hands. When Marna comes of age and into her holdings, she and Haftor together will control a full half of the original holding, while you and Rufus will hold two sixths. . . ."

"It is a family matter, for family to consider. Unlike Rufus, I foresee no problems with it. It would not be the first time the holdings were run by weighted votes." Lars's voice was curt, a polite reminder to her that although he spoke to her he regarded the matter as private. He no longer pretended to work at the crystals.

Ki watched Katya's chin come up at his tone. She shifted her hands to her hips. She towered over him as he crouched beside the pin and bucket. Her breasts rose as she took a deep breath. "A woman would want to know these things before she joined a family, so that she would know how her offspring would fare. She might consider it more advantageous to find a man willing to join in with her own family, and she thus would retain her own inheritance rights."

"I agree," Lars replied evenly. "She would be a fool not to consider alternate moves. And alternate mates."

He rose and shouldered past her to stride to the next pin. She remained standing on the dock, watching him work. Ki glanced swiftly at her face as she moved to her next pin. Katya seemed to be regretting her words.

Slowly Katya drifted after Lars to kneel beside him again. He rose even as she knelt, going quickly to the next pin. Undaunted, Katya followed him. Ki moved on reluctantly to her own next pin. Every pin was bringing them closer to the junction of the floating docks.

"Did I tell you that I just came from taking a lamb to the Harpy Platform?" Katya asked in a girlishly contrite voice. Lars moved silently to the next pin. She trailed after him. "Father asked after you first, as he always does. He was pleased to hear how well—how well you wear your manhood."

"Katya," Lars groaned warningly.

"And he was full of news of his precious Harpies, as always," she went on hastily. "He hasn't changed a bit. When he was with us, he always knew all the news: joinings, births, quarrels, deaths. Father was always talking of it, almost before it happened."

Lars picked up his bucket, moved to the next pin. Ki tarried at her own pin, pretending to be having some difficulty with it. But Katya's voice carried as clearly as ever.

"There has been a tragedy!" She offered it most pleadingly for his attention. Lars gave in, rocking back on his heels and turning martyred eyes up to her.

"Not in our own aeries, I am relieved to tell you. It was in a lone aerie far to the south of here, a good week's travel away, though only a few days for a Harpy on the wing. It was a renegade aerie, the Winged Ones there raising a brood alone. Father said they were a loning pair, caring little for keeping peace with other folk. Their attitude in this is not condoned by our own Harpies. Indeed, some of ours are saying they brought it upon themselves. For all that, they still have our sympathy and a promise of aid in their search for vengeance."

"Vengeance?" Lars asked slowly. His voice was troubled.

The buzzing in Ki's ears suddenly rose in volume. Premonition leaned cold on her.

"A nest destroyed within days of hatching! Done by a Human, too, by all the signs. Someone scaled the cliff to torch the nest. The mother was heartlessly slaughtered, her body flung to the base of the cliff. The father was hideously burned in a vain attempt to save the eggs. He may never wing again. He is so scarred he has lost much of the movement necessary for normal flight. But he will live."

Ki watched the cord slip from her lax fingers to vanish in the murky water. Her head whirled with sudden vertigo. She could not seem to get enough air into her lungs.

"Of such stuff is nightmare made." Lars's voice was haunted. "When did it happen? It must have been some months back, at the end of hatching season. Or was it a late brood and it happened but days ago?"

"Father did not say." Katya seemed pleased at Lars's response and interest. "I understand that the father was not found for some days, for he could not fly for help. He was near death when he was rescued. They say he is partially blinded, too. Our Harpies are sympathetic and have been taking food to him. But he was a militant and a renegade. They will not take up his revenge for him, though they speak of the deed angrily and listen for news of such a Human. One such as that makes me ashamed to be of the Human race."

"In that, you would not be alone," Lars replied. Katya carried the heavy bucket as they moved to the next pin. Ki, drawn by horror and fascination, picked up her own bucket to move down another pin, where she could pick up their voices.

"Is it true, Father wished to know, what we are hearing? That Haftor seeks to win favor with Ki?"

Lars stabbed an angry look at Katya. "Are you taking up your father's hobby so soon?" he asked in a deadly voice.

Katya flushed. "It is not for myself I ask, Lars, but for my father. You know how he thirsts for news. He says he has heard it from others on that side. That Haftor will try to win Ki, and with her Sven's lands. The family holding is large. It is natural that there would be much curiosity, and even alarm, to see the ruling share of the holding fall to new hands."

A dull, aching anger rose in Ki. She felt herself a tally bar, a reckoning piece in this game of balancings they played. She, Ki, reduced to a measure of land to be controlled. But she did not move or speak. She set an orange crystal gently in her bucket, drew out fresh line for the pin.

"I fail to see any reason for alarm, Katya. You sound like Rufus when you have so much suspicion in your voice. Haftor is cousin to me. We fear no treachery from him. Given some time, he might well prove a good leader for the holdings. But I doubt that it will come to pass. I am as close to Ki as any, and I can tell you that she has no soft feelings for Haftor, regardless of how he may see himself or what ambitions he may have. Haftor and I have had our differences, but he is a good man. When Haftor makes a joining, it will be to a woman he cares for, regardless of what she may or may not hold. Mark my words, and see if I am not right."

"There are even those who say . . ." Katya hesitated, but the look in her eyes was more catlike than uncertain. ". . . those who say that Lars would profit more to take Ki to wife than if he took Katya."

"Lars!" Ki called it twice as loudly as she needed to. "I've a full bucket. I'm going up to the hanging shed."

She sent Katya a warm smile under cold eyes. Lars did not look at her or reply. Ki rose, heavy bucket dangling, and thumped up the floating dock to climb the steps to the bank above the marsh. She followed the beaten track between the banks of coarse, waving grass. The sun beat on her aching head, and her mind could find no safe place to light. The blue Harpy lived, and lived to seek revenge. Other Harpies would aid him. Tongues wagged about what bull would next be put to Ki the cow. Her pace quickened, her scowl set deeper.

"Race along like that, and every crystal will be shattered before you get to the shed," warned a voice behind her.

She slowed her pace and looked back. Haftor toiled along, a bucket dangling from each hand. He looked out at her from his dark, beetling brows and grinned to soften his words.

"Do you know how they speak of us?" Ki found herself asking him angrily. The dammed-up anger burst in her. She let it flood her mind with the more personal affront she felt, letting it wash her thoughts away from circling Harpies and sharp talons.

Haftor shrugged under his burden, allowed himself a small chuckle. "Does it bother you, Ki, to have your name linked with mine? You have never spoken of it before. I thought you were unaware of it. A vainer man would believe that you approved the talk. But it is easily resolved. Wait until you've an audience, then put your fist in my ugly face. No woman will blame you for it. It will give them something new to talk about."

Ki looked at him incredulously. "Does it not bother you, Haftor, to have every tongue forking over your personal life as if it were their manure pile?"

Haftor stopped, set down his buckets to get a fresh grip, and then moved on. Ki followed him.

"People have 'forked over' my life since the day Marna and I were brought here as children. Most felt that Cora took us on out of the charity of her heart. Only Cora seems never to have seen it so. So, walk with me or poke me in the eye. They will talk about us, either way. Only the tone of the gossip will change. So," his tone suddenly became lighter, and he turned to toss Ki a smile, "why not give them something to jabber about? When will you come to my sister's house to visit and admire the work of her hands? From her forge and anvil come the best metal-working the family has ever seen. *She* has never given them cause to regret taking us in."

"I am sure neither of you has ever done so," Ki hastened to reply. It was the first time Haftor had ever spoken openly to her of the matter. Ki had never understood what there was about the subject that made it seem forbidden. But she felt the mention of it drew her onto shaky ground.

The hanging shed loomed up before them. The door was ajar, and Ki could see within to long poles that spanned the interior and supported the glistening crystals on their cords. "I will come to see you and Marna when Rufus leaves me time free. Perhaps Marna would work some metal for me? I've little to trade, except a share of the metal itself. It's silver, and fine, but I've no use for it as a silver mug. It takes the heat of the drink too well and burns my hand."

"I'm sure she would be pleased to do it for nothing. She gets little chance to work with fine metal and takes pleasure in good materials. What will you have her make from it?"

They had reached the door of the hanging hut. Ki set down her heavy bucket. She folded her mouth, her face thoughtful. "Almost, Haftor, you make me forget who I am, and when. I had the mug for a long time, and often thought of a hair comb for myself and a wrist piece for Sven. Now I've no use for either. My hair is bound back in widow's knots, and I shall not see that metal shine on Sven's arm. Almost, almost, you make me forget."

Haftor flushed unexpectedly at her words. A smile gentled his homely face. "Fetch the mug anyway, and bring it tonight to my sister's house. Have your hair comb, and a wrist piece to fit yourself. Surely you shall not wear widow's knots to the end of your days?"

She looked at him silently. She stooped and took a crystal on its line from her bucket. She reached to an empty spot on the pole and knotted the line about it. "I shall ask your sister to make me only the comb, and a wrist piece to fit herself. Or her brother, if she has no vanity for jewelry."

Haftor looked deep into Ki's eyes. Gentleness mellowed his face. "Ki, will not you tell me what troubles you today? A spattering of gossip, no matter how distasteful to you, could not pale your face this way."

Ki folded her mouth narrowly. She stooped to her bucket for a fresh crystal, took her time to hang it. Where was her mind today, to let her face so mirror her distress? Damn Harpies and everything to do wih them! She tried for a weary smile.

"I am but tired, Haftor, in a peculiar way. The odors of the marsh make my eyes sting and my nose run. They make my head pound until my ears are filled with the sound of a thousand bees humming. I do not think this life suits my body. I find myself longing for the coming of the Rite Master, so that you all may make your Rite. Then I can go on my way with a good conscience."

Haftor looked at the empty path behind him. He stepped inside the small hut, close to Ki. His eyes were darker in the dimness of the hut's interior. His voice was low and urgent.

"Go now, Ki. Go now!"

She stepped back from him, bewildered and frightened by his sudden intensity. He did not look completely sane, with his mouth set and eyes glowing so. She licked lips gone dry. "I cannot go now, Haftor, and keep my honor intact. I have given my word to Cora that I would stay. Would you have me break it?"

"Yes! I would. But you, I fear, will not." He shook his head and cast his eyes down. The fierceness seemed to ebb away. "For your sake, I hope the Rite Master hurries. But he is an old man, and he will not hasten his rounds. He travels from town to town in the valley, catechizing the children and presenting them to the Harpies. As he did to me once." Haftor's voice trailed away uncertainly, and he seemed lost for a moment in a memory. "Another month will find him with us."

Ki wondered what he had recalled. Had older memories haunted Haftor as memories of him haunted Ki now?

A jolt to Ki's ribs recalled her to the present. Vandien had stirred himself in his coverings to nudge her. Ki glanced up at the sky. No Harpy. And the sun was still high enough for them to travel yet a ways.

"What's the matter?"

"Tonight's camp." Vandien had settled back against the cuddy door, but he pointed a gloved hand.

Ki looked. She saw no more than a wide place in the trail. True, the rock there overhung the trail a bit and was free of blue ice. But it was bare to the sky, a bad place to have to defend.

"And if we push on past there—use up what daylight is left to us?" Ki asked over the wind.

Vandien shook his head slowly, not even bothering to straighten up on the seat.

"A narrower, more treacherous trail ahead, one best seen in full daylight. And no place to camp for the night, unless you want to light your fire on the trail before or behind us. Here at least you may unharness the team in a level spot and let them take shelter between the wagon and the cliff. Ahead, nothing."

Regretfully, Ki pulled the wagon up in the wide space. She wanted to flee from the Harpy. Hopeless. It had always been hopeless. Even at a dead run on level ground, the team could not outdistance that winged death. Ki prayed for strong winds as she moved to unharness the team. A bitter smile twisted her lips. Did she think that Keeva would hear one who had forsaken the Romni ways?

The rhythm of camp-making took over her mind. Rub the team, blanket the team, shake them out a double measure of grain. She leaned on Sigurd a moment, feeling and hearing the steady munching as his dull teeth ground the grain. The inevitability of her own death settled over her like a cloak. It seemed to make the wind muffled, to make the nasty fingers of the cold more impartial. It dulled the old fear that nibbled at the edges of her mind. It was coming for her, as she had long known it would. Now it would be soon, and the waiting would be over. Ki would be glad when the waiting was done. She was weaponless on an exposed ledge on a mountain face. Let death be mercifully swift for her. She wondered if she would struggle at all.

A grim humor settled over Ki. It was as Haftor had said: You needed the bitter edges of life to make it real, to let you taste what was still sweet. She hugged Sigurd's great shoulder impulsively. The beast veered away from her in surprise.

Six

VANDIEN had already kindled a small fire between the wagon and the bare cliff face. It winked at Ki in the gathering darkness. Vandien moved among Ki's things with sureness now, knowing where to seek for the kettle, the brewing herbs, the mugs. She started to go to the cuddy to gather the makings of the stew, then saw that he already had it beginning to bubble on the fire. She was torn between displeasure at his free ways with her possessions and relief that it would be ready to eat soon. Impulsively, she changed her pace, came up behind him silently over the snow. He poured tea steaming into a mug and turned to present it to her. "You've keen ears," she said. He shrugged and poured a mug of tea for himself. She watched him over the rim of her mug as she sipped. *Who the hell was he?* What fate had slipped him into her life, sandwiched between a late cargo and a Harpy bent on revenge? It did not seem at all fair that she must be burdened with him when there was already so much hanging over her. She watched him narrowly, seeing for the first time the precise way his hands moved as he did things, the smallness of his hands and feet that moved so economically to every task. Even in his unkempt state, there was an inborn tidiness about him that refused to be quenched.

He took the kettle of stew from the fire. Ki followed him as he carried it to the wagon seat, and then into the cuddy. Two bowls were set out on the small table.

"I saw no sense to eating in the wind," he explained as he poured two equal portions that left the kettle empty.

Ki took out hard traveler's bread from a cupboard to add to the stew in their bowls. They ate silently. Ki tried not to watch him. When the meal was finished, she pushed her bowl aside. Their body heat and the single candle had warmed the cuddy slightly. Vandien had pushed his hood back.

As they sat silent at the small table he seemed to become more and more uncomfortably aware of Ki's gaze. Before it, he seemed to withdraw deeper into himself, as if he could vanish by being still and silent. Ki tried to put her eyes elsewhere—on the toy horse on its shelf, on the handle of Sven's cupboard—only to find her eyes fleeing from her past to rest on the dark little man.

Vandien fidgeted. Reaching into his tunic pocket, under Sven's cloak, he drew out a fine, thin piece of cord. It was creamy white and silkily smooth as he drew it over his hands. He tied the ends of it together with a small, peculiar knot and then began to loop it in an intricate pattern over his fingers. Ki found her eyes drawn away from his face and to the moving string. She watched as his fingers looped the string about themselves, built patterns that faded and melted into other patterns. He glanced across at her from under thick eyelashes. She became aware of a small smile that hovered at the corners of his mouth.

"It's a story string," he said in reply to her unasked question. "Haven't you ever seen one before?"

Ki shook her head, watching his fingers deftly loop and throw the string about in melting shapes. He transferred a loop from the thumb to the finger of the other hand, made a pattern of diamonds, and now a shape of rectangles. With a sudden snap of his narrow hands it was a loop of soft string again. He untied his knot and passed it to Ki for her inspection.

"It seems like any other string," Ki observed, as she let it trail across her hands. She tugged it gently, feeling its limber strength. Vandien reached to snag it back from her loose fingers.

"Where I come from . . . on the other side of these mountains, and then a ways north . . . they are taught to all the children. From this string I have learned the history of my people, the genealogy of my family and of other families that touch mine, to say nothing of the doings of many heroes."

"From a string?" Ki asked, half in wonder, half scoffing.

"Here's a tree," Vandien said, and with a flicker of his fingers he held before her a tall triangle of string stretched on the fingers of both hands while four fingers of one hand held the rectangle that was its trunk. Another flash of his fingers, and the tree disappeared. "A star!" This took a moment of loop-

ings before he held up a five-pointed star on the fingers of one
hand. "The Hawk!" An abstract, graceful figure that suggested open wings. "My name!" This seemed to be two separate abstract figures, one on each hand, held up side by side for
Ki's inspection.

"Do the shapes form a sound, like the characters linked on
paper?"

Vandien shook his head. "We have that type of writing also
for things that must be recorded, sales of land, the pedigree of
a bull, public announcements—but these are older by far than
those symbols. No, this is *Van*," he nodded to his left hand,
"and this is *Dien*," with a nod to his right. "Vandien.
Myself."

"What does your name mean?" she asked him.

He shrugged at her question, his dark brows drawing a little
closer together in puzzlement. "It's a name, like any other,
given by my parents. No meaning."

"My father named me as the Romni do; making the name a
reason to remember the time of birth, 'Ki, Ki,' a bird called to
him on the morning I was born. And so I was Ki."

Vandien looked scandalized. "Among my people, that is
how we might name a horse or a dog. Not a Human. Your
name should bespeak who your parents were and the order of
your birth. I sang—croaked might be a better word—to you
of Sidris today. Her father was Risri, her mother Sidlin. She
was their first-born daughter, hence she was Sidris. You see?"

Ki shook her head. "I do not follow it."

"It is simple. If she had been the first-born son, she, uh,
he would have been Riscid. Their second-born daughter was
Linri, their second son is Rilin, and so on."

"And if they have more than two daughters?" Ki asked.
"What do they do when they've run out of names to share?"

"A Human's name does not run out, unless there is a time
when he had no forebears. For convenience, we use but the
first two parts of our names. I know my own to thirty-six forebears. There is more to it than that, of course, but the rest is
for the keepers of the genealogies. A girl adds to her own
name the entire name of her mother. A boy takes his
father's."

"Who could ever keep it all straight? And, more to the
point, who would want to?" Ki's tone was lightly mocking, but
Vandien's face went dark at her words.

"There are some to whom such things matter. They used to matter to me, once, but no more. It is, as you say, a silliness." He snapped the string free of his fingers and pocketed it. He rose to take the stacked dishes and clamber out of the cuddy with them. Ki wondered what had offended him. Her pleasant mood evaporated, leaving darkness inside her heart. She wondered at her own foolishness, to sit and talk on trivialities while death stalked her from the skies. She sat still, harking to the wind. *Blow long and hard,* she urged it.

Through the wind she could hear Vandien outside the cuddy, heard him speak to the team, felt the slight movement of the wagon as he put the dishes into their chest. Idly she wished she were alone tonight, to sort out her memories, to handle the good ones and set aside the bad ones. To look back on her days. Instead, she must deal with this peculiar dark-haired man, so foreign to her experience. He made Ki aware of him and drove Sven back into the shadows. She did not like the way he stung her out of her solitude, didn't like the way he made her ask questions and wonder. She didn't want to consider the way his body moved or guess the lively thoughts behind the movements of his features. She liked her silences. She missed her solitary routines.

Her fingers moved idly to her hair. Out of long habit, she let it down and combed her fingers through the brown strands until they lay flat and smooth down her back. Then, with the swiftness born of habit, she put it up again into her knots and weavings. She removed her outer cloak and spread it over the bedding. She was kicking off her boots when Vandien returned. She slammed the sliding door shut against the rising wind that tried to follow him. Without a word, he shook out his cloak and spread it over the bed. He began to remove his boots.

Ki sat staring. Cloakless and bent over, the arch of Vandien's neck was curved. A marking was on it, small, almost hidden under the hair that straggled there: Outstretched blue wings.

Ki's heart went cold. She met his gaze with stony eyes as he straightened. He looked at her, perplexed. Then his dark eyes fell, and he shifted his feet in embarrassment.

"When I am weary," he said softly, "there are subjects that come to my mind. Things that pain me. And when those subjects are touched upon, I become abrupt and rude, taking

offense where none is meant and forgetting where courtesy is
owed for hospitality shown."

He stood before her, seeming to wait. Words struggled in
Ki. Should she demand to know the meaning of the mark on
his neck? The candle flickered in the cuddy, the lighting was
uncertain. Was Vandien to be accused and suspected because
he had a peculiarly shaped birthmark? Her logic fought with
her wariness. Courtesy intervened when she realized that
Vandien was still standing before her, waiting.

"We are both tired," Ki said. The words were enough. He
sighed as she blew out the candle. There was less awkwardness
as they crawled under the covers, but more watchfulness on
Ki's part. He did not seem to notice. He stretched his body out
beside hers, full-length, yet he was careful not to let any touch
occur. He was still and silent except for one spell of coughing.
Yet Ki could not lose her awareness of him. Anger rose in her.
She was sick to death of her fears. Enough that she must watch
the skies all day for death. Now must she fear that the man
stretched beside her was a servant of the Harpies, an instru-
ment of their revenge? She cautioned herself that she must
wait and see. She would not let her hastiness hurt an innocent
man. She would never be guilty of that again. And yet she
chafed to know, to have her final encounter with the Harpy
above, to know what this man beside her was. But she must
wait. And waiting was the thing she was worst at. Her last few
days at Harper's Ford seemed to have been years in her life, to
have aged her as years on the road with Sven had not.

Her short knife chewed slowly through the tough stem. Already it needed sharpening again. A poorly forged tool, even
for this job. Ki squatted, seized the large orange fruit, and
lifted it. Moving carefully to avoid the plants that still bore rip-
ening fruit, she lugged the punker over to where the beaten
cart track wound through the field. She stacked it with the others. She stopped beside the pile, arching her back to stretch
her aching muscles in a new direction. About her the hills were
beginning to turn from greens to yellows. Leaves of birch were
yellow-veined. Alder would be scarlet soon. The summer was
dying. The Harp trees played a sadder song. Or was it the
humming of her ears?

Ki returned to the row, stooped to saw free another large
punker. So this was the life of the landed, she reflected bitter-

ly. Now she knew what it was to belong to the dirt under her feet. With a twinge of despair, she thought of her wagon gathering dust in the barn. Her heart yearned for the road. Soon, soon, she promised herself, wondering if she lied again. Soon.

She lugged the punker to join the others in the pile. She worked alone. Time had not brought her acceptance. There were still those in the family who would not concede that ignorance had brought about that disastrous rite. There were some who would never forgive her for shattering their ideals, even though Cora often told Ki that all was not as bad as they made it out. Ki still did not know what to make of Cora.

Why did she wish to keep Ki here, and go to such lengths to try to make her happy? Ki herself was willing to admit she was a good worker. She had nearly finished harvesting the field of punkers by herself. Rufus had wanted to put three workers on the field; Ki had done it alone in a single day. There was a simpler answer: Cora loved her as she said, and wished her to stay for that reason only. Ki grunted as she lifted a large punker. She hoped that was not the reason. For, then Cora might never be willing to let her go. And she hungered for the road. Here in the fields, she could not dream of Sven and her children, she could not pretend them here beside her. They had belonged on her wagon, by her fire at the close of the evening. Ki grieved because she could not grieve for them. Cora knew it. She would come upon Ki, silent at some task, and give her a nudge or a shake as she passed.

"Let them go," she would plead, a sorrowful look in her eyes. "We do not speak of our dead here, lest we draw them back to us from a better place. And what you are doing is worse than speaking. You clutch them to yourself. The Rite did not loose them from you, Ki. Now you must loose them on your own. Let them go, child. Begin to live your life again."

Then Cora would leave, hurrying to some task of her own. Ki envied her that bustle of life. She looked so purposeful, so certain of the importance of what she did. And lately she looked at Ki with more speculation in her eyes than before. Ki dreaded the moment when its purpose would be revealed. She did not wish to have anyone thinking of her, making decisions that included her. She only wanted to be on her road.

Ki watched her hands sawing at the stem. They were thinner now than they had ever been, but just as strong. The calluses were in new places now. Ki felt as if she were drying up all over, hardening in spots where once she had been soft. She did not mind. She just wished the process would hurry up. Maybe when she was completely dried and hard she would accept this new life. She might stop wondering hopelessly why she lacked the force of will to leave.

A shadow fell across her hands. Lars bent and took the punker from her.

"Must you always work so diligently?" he asked, laughing weakly. "You leave me no excuse to idle!"

Ki made a smile for him as she rose. "I didn't even hear the wagon come. We may have to make two trips with this field. It bore more heavily than the other."

"I didn't come on the wagon," Lars said. For the first time Ki took note of his appearance. His blond hair was still damp and curling at the ends. His yellow shirt was of a finer weave than usual, and it bloused over clean trousers. He wore his good boots, not his rough field clogs. Ki smiled in spite of herself. He smelled like Cora's herb water.

"What occasion makes such demands on you, Lars?" she asked teasingly. "You'd put to shame a Romni bridegroom. Will you ask Katya to bind back your hair this night?"

He gave her a long-suffering look and shook his head. "We've a guest, to arrive late this night. I don't know how you missed hearing of it. Cora sent me to fetch you. The punkers will keep. A night or two in the fields will not harm them. She knew you would want to be cleaned and freshened for the gathering."

Ki followed Lars as he lugged the punker over and deposited it on the top of her pile. Then she fell in beside him as they followed the cart path across the fields and back to the house. His hands swung as they strode along, once lightly brushing against Ki's.

"Who is this guest, so important that we must be scrubbed for him?"

"Cora has not told you?" Lars asked her with a sideways glance. "I am surprised. One that will lighten your heart a bit, I think. And, as I was the one to scold you so for your errors, I will take the happy chance of being the first to tell you good news. You took it sore-to-heart, Ki, when I told you what your Harpy emotions had taken from us. Afterwards I was disgusted with myself. What good had it served to tell you such things? And when my mother knew what I had said! She made my remorse the thicker with a number of names she had not called me since I was a thick-headed child of nine. To lay such a burden on your shoulders was not to my credit. But now we shall both be freed of guilt.''

"What are you saying?" Ki demanded. "Come to the point, Lars!" She found her heart beating strangely faster. It had rested heavily on her that she had denied the family the comforts they took from their religion. Disgusting and morbid as she might find their Rites, she had no reason to snatch them away. When Ki had felt the most oppressed by the passing of Harpy shadows overhead, when she had longed most for her wagon and the freedom of the road, she had reminded herself of what she had stolen from these people. She felt she owed them. Was Lars hinting that the debt was nearly paid?

"The Rite Master has come," he told her. "He has traveled far out of his road to come to us at this time of year. He makes ready the Rite of Cleansing. We shall renew our bonds with the Harpies! Do not stare at me so! I have not held back news from you. It was only a short time ago that my mother told me of his coming. No doubt you would have known also if you spoke to people instead of moping about the fields. For three days we will meditate and repent. On the fourth day he will work the Rite for us, to lift from our minds the poisons that separate us from the Harpies and to visit again their . . . their dead." Lars faltered at the last words, as if he touched too close to a wound. Ki's face did not change.

They walked on in silence. Lars's hard-soled boots thudded on the packed earth of the cart track. Ki's own softly shod feet made no sound. With the sweat of her earlier work drying on her back and neck, Ki began to feel the chill of the fall day. The light wind that blew had an edge to it. The autumn restlessness she knew of old settled on her. It stirred her like it stirred the water birds, the migrating herd animals. She had an urge to be moving, to be leaving behind the too-familiar fields here, to be leaving the Harpy-studded sky. She was thirsty for a cool newness. Soon she would return to her roads, to her old routes, go through towns where the stable folk remembered her team and called her by name. But just as her heart lifted, a darkness seemed to brush across her eyes. A Harpy had flown across the sun. A deadening doubt fell on her. She tried to shake it off. Indecision.

She felt the sweat-caked dirt about her ankles. Her feet inside her shoes would be filthy. Dirt was under her nails, ground into her skin. The land had seized her, left its mark upon her. It would never let her go. She could not tell them no.

Lars slipped a hand lightly under her elbow. "Must you look so glad at my news?" He gave her arm a shake. "Look out of your eyes, Ki! For too long you have worked alone. Your eyes look only inside you."

Ki lifted herself away from his touch, gentling her action with a smile. "When this old man and his rite are through, you will all be healed of the harm I have done you. My own healing must come from another source, I fear."

"Perhaps we must find another man and another rite to heal you," Lars countered.

Ki smiled, but did not understand his jest. Lars seemed to search her face and eyes for an answer to some question. They walked on, but Lars went more slowly, and finally stopped altogether. When Ki turned to face him to ask what was wrong, the strange look on his face stopped her. His eyes told her that he was going to ask something of her, something very difficult. Ki steeled herself.

"Will not you make the Rite with us, Ki? No one excludes you from us but yourself. The way you spoke just now, it is plain you have no thought for joining us in purification and atonement. Yet, all would welcome you."

Ki shook her head slowly. Her eyes were hard. "I have done nothing to be purified of; I have sinned no sin to atone for."

"No, of course you haven't. Don't take my words to mean that. But, for you to go through it might make you feel more at ease here. Every day you go off to a task and work at it alone. It isn't right."

"It's what I'm used to," Ki broke in. She didn't want Lars to speak any further. The truth rose up in her, burst from her lips with a strength she thought lost to her. "I don't want to join you. Please, don't look hurt. I would not hurt you any more than I have already. I have stayed on at Cora's request, bound by my own word foolishly given. I have lived your ways and tried to make them my own. But they are not. I have pulled weeds and gathered crystals, salted fish, and tanned hides. I've put my team to pulling a cart of manure across a field and used them to drag logs for Haftor to make into lumber. I've done all you asked me to. But there is no joy in it for me. Every day my life meshes more closely with those of a dozen others about me. I must do one task, or another task cannot be started. I must haul the logs, or the lumber cannot be sawed to build the new grain shed. I do not like it, Lars. With my wagon, it rests on me. I can fail no one but myself."

"What about Sven?" Lars asked bravely, bluntly. "You bound your life to Sven's, and then to the children as they came. They depended on you."

"And they lie together in a common grave because that dependency was misplaced!" Ki hissed fiercely. "Shall I let you lean on me, to fail you also?"

Lars faced her squarely. "No one asks you to let us lean on you. I invite you to enter our Rite, and to lean on me."

Ki put her hands to her face, to push back from her eyes the loose hair that had pulled from her widow's knots. Her hands smelled of dirt and punkers. Grit clung to her wet face when she wiped her hair back. Her words came cold and hard. "I can lean on no one. I cannot join your rite. I will not consort with Harpies, asking them to show me the faces of the ones they snatched bloodily away from me. Lars, you cannot ask that of me."

She watched his face. His blue eyes were softer than the skies above him. A pulse beat warmly at the base of his throat. Ki watched it jumping. "I cannot ask it of you, Ki. You are right. But I would rather ask that of you than what Cora will ask. I am sickened with anger at what you may meet tonight. I am shamed by necessity. I fear I know what you will choose. I have not the heart to ask it of you. Let Cora do this to you. I have no heart for it. In truth, I am too fond."

Lars walked away. Ki stared after him. When she followed, she took care not to catch up. Her heart was cold with trepidation. She was too heavy with her own pain to ask what pain she might have given him.

He was out of sight when she entered the common room. The room stirred painful memories for Ki. Here again was the long table pushed to the middle of the room, the empty benches waiting. A proud bowl of beaten silver cradled the year's last water lilies in a shining pool. Ki smelled savory odors of meat cooling and heard the noisy bustle in the kitchen. There would be many at this table tonight. Ki passed hastily through the room, down the hall to her own room.

The room she slept in now was a smaller, simpler one. Cora had moved her into it, hoping to put Ki more at ease in the house. Ki had tried to arrange it to her own tastes. She was not satisfied with the results. Her few garments hung on pegs on the wall. The single small window was left open and bare of draperies to let in what light and air it could. A shagdeer rug on the floor, Ki's own bedding on the narrow bedstead echoed the cuddy waiting in the shed to Cora. Ki did not see it so. She knew of no other way to arrange a room. A bare wooden stand beneath the window held a simple jug and bowl of blue earthenware. Lydia was pouring warm, scented water into the jug as Ki entered.

Ki started to scowl, then wiped it from her face. She would never become accustomed to it, never. To Lydia and Kurt fell the simple household tasks. They filled everyone's water jugs, shook and aired all the family bedding, shared the washing of all garments. Ki reminded herself that her privacy had not been violated. Lydia was but doing her task, as Ki had done hers in the punker field.

"Thank you. That smells lovely."

"I'll leave the extra pitcher of water," Lydia replied, setting it down gently on the stand. "Cora said you might want extra water tonight, in honor of our guest. Oh, when I washed your brown shift, there was a seam coming undone. I mended it with black—the closest match I have for it right now. Will that be all right?"

"Of course. Thank you. You needn't have done it, Lydia. I don't mind doing my own mending."

"I know. And I don't mind harvesting my own punkers. But it all goes better if we do our own tasks. Be easy with it, Ki. A person would think she had shamed you by doing any small task for you." With a smile and a shake of her head, Lydia hurried from the room. She would be busy tonight, preparing the house for a large group of people. Ki did not envy her.

When the door shut behind Lydia, Ki stripped off her garments, kicking free of her soft, low boots. She poured water into the basin, dipped a soft cloth in it. She began with her sweaty, dusty face and worked down her body past small, firm breasts that no longer served any useful function, over a flat, muscled belly that bore the rippling scars of two children's passage. She had to change the water in the basin twice as it became brown with suspended dust. The grime on her feet had been worked into her skin by the pressure of her boots. Ki scrubbed them, soaked them a bit, and scrubbed them again before her feet emerged small and pink as a child's.

The cool wind from the window had dried her body as she worked. Now she seated herself on the bed to unbind the complicated knots and weavings of her hair. Loosed, her brown mane fell nearly to the small of her back. She curried it thoroughly, listening to the soft ripping sound the brush made as it smoothed her hair and took the dust from it. When her hair finally swung smooth and shining, she bound it up swiftly again into widow's knots.

When her hair was a woven net that bounced against the back of her neck, Ki moved to the pegs where her clothing hung. The choice was not large. The simple brown shift was presentable. Lydia's skillful mending scarcely showed. Next to the shift was a pair of loose blue pantaloons and a gaily embroidered vest. This was acceptable wear by the mountains and on the other side of the range, but slightly scandalous in Harper's Ford. Beside it was the green shift with yellow flowers that Ki had worn the night of the Rite of Loosening. She had not touched it since. Now she let the fine weave of it slide over her fingers softly. She had refrained from wearing it lest it remind the others. She lifted it from the hook. They would be thinking of it tonight no matter what she wore. It might as well be the green gown. She slid it coolly over her head. It was still too long for her, even with the heavy sandals she strapped on her feet.

People had begun to gather in the common room. Most of them greeted Ki with a modicum of kindness. Some still nursed the psychic bruising she had given them. Holland was speaking quickly and softly to a woman who stood beside her nursing a child. Ki guessed what they spoke of. She deliberately walked over to them and touched one of the baby's rosy bare feet.

"Healthy as a little pig, isn't she?" Ki smiled hard at them both. The woman nodded hastily and turned to admire a nearby wall. Holland did not attempt to disguise her glare. Ki's smile curved a little deeper as she walked away.

"For shame!" muttered a low voice beside her. Ki turned quickly to find Haftor grinning behind his hand at her. He shook his head. "Shame on you for waiting so long, that is.

You should have begun to bait them a long time ago."

"To what end?" Ki asked curiously. Haftor's good humor gleamed through his homely face. Lamplight outlined the high cheekbones, glanced from his gleaming black hair. His dark blue eyes were full of merriment.

"To force them to deal with you. While they can gossip about you in corners, and you stroll by as unperturbed as a hunting cat, they have no reason to respect you. Or to change their minds about you. Give them a taste of your wit now and then. They'll either come to fear you and leave you alone, or recognize your worth and let you become one of the family."

Ki smiled in spite of herself. "You and Lars have had your heads together?"

Haftor knit his dark brows. "Lars? He doesn't indulge in long conversations with me. Saves them all up for you, I suppose."

"Meaning?" Ki asked bluntly.

"Meaning . . . nothing. Except that Lars seems to find himself more in your company than any of the rest of us do."

"That's Rufus's doing, I guess." Ki wondered where this strange turn of the conversation was taking them. "He told Lars to show me how to make myself useful. Lars has done so, giving me the same tasks he does himself. There's nothing strange about that."

"Nothing at all, Ki. As anyone with half an eye would see. Rufus would be a fool not to arrange it so."

Even as Ki tried to make sense of his remark, she felt a light touch on her sleeve. Lars smiled at them both.

"Speaking of Lars, here he is, to snatch you away for some doubtless important reason."

"Extremely important," Lars agreed blandly, ignoring the acid edge to Haftor's voice. Ki wondered what fey spirit had taken them both tonight. "My mother, Cora, requests that Ki come to her to meet our guest. You will agree to the importance of that, Haftor, will you not?"

"Certainly, Lars. In fact, I find it so urgent I shall escort Ki to your mother myself."

Ki moved lithely away just as Haftor would have possessed her arm. "I shall escort myself there, thank you. Whatever tussle you puppies have going, you had best leave me out of it." Ki moved swiftly away, leaving the two eyeing one another.

Cora was seated in a throne-like wooden chair to one side of the fireplace. On the opposite side of the hearth was a matching chair, empty. Ki moved to Cora's side with a smile.

"You sent for me?" Ki's eyes touched Cora's hair, glinting silvery from the fire's light, then fell on the worn hands folded idly in her lap. How strange to see Cora's hands still! Ki's heart went out to her, resting for a moment in Cora's quiet strength. If Ki had ever had a mother, she would have wanted her to be a woman like this, full of quietness inside however she might chatter on the surface, loaning her strength to any that might need it. Cora had constrained Ki to stay here; Ki disliked that act. Yet, she could not dislike the woman who had done it. In Cora's presence she felt that, for the moment, she could relax her grip on the reins, knowing that a woman fully as capable as herself was in charge. Ki could feel safe with Cora, for as long as their interests ran in the same direction.

Cora smiled up at her, reached to pat lightly at Ki's hand. "I wanted you to meet our guest. He's had to go to the back-house again. He's an old man, troubled by his stomach. Nils is his name. He has come from far to help us. Lars has told you this?"

Ki nodded and gathered her courage up. "Did Lars tell you that I would not enter into this rite? For, I am sure that idea came from you, not Lars."

"He told me," Cora admitted serenely. "And I told him that he had not asked you sweetly enough. He can have a charming tongue when he wills it, that boy of mine, but he will not always use it when I request him to. So, I suppose I must ask you myself. Ki, why will you not make this Rite with us? It would show the others that you have determined to make your home with us, to share our ways and enter our family fully."

"Then, I would be lying to them," Ki said firmly in a quiet voice. She and Cora both looked about the room, smiling at any who might mark their conversation. Lydia held up a wine glass to her, and Cora smiled and nodded. She came promptly to serve them red wine in ancient glasses. Cora complimented Lydia on the table flowers. Ki smiled and nodded her thanks to Lydia as she received her glass of wine. She held it, untasted, as Lydia moved away.

Cora sipped at hers and fixed bright dark eyes on Ki. "You do not wish to be one of us, do you?"

"I do not," Ki answered. "Though I thank you for the offer. Cora, I have stayed as you asked me. I have tried the life
you offered me. I cannot make it mine."

"The time of healing is not finished," Cora reminded her.

"I shall stay it out," conceded Ki. "But then I must be on
my way, with no hard thoughts between us, I pray. You will
let me go then, Cora."

It was Cora's turn to bow her head to Ki's will. She did so
with a slight slumping of her usually squared shoulders. Ki's
heart smote her. "I will let you go," Cora said. "If by then
you have found nothing here to hold you, I will let you go.
There will be no hard thoughts between us, but on my part
there will be regret. When I was a girl, Ki, I found a
wounded hawk, little more than a fledgling. I nursed it and
coddled it back to health. It rode about on my wrist and
fetched birds from the sky at my command. But I knew its
heart was not in it. So, to my father's disgust, I one day set it
free. I know how to let things go, Ki. Do you?"

Ki looked at her hard, uncertain of the question. Before she
could speak, Cora was nodding a greeting to an old man
who was settling himself in the chair opposite.

Ki marveled at him. His smooth white hair was knotted at
the base of his neck in the old way. His eyes were winter-blue
under finely drawn white brows. The rest of his features were
equally precise—the straight nose, the small mouth. He
looked like a carefully preserved statue of an earlier type of
Human, a man whose muscles were not nearly so important as
his mind. He was slight of build, coming little higher than Ki's
shoulders. Age had stooped him, making his narrow shoulders
curl toward his chest. And yet, despite his small build, he had a
carriage of power. Ki dipped her head to him instinctively.

"Nils, I present to you Ki, my daughter chosen by Sven."

The old man sat calmly, nodding at Ki. "I've come to undo
your mischief, Ki. What do you think of that?"

Nils spoke as if she were ten seasons old. Ki refused to take
offense. "I welcome you here as no other could. I see you as
the key to my freedom, old man."

Cora frowned at Ki's rough form of address, but the old
man put his head back and laughed. He had small, even teeth
and a laugh that seemed bottomless. The room about
them quieted as attention fixed on Ki and Nils. Ki's ears
burned.

"I feared an adversary here," Nils said loudly to Cora. "You warned me of a spirit that had wrested control from you during a Rite. I thought to find bitterness, anger, and a sly mind. Instead, I have this puppy telling me to do my best to put things to rights; she will be grateful. Ki, you make an old man young again."

The room had begun to buzz about them. Ki wondered at Nils's motives. His little blue eyes gleamed bright as a ferret's. They seized Ki in their gaze, and he gave a barely perceptible nod.

"I claim your daughter's arm to help me to the table, Cora," Nils announced. Ki stepped to his side uneasily. Never had she seen an old man in less need of physical assistance. Yet he gripped her arm hard above the elbow, and put enough weight on it that her body was forced to sway close, her head above his. He took small, slow steps, as if he found walking a labor.

"You're a bright one," he whispered as Ki helped him to the table. "Hiding from you would do my purpose more harm than good. Cora is right. I must tell you. You'll be in for a rough time of it tonight. You've scared these people half to death. To rejoin them to their Harpies, I must unscare them. I must make you appear less formidable, more of an incompetent child and less of a strong counterspirit. You could resist me in this. You could stand firm and young and strong, making a mockery of their beliefs, forcing us to see the uglier side of that race that has befriended us. Or you can let me make a mockery of you, belittle you, turn you from the specter in the corner to the shadow under the bed. Which will you?"

Ki thought rapidly as she drew out the old man's chair for him. "And if I choose to withdraw completely? I have already told Cora that I will not join you in this rite. What if I should seek the privacy of my room?"

"The fears these people have built up will stay with them, daunting them until the end of their days. My rite will be powerless against it. No one will again see their dead. There will be no more Rites of Loosening. One more rhythm will pass out of their lives, and they will be the poorer."

Ki gently pushed the chair toward the table. She curbed the pride that rose in her. She had said she wished to make amends. So this is what it would take. "Do your worst, old

man," she replied. Nils chuckled and sent her a bright glance.
"Remember your resolve, girl. You'll need it."

Ki stepped back from the table, uncertain of where to place
herself. She looked to Cora. The glance Cora shot her
pleaded. For what? Then, as Lars moved to silently escort Ki
to a seat far down the table, away from the adults and people
of import, Ki understood. Nils had primed Cora to what must
be done. Cora, ruthless as a wolf when her family was threatened, had taken the necessary action.

Others were moving into their places about the table. Kurt,
Rufus's eldest son, took a seat beside Ki. He glanced at her,
abashed to find her seated so closely, and then looked away.
Edward took the chair on the other side of her, and other children filed from across the room to fill in the empty places. Ki
sat gravely, her dark head raised above theirs, looking up the
table to where Haftor, Lars, Lydia, and the others were being
seated. Haftor stared down the table to where Ki sat. The
muscles of his jaw clenched, and he spoke some short, angry
words to his sister seated beside him. Embarrassed, Marna
hushed him. Haftor's dark blue eyes met Ki's in a pledge of
loyalty. Ever so slightly, Ki shook her head. She hoped he understood the message. Lars, Rufus, and Cora did not even
look her way. Their attention was fastened on Nils, as was everyone's. The little girl across the table from Ki giggled nervously. Her seating was so inappropriate that even the youngest
child was aware of it. Ki took a slow, deep breath and turned
her eyes to Nils.

Nils did not need to make any gesture to gain the full attention of the table. He simply began to speak.

"I have come to you here, at Cora's request, to repair a rift
between you and the Harpies of Harper's Ford. We shall not
speak tonight of ignorance or pettiness." Ki's face reddened.
Haftor's knuckles showed white on the edge of the table. "I
am not here to instruct you in what you already know. You
have been raised to certain ideals. You have enjoyed the com-
panionship of beings better than ourselves, creatures closer to
the Ultimate. But your regard for them has been soiled, your
image of them spattered with the mud-throwing of a hurt and
angry mind. You were wise. You did not go to the Harpies and
defile their gifts to you by exposing them to these unfitting sen-
timents pressed upon your unwilling minds. You have chosen
to wait, for atonement and reconciliation. You will return to

the Harpies as unsoiled as when, in childhood, you made your first encounters. Tonight we begin."

Nils paused. It seemed to Ki that he paused so that every person at the table could shoot her at least one look. She read every conceivable emotion in them. From Cora, a plea for understanding. Rufus was cold, Nils knowing. From Holland came enmity and a thirst for revenge. Marna's was wonder, Haftor's a grim sympathy and an unreadable promise. Lars's eyes were hooded, careful blanks. But his mouth was small as a stricken child's.

"Tonight we eat together," Nils reclaimed their attention. "We talk, we drink, we speak no words of sadness or misfortune. By each plate Cora has placed a bit of dried kisha fruit wrapped in toi leaves. Take it with you tonight. Chew it slowly before you sleep, and think as you chew it of pleasant memories of happy intercourse with the Harpies. It will help you to recall those meetings in detail, and the feelings of peace and wholeness they gave you. Now, let us eat and speak to one another as if this misfortune had never befallen you."

Nils fell silent. Basins and platters began to be passed at the higher part of the table, and the murmur of polite voices rose. Around Ki the children were silent, waiting anxiously for the dishes to work down the table to them. Ki ate, as the children did, whatever the adults had left to be passed. The children, warned, no doubt, to be on their best manners, spoke little. Ki was at a loss. She could not pretend to be interested in their short comments on the food, and she would not supervise their feeding. Young Edward dropped a piece of meat, retrieved it calmly from the floor, and ate it. Ki pursed her mouth and glanced up-table. Hastily she returned her eyes to her plate.

Nils had effectively drawn out her claws. For the first time since the Rite of Loosening, people were looking at her openly. Nils, by placing her far down the table, had made her an appropriate topic for conversation. He had told them all not to dwell on that mangled Rite of Loosening. Ki guessed that they had found other topics. She ate slowly, in small bites, keeping her head bowed and her eyes on her food. She tried not to care that it made her look like a guilty child to sit so while her "elders" discussed her. She marked the absence of Haftor's deep voice in the conversation. She could hear other voices, but not enough of the softly spoken words to make sense. Only enough to sting. "Romni" she picked out several times, and the phrase "Sven too young" once.

Ki's mind cast about, traveled back through the years. Rufus knelt in the yard, blood streaming from his nose, with Sven towering above him, outraged and weeping in frustration. Lars was a white-faced little boy peering from the door. Ki had been sixteen then, and Aethan a year dead. She had wanted to flee back to the shelter of her wagon, to whip up the tired old team and disappear from Harper's Ford forever. But Cora had been standing in the bright sunlight, wiping earth from her hands, demanding to know what went on. And Sven, a fool in his righteousness, told her.

"I said to him that Ki may stay her wagon in our fields, in the fields that will come to me when I am a full man. I say she may, for I am decided that we will be joined together. He says I let her stay because she pays me in the coin that Romni girls love best to give away. So I struck him. I will strike him again if he tries to rise before he apologizes to her."

Cora had not only made Rufus apologize, but she had forced Ki to eat inside, at the table beside them. Ki had hated her for it at that moment, not understanding why she did it, and not wanting to. This meal was like to that one, with emotions simmering but not voiced to Ki. But here was no Sven to press her hand under the table, to put the choicest bits before her. Seven months later Sven had attained his manhood, claimed his lands, and taken Ki to his bed. He had been young for it, and Ki scandalously so. All talked of the outlandish joining-gifts he gave her. Sigurd and Sigmund were then gray three-year-olds, scarcely broken to pull, nervously prancing at the ends of the new lead ropes that Sven proudly placed in Ki's hands. And their bed had been in the front of a new wagon, built by Sven's hands with the best materials he could muster. He had painted it blue, with apple blossoms about the windows and cuddy door.

Cora had tried to dissuade Sven from making the joining formal, Rufus had mocked him, and Lars had been fascinated by his older brother's daring in bringing this wild road woman to their home. But when Cora had seen that Sven was not to be budged, that he would leave with Ki forever, she had yielded graciously, recognized their agreement formally, and made her tribute to the Harpies in their honor.

So, let them discuss it yet one more time, Ki whispered to herself as she ate. Let them rake and sort the facts, commiserate with Cora over this outsider forced into her home, over the waste of a fine son who could have joined farm lands or timbered country. Ki felt only tired. But then a sudden wail of loneliness snaked up in her, so strong that Ki wondered if she had cried out loud. Sven, Sven, gentle of hand, always giving her too much, giving to her before she thought to ask, always thinking of her, making her way smooth before her. Sven, his wide hands bloody as he received his son from her body; Sven, sunlight on his face, making him squint as he rode beside the wagon; Sven, firelight on his shoulders and back as they made love beside the fire while the children slept safely within the wagon.

In the wake of her silent agony came rage. Sven would never have permitted this to be done to her. Why did she sit here humbly through this insane meal? Why sympathize with their ridiculous need to cozen themselves with images of their dead renewed by Harpy magic? A surge of angry strength went through Ki. She wanted to rise suddenly, to send her chair flying, to sweep from the table the dishes and food. Her darting angry eyes crashed into Cora's agonized look. Cora knew of her internal tempest. Knew it and feared it. Ki felt the power surge within her. She held it all in her hands.

Strong hands pressed down on her shoulders.

"I've finished all I can eat of this meal. And I've not seen you touch a bite for some minutes. Won't you take a piece of fruit to finish on and walk outside into the cool with me?"

Ki had never heard Haftor's voice more tender. She looked up into eyes that seemed to suffer her humiliation as keenly as she did. She began to rise, then checked herself. She looked to Nils.

It irritated Ki that others might interpret her glance as requesting permission. Cora also looked to Nils, who muttered something to her, and Cora sent Ki the barest of nods. Ki rose, wondering at the wounded look that Lars sent her. Haftor leaned past her to select two perfruits from a bowl on the table. He presented her with one, and then followed her as she moved to the door.

Outside she found a smoky autumn night. The smells in the air told Ki that the leaves were loosening their holds on the trees. Soon they would carpet the ground of this river valley with yellow birch and cottonwood leaves, with here and there a sprinkling of red alder. The ground would grow hard with frost, and the wagon roads would be very good to ride on early in the morning, before thaws could soften them to muck. Ki wondered how soon she would be on those roads. Cora had promised to release her as soon as the healing was done. Ki would have to speak to her privately. Would she be able to leave in three days when this Rite of Atonement was over? Or must she wait until they had actually paid their Harpy visits and been satisfied? Ki bit deep into her perfruit.

"It's bitter," Haftor said in a low voice beside her. She had almost forgotten him. She shook her head in denial.

"Mine's sweet," she contradicted, holding it out so that he might sample it also.

"It's not the fruit I was speaking of. Ki, why did you endure that dinner tonight?"

Ki bit the perfruit again, chewed slowly. She did not know how to answer him. If she confided to Haftor her true reasons, would that negate this rite for him? Would it jeopardize her freedom to leave? "It was Cora's will," she ventured.

"Cora's will!" Haftor snorted. He spit the pit of his fruit across the darkened yard. "So they will tame you, make you meek for the good of the family? It's as fitting as putting a deer to the plow."

"It . . . . it isn't what it seems, Haftor."

"It never is, Ki. Not what it seems to me, nor what it seems to you. Take to your road tonight, Ki. I'll help you harness the team and provision your wagon from my own larder. Leave now, while their tongues wag over you. I'll speak not a word of your road to anyone. And I know a way that none would guess. Go while you can. My father did. Sven did. This is not a good place for you."

"What of you?" Ki asked, puzzled. It was the second time Haftor had voiced these feelings.

Haftor laughed a small, hard laugh. "Me? I'm a coward. Sven refused to ever visit the Harpies. Did Cora ever tell you that? I think not. She felt it keenly that he would not go with her to meet the grandparents that died before his birth, that he did not visit his dead father. Sven was willful, even as a boy. I always wished for his courage. A visit to the Harpies cannot be forced, you know. Sven never went. So he was really alive, just as he is really dead now."

Ki averted her face from the hardness of his words, but Haftor boldly seized her shoulders, turned her back to face him.

"It's like a poison, Ki. No, not a poison. It's . . . when you have it, you feel you would die without it. Only since your rebellion made me stop going have I seen it. There are others that know it now, too, I'll wager, though few will speak it to Cora's face. Do you think many of them will return to the Harpies, Rite or no Rite? They have been coming to life, Ki, these last few weeks, and finding it precious. It's becoming real for them. For some it is heady. Rufus has found that he runs the holdings well, even when he cannot go to his father for advice on a field or the selection of a bull. Lydia holds her head high at last, finally freed of her mother's nagging tongue, that had belittled her for seven years beyond her deathbed. And Lars. Poor Lars has discovered that he has a heart that must be joined, as well as a body and lands. You've put the bitter edges back on our lives, and now we see the sweet ones. You've awakened me from a dream that has lasted sixteen years, since first they brought me here, and Cora, to comfort me in my orphanhood, took me to the Harpies to see my father again. With that visit, I was bound. How could I ever leave the one place in the world where my father was still alive to me? And yet . . ." Haftor struggled a moment. "She never realized what she did to me. She thinks I have forgotten how it was. I have not. I do not hate her, Ki. But I can never love myself as once I did. The things I did at her bidding, the things I accepted . . ." Haftor shook his head as his voice trailed off. He coughed, clearing his throat.

"Ki, Cora asked you to make this Rite, did she not? She seeks to lure you to the Harpies. Answer me this, Ki. If you could embrace Sven again, could cuddle Rissa's warm little body against you, tweak young Lars's nose for his nonsense . . . would you ever leave Harper's Ford?"

Haftor's eyes were dark holes in a white face inches from Ki's own. The darkness was cold about her. The lonely wail that had sounded inside her echoed again through her. To have them back, to hold and be held, to feel Sven's warm breath on her face.

"Bones," said Haftor. "Bones and meat nibbled by worms. But the Harpies dress it anew, sell it to you for more meat, and direct your life to their best advantage. 'Build up your flocks,

Rufus.' So your father tells you. Harpies are ever hungry. Open more land to pasture. Bring in more cattle. Why waste your time on sheep? A calf is bigger than a lamb, more satisfying to a Harpy's hunger."

Ki's heart thudded. She wrested herself free of Haftor's grip, then stepped away from him.

"Cora would not do this if that were true."

"Cora would never do a thing this evil," Haftor agreed. "If she *knew* how evil it was. But she is old, and she has never known any other way. Shall she deny it, admit that when she dies a few years hence she will be truly dead?" It might have been a sob that caught Haftor's words in his throat. "Who among us can resist such pretty lies? I don't believe in myself. I don't believe in your will, either, Ki. So I tell you to go. Go now as I would go myself, were I a stronger man."

"I gave Cora my word." Each word dropped from Ki's mouth like an ice-covered stone. "I cannot go yet."

"Then, you will never go." Haftor's voice fell. "I waste my words, and the courage to tell you to go has been used up. If I left Harper's Ford, I would have to be responsible for my own life. I could not blame my decisions on my father's ghost. I would have to answer for all I did, and for all I did not do. So Ki will stay. I cannot say it makes me sorry. I should miss you sorely and grieve at your leaving, even as I shouted to hurry your team into the dark."

He rubbed his face with both hands as if he were awakening from a long sleep. He stretched wide, and then made a grab at his belt pouch.

"I had forgotten. Marna is too shy, so she sends me back to you." His fingers fumbled clumsily at his pouch in the dark. There was a glint of moonlight in them.

"A silver comb to hold back your hair. And a wrist piece."

Ki took the exquisitely worked silver from his hands. It was warm with his body heat. The comb had been worked into a symmetrical, branching vine. Ki held it to the light that escaped around the door, shifting it to watch the silver shine in her hands. The wrist piece was more massive, like a forked bolt of lightning twisted into a curve. Ki hefted them both in her hands.

"I've an expert touch at judging weights, Haftor. The full weight of my silver cup is still in these two pieces. Marna has taken nothing for herself."

"She would not. She took all her pleasure in the making, indulging her fancy for design as usually she cannot."

"Yet one of the joys of creating is in seeing the thing you have made enjoyed, every day." Ki bobbed her head to kiss the silver wrist piece. Then she caught Haftor's thick wrist and deftly imprisoned it in the silver's curve. He shook his head and tried to draw it from his arm, but Ki held it there firmly.

"It's an old Romni trick. A good one. If you give me back this gift, you are returning my love to me as something also you will not take."

"That was the kiss?"

Ki nodded. It felt good to smile, good to give freely again. She wondered that she had not done it in so long.

"Then you have trapped me into accepting it," Haftor conceded.

"As I intended. And I hope it will remind you and Marna of me after I am gone. For, go I shall, Haftor. You will see."

A rectangle of light opened in the night. Edward came pattering out onto the porch.

"Ki!" he called imperatively. "Nils bids you to come that he may wish you good evening."

"I come," Ki replied. Edward remained standing on the porch, staring at her. Ki shook her head resignedly at Haftor and followed the child back into the house. She heard Haftor's boots come behind her.

The room was dazzling after the night, the mumble of voices an assault after the quiet of the porch. The eternal humming in Ki's ears rose suddenly to match it. Edward threaded his way between knots of talking people to where Nils still sat alone at the head of the table. Nils dismissed the child and nodded Ki to a seat beside him. Ki seated herself, pushing aside used plates and utensils to make a place to rest her elbows.

"Well, old man?" she addressed him directly.

Nils chuckled. "You did very well. No, do not smile at me. Keep your eyes down on the table as if taking an instruction. I congratulate you on your will. Cora thought that surely your pride would send you from that seat. And you left with that young man at a perfect moment. You are a woman among them again, one who can be wrong, one who can be gossiped about and courted by men, and even one who can indiscreetly leave a dinner gathering to be alone with a man."

Ki hissed at the insulting import of his words, but Nils's

laughter covered the sound. "You did not plan it so, then? No matter. It still set the table to buzzing and speeded up my work immeasurably. And that pretty comb in your hand will set the tongues to wagging all the more merrily." He laughed again at her discomfort.

Ki raised her lowered eyes to pierce the old man with coldness and contempt. Nils snorted at her and shook his head, letting his own contempt show. "Go to bed, Ki. You are of the ones that cannot be saved. You will ever prize the freedom and honor of one over the good of all. You will never learn by experience. Why Cora seeks to keep you here, I do not know. You will spoil them all with your poison, like a piece of rotting meat thrown into a clean spring." His old hand angrily waved her away with the gesture one would use to flick away an annoying insect. But even as Ki scraped her chair back, the old hand seized her wrist in a grip of iron.

"What will you do now, Ki? Will you work to undo what we have wrought at this dinner tonight?"

A quick twist of Ki's wrist freed it from his grip. "You have said it yourself, old man. I value my honor as one over what may be the good of all. My word was given. I will not go back on it. I will let you make this rite. But I do not think it will be as effective as you hope it will be."

Ki stormed away to the privacy of her own room. All marked her passage, none thought to impede it. But Rufus's quick eyes flicked to her as she passed. He swayed forward from where he leaned beside the hearth. He gave Lars a rough shove with his elbow. Lars glared at him, annoyed at having his morose thoughts so disturbed. Ki could not catch the words, but she saw Lars scowl and redden. She hastened to her room.

Ki frowned into the darkness. Sent to bed like a naughty child after being humiliated. Defiance and anger blazed up in her, hotter than any she had felt on that night long ago. A sudden hatred for Nils and all he stood for ripped through her. She should have fought him then, should have ripped to shreds the fabric he sought to weave. Slowly, she sat up in the darkness of the cuddy. She paid no heed to the cold that stroked her as the covers slid away from her body.

She settled on an elbow and stared down at Vandien. His face was a mask. Hollows full of shadows marked his eyes. His body was a mound under the covers. Those many years ago, Ki had been paralyzed by indecision, had been made a game piece in ruthless hands. But no longer was that so. *She* would be the one now to take the actions, shape the circumstances. If Vandien was in league with the Harpies . . . She growled soundlessly in the darkness. She could kill him now, put that suspicion to rest. It would be an easy task to cut his throat now as he slept, to drag the body from the cuddy and leave it beside the frozen trail. If he were the vagabond he claimed to be, no one would miss him. And if he were the Harpy's servant, she would have struck first to even the odds.

His chest rose and fell hypnotically under the shagdeer cover. She did not reach for her knife in the darkness. Instead, she sank slowly down beside him once more, entering again the warmth their bodies created under the coverings. There was a hoarseness to his breathing; he coughed lightly in his sleep. Ki closed her eyes tightly against the sudden sting of tears. The vulnerable eggs of the Harpies came to her mind. It was the same. No matter what future evil the man might hold for her, she could not strike in this manner. She would be wary, but not rash. She would remember.

She tried to be coldly logical. She listed her doubts. What chance had sent him to attack her that night by her fire? What were the odds of meeting a man in such a desolate place, a man marked with a sign of spread wings. He had precious little to recommend him. And yet . . .

Ki eased deeper into the bedding. She let her eyes trace the lines of his nose and mouth. She could see those bearded lips smiling, tossing quick mocking words at her. She liked his hands holding a mug or weaving stories on his ridiculous string. There was the way his stride matched hers as they tromped before the horses, the easy way he had fit himself to her life. An old feeling stirred in Ki, one so long-unused that for a moment she did not identify it. And when she did she felt only disgust for her own fickleness. She doused her thoughts, flopping over to put her back to Vandien. She closed her eyes and did not stir again.

Vandien lay silent, staring at the ceiling of the cuddy. He wondered.

SEVEN

Ki awoke to the beginning of gray daylight. In the cool air, her memories and dreams of last night came swirling back to her, mingled to incoherence. She flinched at her own emotionalism. She pushed the covers back experimentally. The cold touched her and she slid silently from the sleeping platform to hastily pull on her outer garments. Vandien slept on, an arm flung over his face. Ki dragged the cuddy door open. It slid stiffly.

The wind had ceased in the night. Snow was blown up against the wheels of the wagon, was smeared across the wagon seat. But now all was still and calm, and the cold pressed down harder than ever. The arched sky was a far and pale blue. Empty. Ki scanned it from the cuddy door, then climbed out on the seat to stand on it and survey the whole sky. Pure it was, no clouds, no far dark wings.

She breathed in relief. Then her eyes fell on the gray huddle of horsehide in the snow, the crumpled fallen shapes. "Damn!" she screamed, and leapt down to run to them. With a lunge and a snort, the horses rose, shying away from her sudden movement. Ki laughed in relief. They had been sleeping, legs folded beneath them for warmth. She called them back with gentle words and a handful of grain. They came, shy at first, then eagerly, to munch from her hands. She slid their blankets off and led them to the traces. She harnessed them quickly.

Some time in the night an iron determination had been born in her. She would be on her way, right now, to conquer this pass and take her freight through. Woe betide any Harpy that tried to bar her way. Or any man. She heaped the team's blankets about her on the seat, wondering if it could get any colder.

The wind had erased the wagon tracks behind. Before her the trail wound across the face of the mountain, rippling with tiny low drifts. It would give the team no problems. Ki stretched, feeling her shoulders pop and crackle. She started the team. The wheels rolled almost silently, cutting their narrow grooves through the white snow. The team needed little guidance. On one side of the trail, the ground dropped away abruptly. On the other, the bare stone reared up.

Ki heard the cuddy door slide open behind her. She turned quickly to face Vandien as he emerged, blinking at the snow-brightness and rubbing his face. "By noon today we shall pass the Sisters," he said with satisfaction. He began coughing, shaking with the effort it demanded. He settled down hastily on the seat beside her, tugging at the blankets and arranging them about like a nest. When he was settled and had his breath, he pointed a hand ahead to where the trail seemed to go off into empty space. "Around that bend of the mountain, and we shall be able to see the Sisters. Though, from this close they won't look like anything more than a rise of black rock on the cliff face. Once we're past the Sisters, we travel a short way more across the face of this mountain. Then the trail begins to take us around the side of the mountain, and down. I shall be glad to see the other side of this pass." He whistled tunelessly for a moment. "Hungry?" he asked Ki suddenly.

She nodded, and he dove back into the cuddy. She could hear him opening cupboards and rummaging in drawers. Ki called back, "There's cheese wrapped in cloth on the shelf above the window."

He pushed the laden platter out onto the seat before him. He had heaped it with chunks of cheese, slices of sausage, and two pieces of hard bread. It was all cold, making it harder to chew. Ki ate absentmindedly, one eye on her team and one on the trail ahead. The sharp curve Vandien had pointed out to her was an illusion. As they approached it, Ki found the bend was gradual, following the rounded flank of the mountain. Around the bend the snow began to grow perceptibly deeper with every turn of the wheels. Here the wind had not swept the snow from the trail but had heaped and packed it on the ledge. The grays plowed through it gamely, but Ki felt growing apprehension. All morning she had marveled at the good fortune that had given her a road clean of snow and a sky clean of Harpies. Now she decided that the Harpy knew this pass, and would wait until she was mired in snow before he struck. Ki set her teeth. She squinted her eyes against the snow's brightness.

Her face felt stiff, her nose was prickly with cold, her eyelashes clung together when she blinked. The deep cold, the heaped snow, and a Harpy overhead. Ki spurred herself with her own desperation.

The snow was the worst right now. The team could barely lift their heavy hooves clear of it to plunge into the snow ahead. With every step it grew deeper. The tall wheels began to stick and jerk, and Ki could hear the brushing of the snow as the wagon bed passed over it. Soon the wheels were sliding as much as they were rolling. The team floundered and bucked along, no longer pulling smoothly as a team but seesawing the wagon along as best they could. Ki halted them, and steam rose from their huge bodies in whirling eddies.

"The Sisters!" Vandien's voice was muffled. He had pulled his hood up as far as it would go and held it mostly closed across his lower face. Ki looked up.

They loomed ahead over the trail. Soon the wagon would pass directly under them. As Vandien had said, they were no longer the two embracing women they had appeared several days ago from far down the mountainside. Now they were a slight outcropping of shiny black stone towering high over Ki's head. The snow reached nearly to the base of them. A chill not of cold swept Ki as she looked up at them. They brooded above her, perfect in their endurance and vigilance, guarding their pass eternally. Watchfulness—that was the emotion they conjured in Ki now. None of the beauty and love she had glimpsed below shivered through her. She dreaded passing under their close scrutiny. She sensed the rightness of Vandien's anxiety to be past them, to be going down the other side of the pass.

Ki started her team again. They had gone but a handful of paces before both horses stumbled. They recovered swiftly, but only by stepping high to get their front hooves onto a hidden ledge before them. Ki watched in some surprise as the grays struggled onto the higher ground, where the snow was shallower. The harness creaked with the unusual strain of having the team on a higher level than the wagon. Then the wheels hit with a jolt, jamming against the hidden ridge of ice under the snow. The team jerked back, nearly snapping the harness. Vandien clutched at the seat and Ki with a surprised yell.

"Why didn't you warn me this part of the trail was uneven?" she snarled at him as she held in the confused team.

"In summer, the trail through this pass is smooth and flat as a causeway. I've no idea what we've struck."

They looked at one another for a moment, then both climbed cautiously down from the wagon and waded forward through the snow. Ki bent down to sweep and dig snow away from before the wheels. Ice. Solid ice, a ridge of it, rose in the trail. Ki frowned down at it and scanned the cliff face above them, looking for some sign of a runoff that would explain the ice. There was none. But Vandien cursed from the other side of the team.

"Snow serpent!" He spat sourly. "It must have come up from the other side of the pass, then doubled back for some reason. Probably for the express purpose of leaving this ridge here to block us. The gods spit upon my destiny."

Ki did not answer. She considered the obstacle. Even under the snow that had masked it, it was impressive. The step up the grays had taken was as high as Ki's knee. The horses shifted uncomfortably in the harness that dragged back and down at them.

"We shall have to somehow chop a ramp in it, so the grays can pull the wagon up onto it."

"And down the other side with a jolt!" Vandien added savagely. "This is the track of a big serpent, Ki. It has ruined the trail ahead of us. This rise of ice here is only the beginning. If it has slithered back and forth across the trail, we can look forward to humping up and down from here to the other side of the mountains. And if it has traveled straight, you will find that it has left a ridge of ice on one side of the trail or the other. Do you fancy riding along with one set of wheels perched up on that ridge while the other side of the wagon sticks and jerks in the deep snow?"

Ki did not reply. She waded back through the snow to the wagon to fetch the horses' blankets and her firewood hatchet. Even her stubbornness had to recognize the ridiculously small tool she had to use for such a job. This would take time.

She unhooked the team from the wagon, leaving their harness on them. She took their blankets and her own worn ones and spread them over the horses. Best not to leave them standing in this cold unblanketed after they had worked and steamed all morning. A measure of grain bought the team's patience. Vandien watched Ki in disbelief. Ki walked ahead of her team for a few paces until she suddenly stepped off into snow that rose to her hips. The team watched her curiously as she wallowed and fought her way back up onto the ridge. "And a ramp down," she said drily.

"You're mad. You're absolutely mad, woman. You still think to force this wagon through? There, she nods! I call the gods to witness that she nods!"

Ki ignored him. She moved back, hatchet in hand, and began to kick and stomp the loose snow away from the front of the wheels. On the box, Vandien was speaking softly in a tongue she did not recognize, but the flavor of the curses still came through. She paused to admire his fluency and then went on doggedly with her task.

The hatchet bit into the ice, but not deeply. The size of the chips made Ki at first despair, and then increase her speed. She heard Vandien climb off the wagon. She ventured a look at him. He glared at her ferociously, and then bent over to begin sweeping snow and ice away. They did not discuss the arrangement, but tacitly began to take turns with the hatchet. Ki chopped with it for a while, then passed it to Vandien while she cleared her chips away. While she waited for him to pass it back, she scanned the chill blue skies.

The sun was overhead when Ki hooked the team to the wagon again. The ramps they had cut were steep. The team hunched down and all but crawled on their knees as they tried to get the tall wheels started up the incline. Ki was at their heads, tugging and encouraging. Vandien went around to the rear of the wagon to add his puny strength to that of the grays. The team pulled, eyes rolling, nostrils flaring, heaving against the harness. Then Ki halted them, petting and gentling them down, and had them try again. She had lost count of their efforts when, suddenly, incredibly, the wagon moved forward. She didn't dare let them relax, but urged them on swiftly, building up momentum so that the rear wheels stuck for only a second before they, too, came sliding and turning up the ramp. Ki halted the blowing team.

"We're up!" she called. She ran to the back of the wagon to be sure it was safely up on the ridge. Vandien stood in the deep snow they had just emerged from. His arms were folded on his chest. He looked triumphant and challenging. Behind him in the snow were three sacks of salt and the remaining load of grain sacks. Ki spun, unbelieving, to stare at the back of her empty wagon. Now she understood why the last effort had seemed so easy.

"My freight!" she hissed, advancing on him.

"Would be better off in your pocket. Why risk your life for this masquerade? I left two sacks of grain in the bottom of the wagon, and the firewood. It should be enough to get us through the pass. Alive." Vandien's dark eyes met her angry ones squarely. Ki saw a glint of humor vying with the challenge in them. She tried to keep her eyes from flickering back to her wagon. Vandien fought a grin, lost the battle.

"It's still there. If I had wanted to steal it, I could have done so long ago. And I certainly wouldn't be telling you about it now. I've told you before, I am not by nature a thief. But go check it, if you wish. I shan't be offended."

Still Ki looked at him. Damn the man!

"I've no objections to pretensions until they endanger a life. And when it is *my* life they endanger, then I become a man of action." He cocked his head at her, raising his eyebrows appealingly. Ki met his look without a smile.

"Put one more sack of grain back in. When it comes to my team, I like a large measure of safety. Shorting them would be another way to endanger your life." She turned on her heel.

She was already at work chipping out a down ramp when Vandien came forward again. The still-blanketed horses watched the Humans who had gouged a steep ramp in the ice. They both turned wary eyes up to the sky frequently. Vandien scowled at the passage of the sun, but Ki looked cautiously grateful for the emptiness she found overhead.

When at last the ramp was ready, Ki led the team down in just a few steps. She set the brake on the wagon, and Vandien on the seat fought to keep it on as the wagon lurched and skidded down the ramp. The snow beyond the ridge was deep, and the team floundered frantically ahead to keep from being run down by the wagon. Ki winced at the beating her team and wagon were taking. Safely down, she halted the horses to make a brief check of the wheels and axles. It was difficult to see much; the snow rose nearly to the bottom of the wagon.

Ki took the blankets off the team, and she and Vandien remounted the wagon. She shook the reins. The shadows of the team were blue on the snow. They leaned into the harness without spirit, and the wagon began to scrape forward again. With a lifting of heart, Ki found that a slight breeze stirred against her face. She prayed it was the wind rising again. She preferred heaped and drifted snow to a single Harpy sliding down the sky.

For a time, all went well. The team hugged the cliff face, where the snow seemed shallowest. By the edge of the trail the snow was heaped high, a wall that blocked Ki's view of the drop-off. Mercifully, it cut the wind as well.

They drew closer to the Sisters, until at last the wagon was creeping past them. Ki craned her neck back, looking up at them. The cliff was too vertical and the sun was in her eyes. She could not see the top of the Sisters' heads, let alone the top of the cliff. At a lower level, she could look up at the stone the Sisters were made from. Shiny and black, it took no reflections of light from the snow. Its smooth glisten reminded Ki of a finely polished piece of wood. She felt she could look into the depths of that shining stone.

The reins jerked in her hands, brought her mind back to her driving. Sigurd half-reared, bringing Sigmund to a forced halt. Sigurd was crowded back in the harness, his hindquarters cramped almost against the wagon. Ki looked across to Vandien. His mouth was folded tightly. He seemed to be making an effort not to speak. Ki dropped down off the wagon again to wade forward through the snow. But she did not sink as she had expected. Instead, she found herself standing nearly on a level with the bed of the wagon. What she had taken to be a higher drift of snow by the edge of the trail was actually an overlay of snow on a ridge of ice. She walked along it to where it swayed suddenly in front of Sigurd. Ki looked ahead. The ridge dominated the center of the trail now. It had channeled her team closer and closer to the cliff face, until now there was no longer a wide enough trail for the wagon to pass.

"The serpent," Vandien began instructively, "evidently traveled down the outer edge of the path this far. But at this point, for reasons unknown to us, he decided to make his way down the center of the trail instead. If I stand on the seat"— which he proceeded to do—"I can see that the hump of ice the serpent created by his passage now extends down the center of this trail as far as my eyes can see. Which isn't far, in this fading light. One could note, in passing, that the area left to ei-

ther side of the hump of ice is too narrow for a wagon. A wagon cannot get through this pass now. But a man, or a woman,
on horseback could. As someone said to someone else, some
days ago."

"Shut up!" Ki said with savage fury. The horses jerked in
surprise at the venom in her voice. She kept her back to
Vandien and the team and looked wordlessly down the ruined
trail. She stood on a giant hummock of ice that, as Vandien
had said, writhed down the center of the trail. The wind wandered past her, stirring her garments slightly as it went. She
wondered if it would rise enough to keep a Harpy out of the
sky.

"A rising wind may sweep even more snow upon us,"
Vandien said, as if he could read her thoughts. "The skies may
be clear, but the wind will lift snow from higher areas to de-
posit it on us."

"Shut up," Ki repeated, but with less energy. Suddenly,
she was tired, weariness clogging her brain. The shadows
loomed ever darker, the Sisters more awesome. She looked at
the drooping heads of her horses. She could ask no more of
them today.

"Make camp," Ki conceded. In the night, she would think
of something. Right now, they all needed rest. She tromped
back to the wagon, tugged at the horses' blankets. Vandien remained seated on them. He looked down at her with eyes that
were bleak in his white face.

"Ki," he said softly, almost pleadingly. "We cannot camp
here. We are in the shadow of the Sisters. Even pausing this
long invites their displeasure. Every loremaster on the other
side of the mountains has tales about this place. I told you the
legends. I swear to you they are true. To stay here means
death for us all."

"Only if we freeze to death, or if an unblanketed horse
takes a chill and a cough. That's probably how folks die here—
they talk themselves to death."

"Ki." Vandien was shaking with earnestness and cold. He
held his arms tight to his sides. Ki wondered if he was resisting
the cold or an urge to slap her. I ask you one more time . . ."

"The wagon goes through," Ki cut in harshly. She saw his
eyes widen, watched his facial muscles tighten. She pulled
hard on the horse blankets, suddenly furious with him. She
raised her flaring eyes to his just as his clenched fist fell from

the sky. The blue lightning hit her. From far away, she heard Vandien's fading voice: "What becomes of a sentinel when the need to guard is gone? What happens to a watchdog when the family moves away but leaves it chained in its kennel? Some would die of loneliness, and some would break their bonds and go their own ways. But one that knew **only** its watching, one that came of a line bred for eons to **guard**, one whose only consciousness was of the need to **protect** the gate—one such as that might remain, might go on **guarding** for centuries, long after the folk it guarded had passed into other times. Such a one might stay on. Or such a two."

Vandien's voice faded to a far-off apologetic murmur. Deep waters closed over Ki. She sank. The deep warm waters, full of familiar horrors, swirled about her. She knew these ugly memories well; it was like a grisly homecoming. Ki glided. She had dreamed these dreams before. She knew it. In some other time and place she had been trapped here. But now she knew how to escape. She only had to open her eyes. Just open her eyes. But her head hurt, and she was dizzy, and it seemed to Ki that her eyes were already open. She fell deeper into blackness, into timeless dark. And in the darkness she found her closed eyes, and at last wrenched them open. . . .

Ki awoke to blackness. It was not yet time to rise. The rest of the house slept still. She lay quiet in her bed, staring with relief at the small patch of stars her open window framed. She shifted on her damp bedding and reluctantly explored the dreams that had sent her into such a sweat. They were senseless fragments now, dreams of terror and guilt. Nils had been watching her. She could not see him, but she had felt his eyes, felt his hands trying to force her back. She had thrown him off and run away from him, past black-flapping curtains. She ran down a long, dark corridor that led through a series of doors, slamming the doors behind her as she ran. Then she passed through the last door and slammed it, and she was suddenly again at the foot of the Harpies' cliff.

Once again she climbed the cliff, though Cora clung tightly to her legs, weeping and begging her not to do so. Ki kicked her loose, to watch her bounce and break down the rock face. Ki laughed aloud at the sight and her laugh was a Harpy's whistle. She reached the aerie, saw again the fire, the bursting eggs. But from the eggs flowed, not unborn Harpies, but Sven and Rissa and Lars, in curled miniature form, wet with blood and fluids. Ki was too horrified to touch the cold, wet little bodies. They squirmed in the liquids and shell fragments and expired before her with small, gasping cries. Ki had killed them all. The mother Harpy appeared, to sit on a ledge above Ki and weep, in Ki's voice, for their passing. Ki tried to cry out that she was sorry, so sorry, but from her throat came only the whistling laughter. And through it all she heard Nils's footsteps and heavy breathing as he searched for her in the dark passageway. He did not find her. When Ki had felt him getting closer, when she had heard him opening the final door, she awakened herself. In her awakening she took a sorry little triumph.

Ki rose from her bed, drawing on clothes haphazardly, scuffing her bare feet into her worn boots. A fierceness burned inside her. A premonition weighted her, refused to be denied. The old man was danger, mortal danger to Ki. The sooner she was away from him, the better. She moved about the room, gathering her clothes and small possessions. She dumped them on the rumpled bed, bundled them together. Haftor was right. She had to go now. Not knowing what drove her, unable to find a basis for her presentiment of danger, she made her preparations.

She slipped down the darkened hallway. She passed the ceremonial bedroom where she had slept the night of the Rite. From within came the querulous sounds of the old man mumbling in his sleep. Ki bared her teeth to his sounds in the darkness. She gained the common room and left it, shutting the heavy door softly behind her.

The barn was in darkness. Ki barked her shins on something made of wood, stumbled, and went on. In the dark she climbed her wagon, entered the cuddy. She found the nub of a candle beside her tinder box on its shelf. She dumped her bundle on the sleeping platform to strike her light. With movements that were both frantic and deliberate, she began to set her cuddy to rights. She moved dust, shook blankets out, opened drawers and crocks and bins to see what supplies were still good. There were no weevils in her meal, but her tea herbs were dried to flavorless crumbs. Ki discarded them. There was no meat nor dried roots, no salt fish, no honey, no lard, no cheese. . . . Ki's heart quailed as she mentally listed what she had not. Her head began to ache, her ears to hum. With an almost physical wrench, she shook off her fears and indecision. She was going. She would manage, somehow.

The cuddy seen to as best she could, Ki moved on. The harness had stiffened from the months of disuse. Ki oiled it heavily. Another dollop of grease for each wheel. A check of pins and axles. A fierce joy welled up in Ki at how swiftly she completed each well-remembered chore. She tried to frame words in her mind to make a farewell to Cora. Her affection for the old woman had not dimmed; but Ki could no longer condone her revival of the Harpy customs. She hoped that Cora would understand, and that Haftor would be as good as his word about supplying her with fresh provisions.

The grayness of dawn was beginning to turn to blue autumn skies when Ki returned to the house. She had checked her team. They were fatter than usual, rested by months that had not demanded daily work of them. But they had come to Ki willingly enough, seeming as anxious as she to resume their life on the road.

Rufus stepped from the doorway as Ki approached, blocking her from entering. She regarded him coolly as he stared at her. His eyes flitted over her insultingly. He glanced back the way she had come as if expecting to see someone leaving.

"Your hair is pulling free of your widow's knots," he observed snidely.

Ki touched it self-consciously. "I had given no thought to it this morning." She stepped forward to enter the house, but Rufus did not step aside.

"Perhaps Ki herself also pulls free of her widowhood," he said insinuatingly. "I had heard the Romni were brief about their mourning."

"So they might appear," Ki replied, choosing the pronoun deliberately. "There is no set time to the period of mourning. They know that grief is not measured in days."

Rufus belched thoughtfully. "They are strangely lacking in many rites, are they not? No fixed length of time for mourning, no courtship ceremonies, no rites to precede a man and woman coupling. . . ."

Ki interrupted, eyes narrowed. "Your folk have no mourning period at all, except for your Rite of Loosening."

"By it, there is no death, and therefore no need for mourning," Rufus replied evenly. "Usually." He twisted the word into Ki like a knife blade. He stepped aside then, to thump down the porch and across the yard. Ki looked after him. She was possessed of a mighty anger toward him. But she had no time to satisfy it. Her sensation of danger squeezed her.

She went to her emptied room to smooth and re-knot the hair Rufus had so pointedly commented on. She frowned to herself as she pulled it tight. So Rufus thought she had spent her night with Haftor. From chilling politeness he had advanced to familiar contempt. Ki shrugged. Let him think whatever he wanted. She would soon be free of it all. She refused to dwell on it. Mentally she composed herself, stiffening her spirit for her battle with Cora. She expected it to be nothing less. As her resolve deepened, her spirits rose. She would make her break cleanly and honorably. Cora, she suspected, would prefer it so also.

Ki began to hear the familiar stirrings of the household through the walls. Only now were they rousing. Rufus had been the early riser. Others slept late, past the sun's rising. Ki took a final deep breath and headed for the common room.

Cora was sitting alone at the table, a steaming mug before her. Ki watched her sip at the gruellike grain soup in the mug. It stirred no appetite in Ki. Ki looked forward to purchasing more brewing herbs, to making her own hot aromatic teas in the morning by her fireside. She drew strength from the image as she took a chair opposite Cora at the table.

"Did you sleep well?" Cora asked politely. Her face was still soft with sleep. She took another long sip of the soup.

"No." Ki answered bluntly. She wished an end to courteous words that said nothing. Like a Harpy, she wished to rip to the meat of her discontent. But Cora seemed not to have heard her tone.

"Nor I. The house was thick with dreams. They should have been pleasant ones, as Nils instructed us. Yet, a dark current seemed to flow through the night and pulled all my dreams and thoughts into its murky waters. I am uneasy. My mind tells me that there is an important matter that I have not attended to, a need I have overlooked. But I can call to mind no detail that I have not seen to. It makes me feel old, so old."

"Perhaps I can help you bring it to mind," Ki said mercilessly. "It has never left my mind, all these weary days. Cora, you are close to your reconciliation. I wish to be released."

Cora set down her mug, appearing to notice Ki at the table

for the first time. "Close, but not finished. You remember our bargain."

"I do. I remember it as much as I regret it. I have spent this morning readying my wagon. I wish to leave."

"Ah. And where will you go?"

"Back to my life." Ki watched the old woman's face closely. It did not change. But her bird-bright eyes remained fixed on Ki's green ones, as if probing for secrets.

"And who will go with you?" she encouraged.

"NO ONE!" Ki exploded. "Why must we dance and tiptoe about this? What mean all these questions? I wish to leave, Cora, to be on my road again."

Cora was unruffled. "I had hoped that you might find something, or perhaps some*one*, to hold you here. That has not happened?"

"No. Nothing. And no one." Ki did not try to hide her distaste for the subject.

The expression on the old woman's face grew firmer. "Ki. You will not be pleased by what I must say. It is for your own good. I bind you here until I judge that we have been reconciled with the Harpies. There *is* something here for you, although you will not open your stubborn eyes and see it. It is in the work you do so well, and the way you do it. I know that you were meant to be one of us. I feel it. Sven made you my daughter, and I intend that you shall remain so. If you will only have a little patience, Ki."

Ki rose, her face pale, her eyes terrible. The walls of the room seemed to whirl, to close in about her. She could not find breath to speak, and she felt the walls of her resistance to Cora melt like fog. The threads of her logical reasons for leaving slipped from her fingers.

"Let her go! She is poison to you! Nay, I spoke too gently! Drive her out, stone her forth from the valley! Her soul is a dark and terrible place, full of secrets she will not bare, even in sleep! And you would waste another son upon her?"

Ki and Cora both jerked about to face Nils. This morning he walked like the old man he was. His face was as haggard, as if he had not slept at all. When he reached the table, he placed his fists on the edge of it, knuckles down. He leaned heavily on it, his accusing glance flashing from Ki to Cora and back again.

"She has no wish to be one of you! She left the Kishi fruit untouched on the table, scorning our gift of togetherness! But she had taken of the liquor of the Rite of Loosening, so she could not close her mind to me entirely. It was a sinister place, of foul deeds and fouler ambitions. Things too hideous for me to think of, she has done! And her poison has spread among you. Your own sons I could not reach, Cora! Few among your family came willingly to my healing of dreams. Holland came eagerly, like a hurt child seeking to be comforted. Lydia fought like a wild thing, slipping away from me even as I thought I had her. The dark man and his sister . . ."

"Haftor and Marna," murmured Cora.

"Marna came, but without joy, like a beast to harness. Haftor seized his dreams from my control and twisted them, seeking every chance to turn them inside out and examine the ugly seams. He is a strong, wild spirit, Cora. He remembers things I thought we had cleansed him of, things best forgotten. He is another one best put aside from your household."

Cora's hand went to her mouth, shaking her head, her eyes stricken.

"Do not refuse me, Cora! You summoned me here, did you not, to put things to rights? And even you are not unscathed! Joined as you were to this corrupt creature during that travesty of a rite, you have taken the most of her dark spirits! You too, Cora, were closed to me. You know you were! You stood before a dark place in your mind, a place Ki had put there, and you denied me entrance, even as you would not go in yourself!"

Cora might have replied to his words, Ki might have let herself go and struck him, but from outside the house came the sounds of Rufus's hoarse yells. The words were unintelligible, but the tone of them made Ki and Cora leap up. Ki raced to the door and flung it open. Cora came behind her, Nils on her heels.

From all directions, people were coming—from the barns and cottages, from the fields, all hurrying toward the far corner of the pasture. Ki set off at a run. Holland set down a bucket of milk and a basket of eggs to scuttle from the barn yard and through the pasture. Cora moved faster than her old legs wanted to. Nils hurried after her.

Ki pushed her way through a cluster of people to where Rufus stood red-faced and angry. At his feet was a blood-spattered heap of bones, hide, and tattered meat.

"Harpies!" he was roaring, over and over. Cora reached his elbow. "A decade of breeding went into that bull! Now look at him! Damn them! Damn them!" A wild pulse leaped and hammered on his left temple. His fists were clenched at his sides, his dark hair pulled wild and unruly from his hair binding. His chest heaved.

Holland stared at him in horror, going even whiter at his blasphemy. Ki was silent, in her eyes a green reflection of Rufus's anger and hatred. Their eyes met across the carcass. A jolt of understanding passed between them.

Cora slapped him. Her old hand whipped across his cheek and mouth, making a loud popping sound in the astonished silence. Lars, coming across the field, winced at the wound, but Nils was nodding his head, looking as if he ached to deliver the same blow to Ki's savage face.

It did not move Rufus. It did not budge his head on its neck of standing muscles and veins. The white handprint stood out on his impassioned face. A little blood edged out of his mouth where his lips had been cut against his teeth. Rufus shook his head slowly at her. Anger still reigned in his eyes, but his voice was cold.

"Do you think you can make me sorry for my words, Mother?" He nudged the heaped carcass at his feet. He voiced aloud the comparison that was in everyone's mind. "They left more of Sven and the babies than they did of my bull!" Again that brief eye-to-eye joining of Rufus and Ki. Cora seized his arm, shook it, but his body remained immobile. More folk were coming—young Kurt, with smaller Edward galloping behind him like a colt; Lydia, coming with flour on her hands up to her elbows, dust on her smock where she had wiped her hands—the whole family.

"You have brought this upon yourselves!" Nils's voice rang out over them. Shorter he was than all of them, but he seemed to stand above them as he lectured them all in a patriarchal tone.

"Your blasphemy has severed you from your Harpies, leaving them hungering for the tribute you were unfit to bring! Last night they smelled the stench of your evil thoughts, the depraved dreams you dreamed, when you should have dreamed of sharing and gratitude for the Harpies. Whence comes your anger, Rufus? Is it not a false pride? You would have kept back the best bull for yourself, when it was meet that he be offered to the Harpies! You have no right to anger. They have but claimed their just due! Look within your hearts and be ashamed! You are full of selfishness, forgetful of your dead and your duties to your ancestors and the Harpies. You are far, far from the reconciliation you seek. Your thoughts are evil within you, your minds infected with the poison Ki has spread here! Yes, Ki, I name you by name. Look about you! Do you rejoice in the wickedness you have done, the sorrow you have created?"

Unwillingly, Ki looked about. Holland's head was bowed, tears streaming from beneath her closed lashes. Kurt and Edward remained on the edge of the crowd, baffled by the discord among their elders, afraid to go to either father or mother. Lydia would not meet Ki's eyes. Lars had turned his face from the scene. Many looked at her with eyes that focused all blame upon her. Cora looked at Ki, love and hurt and anger blended in a glance that pierced Ki like a sword. Worst of all, perhaps, was Rufus, who met her gaze squarely with empathy. Rufus stiffened himself in her sight and spoke, deliberately breaking Nils's spell.

"Fetch a shovel for me, Ki. And bring one for yourself. Let us together bury the bull that would have sired calves for us, sturdy ones that would not die in the spring of the shudders, but would have grown to hearty cows that give birth easily and live many a year. Help me bury my dreams, Ki. As deeply as you buried yours."

"Rufus has barred himself from our ceremonies! He is cast out among us, to be one of us only by his Human nature, never again to enlarge his spirits with his Harpy brethren."

Ki wondered if anyone else heard the frantic note in the old man's voice. The elocutionary tones, his imperial stance among them, the hands that pointed accusingly and gestured commandingly; it was not enough to completely overcome the emotion of Rufus's simple words. A few began to drift away from the scene. Ki could feel them slipping out of control, avoiding the unpleasantness, but not swayed to the old man's words.

"In the names of your dead!" The people stopped moving, turned to Nils again. His eyes were starting from his head. His raised hands trembled. All were silent. Nils's eyes worked steadily around the circle, pausing on each face. Some shifted uncomfortably as they met that gaze. Holland looked at him with hungry eyes. Marna bowed her head before it. Haftor returned it boldly, defiantly. The old man continued to extend his scrutiny of the crowd, avoiding only Rufus and Ki. He finished by looking deeply into Cora's eyes. She seemed to lose flesh and shrink in on herself as he looked. "I have walked through your dreams and found you wanting. The poison in you has worked deeper than I feared. If you had a hand that was diseased with rot, would not you cut it from your body? Is not the blighted plant pulled from the field and burned, lest it spread its disease? Do you not remove the afflicted animal from the pens, to be killed and burned lest you lose your whole flock? So must I do now. And those of you who are sound and well must be brave, to endure the knife that cuts away the oozing limb, the brand that cauterizes the festering wound." Nils's eyes stabbed out.

"Lydia!" he accused. She started, gave a half sob. Her thin hands rose to the front of her smock, clung there like tiny animals seeking refuge. "Leave our circle. Your pride and selfish independence have doomed you. Be alone, then! So, your dreams have told me, is your wish. Take no more counsel from your parents. They are lost to you. Go to your home and think on that!"

Dazed and shaken, Lydia stumbled away from the group. Ki glared at Nils. Like a wolf, he had cut out the weakest of the herd first. Lydia's staggering feet stumbled over the tufts of meadow grass. Her hands clung to her throat.

"Haftor!" Marna gasped as her brother raised his head. He gave her shoulder a quick and gentle squeeze, an odd half-smile on his face. Nils scowled. "You grin, do you? You smirk at the poison that sours your soul? Of small importance to you is your sister's pain at this sundering! You are little better than an animal in your desire to follow only your own will. Go!"

Haftor gently freed himself from Marna's hand that clung to his arm. He set her hand gently aside from him. Head up, he strode from the group to catch up with Lydia and gravely take her arm. Her head fell onto his shoulder, and he took the weight of her body. He did not look back.

"Kurt!"

Cora gave a gasp of agony. Holland cried aloud. But the boy stood straight and defiant, as if to mime Haftor's example. Rufus turned slow, amazed eyes to his boy who suddenly stood as a man.

"You are young, boy!" Nils scoffed at his brave show. "No one would suspect it from your face, but I have seen the evil in your dreams. You follow your father. You love your flocks and herds as he does, evilly, as if they were your children instead of mere beasts. When you looked on the dead bull, the flames of your anger flared and blossomed. You love your father and hate the Harpies. Go."

Bravely, Kurt stepped away from the group. He took a hand of paces. Then his squared shoulders began to tremble. Rufus, his hands red with the blood of his bull, looked as if his heart were breaking for his child. Kurt turned. Tears had begun a shining path down his face.

"I am sorry, Mother. But only for how it pains you." He spoke softly, but his voice carried. Rufus stepped past the carcass of the bull, crossed to his son. His voice carried too. "Come, son. Today we shall bury our dreams with a shovel, you and I."

Holland crumpled sobbing to the earth. But she did not follow. Small Edward clung to her, afraid. Cora's mouth opened. She croaked once, but it was no word she made. Old hands trembling, she reached out to the departing men. She took a tottering step. Nils seized both her outstretched hands.

"Do not be weak now, Cora. The Harpies wish you to rejoin them. Have not they already come of their own will to take a tribute from your holdings? Their hidden ears hear our voiceless cries, our distress at separation. Purify your mind. Let go of that which holds you back. Open your mind to me, that I may lance that boil of poison you hide."

No one moved. Nils stared deep into the tortured woman's eyes. She stared back at him, a bird gazing at a snake. Panic was on her face. All the hair on Ki's body prickled up. She felt the danger swirl about her, begin to coalesce. No! she cried wordlessly and, knowing not how she did it, joined her strength to Cora's. They stood together before the black door that Nils sought to open. Ki felt his eyes bore into her own; unseen hands plucked at her will. The buzzing in her ears drowned out all sound. Cora's will began to slip away, to melt like fog in the sun. From deep in Ki's throat rose an animal sound. Her hands hooked into claws. Ki stepped forward swiftly, silently.

Suddenly Cora was gone. Her will had disappeared and taken with it the black door she guarded. Ki recoiled, as stunned as if she had walked into a solid wall. She opened her eyes, surprised to realize that she had closed them, to find that she had not moved at all. Cora was a crumpled heap at Nils's feet. Casually, he let go of her hands, let them fall as if they were pieces of wood.

"The poison runs too deep in her," he intoned. "She will hide in death before she lets it go. Cora is set apart from us."

Nils walked away. The crowd swayed uncertainly, then flowed after him, milling a moment before they parted to go around Cora's body. Ki found herself on her knees beside Cora. She wanted to kill Nils, but found she could spare no time for it right now. Cora's lips were purpling; they puffed in and out with every breath. Ki took one of the cold wrinkled hands. She held it to her cheek. The fingers bent stiffly against her face. Cora was gone, not here. Ki screamed soundlessly, wordlessly, and dove in after her.

She knew not what she did, nor how she did it. A terrible presentiment told her where to seek for Cora. She was behind the last door, the black door at the end of the corridor in Ki's mind. Cora had found at last the despoiled aerie, the dead Harpies. Ki seized her, dragged her away.

It was the deep, warm waters again that Ki swam through. She towed Cora, who did not care to come, who dangled from her hands like a stillborn kitten. Ki fought their way up, past the ugly swirling images, past the dead Harpies that repeated themselves in endless postures, each more ungainly than the last. Ki pushed aside Sven's ravaged body, shouldered away the ruined, crumpled Harpy at the base of the cliff. The wreckage of her children bobbed past her, eyes empty over bloody cheek holes. Ki floundered on. But the water was deep and endless. There was no surface to swim to, no exit that Ki could find.

Someone pinched her savagely, slapped her a blow that rocked her head. Ki cried out in anger and pain. She sprang up at Lars. A rough shove sent her sprawling onto the still wet grass. Lars gathered up his mother's faintly stirring body.

"Sometimes only pain can help you come back," he said briefly. He staggered to his feet, Cora drooping from his arms. Ki looked about her in confusion. No one else was in the field. Ki was shaking with sudden cold, alone, so alone. The morning sounds pressed in on her ears with incredible clarity. She heard the clank of a dropped shovel. She turned to see Rufus and Kurt coming at a run from the barn, their abandoned tools on the ground behind them.

"You two must have an affinity for joining. Usually a feat such as that takes much liquor from the Harpies." Ki dragged herself to her feet, stumbled after Lars who was talking as he walked. "I wonder," he said, "if you two were ever completely parted after the Rite."

"The others have gone."

"You have been gone yourself for more than a little while. I thought you both had gone forever. Nils has taken the others away for meditation, fasting, and purification. Only we outcasts are left."

"We." Ki felt the word gingerly.

Lars wrinkled his mouth at the word. It turned into a small, tired smile. Rufus met them, took his mother from Lars's arms. They hurried to the house. Ki, forgotten now, came slowly behind them. She was drained of all strength. She felt she could drop down onto the dew-wet grass and sleep eternally. Yet within her there leapt up a sudden spark, an alertness. She was awake. She felt a sudden urge to explore every part of her mind, as she might feel her body for broken limbs after a bad fall. She was complete again, once more in full control. No will ruled her but her own. The indecision that had plagued her for the last few months, the feeling of numbness, was fled. Cora. Ki mouthed the word silently. Ki had not realized it. She wondered if Cora had, if she had used it. Too late to worry about it now. She stumbled to the barn, to her wagon, to her cuddy, and into her bed. Sleep seized her.

Kurt had not dared to enter the cuddy. Instead, he had banged loudly on the door of it, communicating his urgency with his frenzied battering. Ki stumbled across the cuddy to slide the door open. His face was white in the light of the candle he bore.

"Grandma wants you. She says you must come now."

He would have scuttled away, candle and all, if Ki had not seized him by the shoulder. He shrank from her touch, and Ki realized with an ache what a strange and menacing spirit she must seem to him. Even now, when he was as outcast as she was, still he flinched from her touch. She did not release him. She would not let him be afraid of her any longer.

"Don't go too fast," she whispered hoarsely. "I'll fall in the dark."

He turned wide eyes up to her. Then he guided her out of the barn and across the dark yard.

Ki was nearly to the door of the house before the reality of the night seized her. She had slept the whole day away. The big house was unnaturally quiet. She entered the common room, to find it, too, in semi-darkness. Its great hearth fire had burnt out.

"They haven't come back," Kurt murmured as she looked about in surprise. Ki squeezed his shoulder gently, meaning to reassure and comfort him. He nearly dropped the candle.

Cora's room was lit with tall white tapers. Death candles, Ki thought. Cora's gaunt hands were claws on the bedding. Her hair was awry, her lips still too dark. But her eyes opened as Ki came in. They were still bright, bird-black. The body might fail, but not the mind. She gestured at her sons feebly as they stood, one to either side of her bed.

"Rufus. To the field and fetch Ki's team. Quickly." Her voice was a cracked whisper, but full of command. "Lars. Take Kurt. Open the barn, and help make the wagon ready for the team. Use no lights! And watch that Sigurd! He's still as fractious as when he was a colt. Keep silent!"

Rufus went, but Lars lingered, eyes full of worry.

"Mother, you are ill yet, and weak. Cannot this wait? Do you cast Ki out in the dark of night? She was sister to us, and daughter to you. . . ."

"Fool!" Cora broke in. She gasped for a breath, and her color became worse. "I have barely enough strength for what I must do, and you wish to complicate it with talk. Long before you discovered her worth, I loved and valued Ki. And though she may not recognize it, no one's love has been truer through these days. Go, Lars. Take Kurt. My words are not for your ears."

They went reluctantly. Ki and Cora listened for the scuff of their footsteps to fade. Cora drew together her strength. Ki moved closer to the bedside and picked up one of Cora's hands. Cold, still.

"No time," Cora sighed, pulling her fingers free of Ki's. "You must leave tonight and travel swiftly. Get over the mountains. I have heard the Harpies don't go there. Soon they will know who killed the mother, who dropped the torch in the nest. The male will demand revenge. Neither Harpy nor Human in the valley will deny it to him. You will be hunted. You have so little time to escape."

"How will they know?" Ki pressed.

"As I finally knew." Cora coughed without energy. "They, too, know without knowing. It was why I could not make them accept you. I hid it from myself, refused to see what you had shown me. I told myself those wild images were what you might do if I did not keep you here, safe, beside me. But the real knowledge was there, closing me off from the Harpies. I will make no reconciliation with them. If I did, I would be your betrayer. I could not hide the knowledge from them. Their minds are strong, stronger than Nils's. No one keeps secrets from the Harpies. Ki, if I know, there are others that know. I was closest to you that night. I received the strongest images. But Marna was there, and Holland, and little Edward. In all innocence, they will condemn you to death when next they offer tribute to the Harpies. There is no way to stop it from happening."

Cora paused, giving Ki time to sort the sense from her breathless words. She took each breath with effort, released each with a sigh.

"After I leave," Ki asked reluctantly, "what will happen here?"

"You mean with the Harpies?" Cora asked. "I do not think they will be harsh with us. They will demand greater tribute. They will make no reprisals, I think. They would not harm Rufus, or Lars, or I, for then who would remain to tend the lands that grow the cattle? Reprisals they reserve for those who leave, or those who speak openly against them. Such as Sven. Such as my brother."

Ki reeled with the impact of Cora's words. "Haftor knows that?" she asked incredulously.

"He was there," Cora replied with an effort. "Just a boy at the time. Turned his mind for a while—he didn't speak for the longest time—but I brought him back from it. It has given him a strangeness. And when you came, with your tidings, well, there's the knowledge in him somewhere, trying to get out. I hope it never does."

"So do I," breathed Ki. She leaned down, put her arms about Cora.

"I shall miss the strength I took from you," Cora admitted softly. Gently, she pushed Ki away. "In the cupboard," she said awkwardly.

"What?"

"The money, for Sven's lands. You must take it."

Ki straightened, looked down on Cora bemusedly. Then she crossed to the cupboard and opened it. The colt-hide sack was heavy. It clinked. Ki turned back to Cora.

"I accept your money for the lands, Cora. You have paid me for it honorably. In the past I have refused the love you offered me, Cora. Now I take it, too, with thanks. And you, in return, must accept mine." Ki raised the bag, kissed it ceremoniously. She dropped it on the foot of Cora's bed. She smiled at the foolishness of the situation. Cora's bird-bright eyes were wet. Ki nodded her head to her and left the room.

Her goodbyes to Lars and Rufus were short and uncomfortable. There was too much to say. It could not be cut to fit into words. Eyes said much that tongues could not form. Rufus hugged her shyly, but Lars's embrace was fierce and hard to break from. Ki scrambled onto the seat of her wagon, refusing to see how Lars wept. She slapped the reins hard on the grays' backs. The night received Ki and closed behind her. When she looked back, not a light showed in the home that had been Sven's.

The road was silent about her, no lights showing in the smaller cottages that she passed. But as her team came abreast of Marna's, a small figure darted in front of it, holding aloft a flickering candle dim as a firefly. Ki pulled the team up short.

"Haftor!" called Kurt's voice softly, and the door of the cottage opened. "She's here!" Kurt said, and then the candle was pinched out, and Kurt darted off into darkness.

Haftor stood limned a moment in the lamplight, framed in the door of Marna's house. Ki sat silent on the wagon. She heard a light footfall behind Haftor and glimpsed Lydia, pale as a spirit as she moved listless to his side, carrying a bulky sack. Haftor took it from her, saying soft words that did not carry to Ki's ears. He pushed her gently back into the cottage, closing the door behind her. He came swiftly, to pass up to Ki the bundle of provisions. She took them without thanks, opening her cuddy door and setting them within.

All words were inadequate. Ki felt she must leave so much unfinished. She climbed down slowly from the seat to stand before him. "I am sorry we make our ending like this," she faltered.

Haftor's eyes were like dark, cold river rocks. He trapped her hands in his, holding them so tightly it hurt.

"This is no ending, Ki. You can't run away from it that easily. Cora will not be able to contain such a secret as she holds. You killed those Harpies. That's a debt paid only with blood. Neither time nor distance will heal it. Harpies don't give up on blood debts. Neither do the men who serve them. A life must be given."

Haftor's eyes had gone deep and mad in the semi-light. Ki tried to step back from him, feeling menaced by his words and the way he growled them. Should he choose to try and kill her, Ki knew she could find no spirit to resist him. He had known, then. As Cora had.

He read the fear in her eyes, understood the way she shrank from him. He released her hands. "They don't know yet. They cannot put the pieces together as I did. To kill a Harpy for vengeance is too foreign an idea to them. They see the pieces, but cannot comprehend the whole. But Nils will. By morning he will know, and there will be no stopping him. He will want your blood himself. If the Harpies do not find you, Nils, or another like him, will. So do not tarry."

He turned to her wagon, surprised her by climbing up the wheel before her. He took up the reins, slapped them against the team. The team started at his unaccustomed hand and stepped out as swiftly as beasts their size could.

"The roads will be watched, by men in the trees and Harpies in the air. So I will show you a way forgotten, branched over by forest growth and so foul and pitted that all think no wagon may pass there. It will take you long to travel that way. But no one will watch for you there."

Haftor hurried the horses, bidding Ki sternly to be silent that he might listen. Ki opened her mouth in alarm when he suddenly turned the team off the road and into a morass. Their hooves sank and made sucking noises as they struggled. A shallow layer of moving water overlay the mud and reeds the team plowed through. The wagon jolted off the solid roadbed and into the mush. The wheels sank. Haftor slapped the reins hard down on the horses. The grays hunched and humped against their traces. Ki's heart sank with her wagon wheels.

"Pull, damn you!" hissed Haftor in a carrying whisper. Their heads went down, their front legs bent, and the team went nearly to their knees. The wagon moved. In sporadic jerks and tugs, the wagon lurched through the mire and onto coarse gravel and then up over deep moss and scrub brush. It was uphill briefly over a slight rise, and then they were descending, and Ki looked down a dark avenue of trees. Tall grass and brush swept the bottom of the wagon. Tall trees had overgrown the unused road and arched over it, sheltering it from the night sky.

"It's going to be bad traveling," Haftor warned her as he pulled the team in. "There may be logs down across the road further on. You'll just have to chop them and use the team to pull them aside. I know that a stream crosses it in one place. It shouldn't give you too much of a problem."

He hugged her fiercely and kissed the side of her face roughly. His silver wrist-piece caught for a moment in her hair. Before she could recover from her surprise, he untangled himself and leapt from the wagon. He gave Sigurd a slap on the rump before he stepped aside, and the spooked horse surged forward in his harness.

The road had been as bad as Haftor had said it would be. The provisions he had given her had run out before she reached a true road again. But she had left that evil trail at last, of that she was sure—she remembered emerging from the forest onto a wide, sunlit road—and she wondered at the darkness about her now, and the terrible jerking and swaying.

It was the swaying that was making her sick. She opened her eyes a little, only to see whiteness rushing past her face far below. She was cold and monstrously uncomfortable; she could not locate her arms or determine what had become of her hands. She had no memory of where she was or what she was doing. The white stuff below her rose suddenly, to strike her in the face with coldness. Snow! She reared back her head as far as she could and let out a strangled cry. Presently, the swaying stopped. With the cessation of the motion, she could separate her body from her discomfort. Her thighs, belly, and chest were pressed heavily to something warm, solid, and living. Her head hung down lower than the rest of her body. That accounted for the throbbing sensation in her face. That much was obvious. The circumstances of the rest of the situation eluded her.

She heard snow crunch behind her. Someone seized her firmly by the hips and pulled until her feet hit the ground. Her hands were loosely but securely bound behind her. She found with the sudden change in position that she was dizzy, too dizzy to stand. She swayed to one side and was caught by strong hands, steadied, with her face nestled against rough cloth.

"Sven?" she questioned blindly, disoriented totally in time and space.

"No, Vandien. I'm sorry, Ki, but it was necessary. I didn't want to do it, but you left me no choice. How's your head?"

It hurt. It made no sense, but it hurt. She tried to raise a hand to touch the throbbing place, but was reminded that her hands were still bound.

"Untie me."

She felt Vandien shake his head. She was still leaning into his cloak, talking to his chest. It was humiliating, but she knew without his support she would fall.

"First we talk, then we untie. I want to be sure you understand my reasons and don't try to kill me."

"What did you hit me with?"

"Not that it matters, but a rock. Back at the time when you were sitting on my chest, looking as if you might arrange my transport into the next world, my hand came upon it. It's been in my pocket since then. Ki, believe me, I hoped never to have a use for it. But you are a stubborn person, the stubbornest I have ever encountered."

"What happened? What are you doing with me?"

"After I hit you, I put you on Sigurd. He has little love for me, I fear, and did his best to stomp me until he realized he could not stomp me without stomping you. The ridge of ice helped; I was above him. Sigmund is a more reasonable beast. Besides, both of them were hampered by their harness. Once I had supplies loaded, I cut us loose from the wagon and got them moving. We have made good time." He paused, waiting, but Ki said nothing. "I could have left you there, you know. It would have been far easier for me. But I didn't. I intend to get you out of this pass alive. I feel that by doing that I will have paid back what I owe you. Even if I do it against your will. Now."

Dimly, she felt his hands fumbling at her wrists. A thin cord dropped away into the snow. Vandien bent and retrieved his story string. Her hands and arms tingled strangely as she brought them up and rubbed at her wrists.

As soon as she felt she could do so without falling, she pushed away from his chest and stood upright. She touched the side of her head gently, still eyeing Vandien resentfully.

There was a swollen lump, but no blood. Still, just to touch it made her feel sick and woozy. Vandien reached out a hand to steady her as she swayed, but she pushed it away and rested a hand on Sigurd's great shoulder instead. Sigurd reached his head back curiously, a shade of reproach in his eyes. She patted him reassuringly.

"They are curious beasts to ride. Willing, but broad enough to split a man in two. Just getting onto Sigmund's back without sliding down the other side took a bit of doing. Even from the ice ridge."

"I'm going back for my wagon."

"Don't be an ass, Ki. It's nightfall already, and your wagon is hours behind us over the worst part of the trail. And it is in the shadow of the Sisters. Besides, I still have my rock. Come, make the best of it, as I did when I had you over me with a knife. Do you need a boost to mount?"

"Without my freight, I have no reason to wish to see the other side of this pass."

"Ah, your freight. A moment." Vandien opened his cloak to the cold, fished inside his shirt. He produced the leather pouch and pressed it into Ki's hand. "It's all there, if you wish to check. I would have put it in your own shirt, but I was afraid it would drop down into the snow. Your riding posture wasn't all it could have been."

Ki clutched her pouch to her chest and leaned her face into Sigurd's warm coat. He shifted, perplexed by her behavior, but did not veer away from her weight. She was silent. Behind her in the snow Vandien moved uneasily. The smile he had attempted faded from his face. She peeked back at him under her arm. He looked vaguely ashamed, but mostly weary. Last night she had thought of killing him. Today he had bashed her on the head, abandoned her wagon, and made poor jokes about it afterwards. She should have been wishing she had killed him. She found that she only wanted to make him understand.

"Rom was the name of Sven's great black horse. Rom came scarcely to Sigurd's shoulder, but he was a stallion and bullied my grays unmercifully. Sven and I used to laugh about it at night by our fire."

Vandien stepped closer to her to catch her muffled words, but made no move to touch her.

"The grays were Sven's gift to me, and the wagon built by his own hands for our purposes. Within that wagon I first knew Sven as a man. Two children I birthed within it, with Sven's great hands to steady me through it. We made our lives as the Romni do, but we were not of them. Sometimes he rode Rom next to the wagon, singing as he rode with a voice like the wind. And sometimes he would put his small daughter on the saddle in front of him, and our son would cling behind him. Then they would tease me for my team's slowness, and race far ahead of the wagon, out of my sight for minutes, and then galloped back, shrieking and laughing to me to hurry up, that there were new lands to see just beyond the next turning. Have a care for your wagon, old snail woman!' he called to me as they galloped past me in the trail of Khaddam past Vermintown. They all three were laughing, and their pale hair streamed behind them and tangled together. They went up a rise and over a hill. I watched them go together."

The silence grew, stretched, and blended with the cold. Vandien cleared his throat. "They never came back?"

"I found the pieces of them when I topped the rise. Just the pieces, and they were only meat in the sun, Vandien, only meat in the sun. It was the work of two Harpies." She turned sick eyes on him, waiting to see if his face changed. But his eyes were closed. Ki swallowed. "I tracked them, Vandien. I climbed up to their aerie. One I killed outright, myself, and by accident," Ki's voice rose higher, "I burned the nest and eggs and scarred the male for life. I put an end to all of them. But it didn't help! Mine were still only meat in the sun." She choked, and it sounded to Vandien like the death of all laughter. "I buried a big black horse and a man and two children in a hole no bigger than the seat of the wagon. Harpies do not leave much when they feed, Vandien. 'Have a care for your wagon, old snail woman,' he used to say. I carry my home with me. I'm going back for my wagon."

She grasped Sigurd's mane and tried to pull herself up. Her body refused. Vandien took her shoulders, turned her gently.

"Tomorrow, then. When we have light. The wind is rising again, and the horses are done in. You stay here. I can tramp out a place in the snow between the cliff face and the ridge of that cursed serpent. We'll be all right."

Ki had not the strength to argue. She did not even watch him. She looked about, but there was little to see in the dimming light. Her wagon was far back, out of sight around some bend or wrinkle in the mountain's face. She couldn't see the Sisters either. The eternal cliff face reared up on one side of her; she and the horses stood on the serpent's ridge; and down the other side cascaded the mountain. Far down in the valley there were darker specks that might have been brush pushing up through the snow. The light was nearly gone. There was no color to anything.

She turned her sore head slowly. It throbbed, and any sudden movement was like a hammer blow. Vandien was unloading the horses. Sigmund had let him take off the sack of grain he carried and the oddly shaped bundles that Vandien had made of the worn blankets. But Sigurd was feeling spiteful. His big yellow teeth closed swiftly and harmlessly on the cloth of Sven's cloak.

"Sigurd!" Ki rebuked him instinctively. His head dropped, abashed, and he subjected himself to Vandien's touch. Vandien did not appear to notice Ki's intervening. She became aware of his monologue, scarcely louder than the shushing wind.

"... left the firewood to bring the grain. So no fire, and so no tea; so I didn't bring the tea kettle. But I took the salt meat and the dried fish and the things I thought would be precious to you: a silver hair comb, a necklace with blue stones, a clean tunic—probably all the wrong things. But we'll get the rest tomorrow. Or die trying." He added the last so softly that Ki was hardly sure she had heard it. He had trampled a spot in the snow. He shook out grain for the horses, twice what Ki usually gave them. He had spread the shagdeer cover out on the snow beside the rising mountain face. He came to Ki to steer her over to it. She sat down on it obediently. Her passivity seemed to trouble him. Ki could have told him that it was only pain and weariness. But that would have taken too much effort. He could be a Harpy's man, or even a Harpy tonight. It made no difference to her. Her strength was spent.

She refused the food he offered. She saw it distressed him and felt a vague sympathy for the guilt he felt. Ki knew guilt well. It made a sorry companion. She dropped over on the shagdeer cover, curled up. The ice ridge provided a small windbreak. The horses knew it and already had moved into its shelter. The cliff towering beside her gave Ki an illusion of shelter. She closed her eyes. She felt and heard Vandien spread the larger, heavier cloak over her. Then he was crawling under it with her, curling his body about hers, his belly to her back. "For the warmth," he whispered, but Ki couldn't care.

The wind swirled loose snow onto them. Ki pulled her head under the shelter of the cloak. She felt the cloak atop her grow heavier with the snow, and she grew warmer with the added insulation. Ki nuzzled into sleep like a blind puppy seeking milk.

Her mind groped. She was awake now, so she must have been asleep. Sven called her. His voice came from far away. It was distant through the strange buzzing in her ears. But it was Sven. Doubt was swept from her mind. She knew every note of that beloved voice. She fought her way up out of sleep. She was puzzled by the warm dark to which she opened her eyes. She pushed the heavy cloak aside irritably. Snow fell coldly on her face and neck. She sputtered and sat up in a mound of it. The blanketed horses looked at her, ears sharp with surprise at seeing Ki emerge suddenly from a snowbank. She grinned at them and stood.

"Ki!" The voice was clearer now, coming closer. Sven strode toward her. The snow offered him no resistance. It did not even slow him. Little Rissa on his arm bounced happily. Lars, blue shirt flapping over his butt, was doing his best to keep up with his father's long strides. He held tightly to one of Sven's hands, and every now and then took a giant stride as he swung on it to gain ground.

Ki's hands flew to her cheeks in joyous dismay. "Sven, where are their cloaks? The children aren't dressed for snow!" She tried to wade toward them. But she sank and floundered in the loose snow. It clung to her, held her back. It was easier to stand still, to let them come to her. Joy washed her, drowning all questions.

"They're fine!" Sven scoffed. "These are tough little Romni brats, these are!" He gave Rissa a bump, and she squeaked delightedly. Ki drank in their presence, luxuriated in the familiar sound of her daughter giggling. She wondered why she had been lonely for them so long. They had been here, all the time, waiting for her. It was simple. She stood, smiling foolishly, and Sven swung Rissa down from his arms and opened his arms to Ki. She stepped toward him.

She was slammed aside, going down into the snow, falling with the sore side of her head punched into the icy coldness.

She was choking on loose snow, gagging. She wallowed up to her feet, wondering what kind of game this was. Sven had been too rough; he should know how big he was, how strong compared to her. She regained her feet, staggering slightly.

"Sven!" she rebuked him gently. The children were laughing. He shook his head regretfully and gave a snort of laughter. He had meant it in fun, a romp in the snow. She saw that now. She smiled her forgiveness and moved toward him.

"KI!" someone screamed. She didn't turn to look. If Sven was here before her, then who else was there in the world? Then it was Ki's turn to scream as Vandien shouldered her aside in his rush, plunging her little sheath knife into Sven's chest.

Sven brushed him aside, unconcerned by him, and Ki saw the blood leap from Vandien's face where Sven's fingers touched him. She did not understand, but Sven was smiling still and beckoning her to come to him. She shook her ears, trying to rid them of buzzing. It only made the sore spot on her head hurt more. She was cold now, too. When Sven had playfully pushed her down, her cloak had ripped wide. The cold air seeped in. But Sven's arms would be warm to enfold her.

"Long have we waited for you, Mother!" Lars called. His hands reached for Ki, grasped her cloak. In his eagerness, smiling, he jerked her to her knees, her cloak tearing like a rotted sack in his grip. Ki looked up at them, puzzled by their roughness. But they were smiling, ever smiling.

Suddenly Sven and the children staggered forward. Vandien had leaped onto Sven's back from behind. Blood masked half of his face. "Harpy!" he roared as he dug his fingers into Sven's eyes. Ki cried out in alarm, sprang up to help Sven beat the madman off.

But Sven shook him off effortlessly. Vandien hit the snow, rolling and plowing it up with the momentum of his slide. Sven disdainfully pulled the little knife from his chest, let it drop into the snow. No blood flowed. Ki looked up into his face as it bent toward her, mouth-close for a kiss. There was a stench nearby, a terrible stench that faded even as Ki noticed it. Sven was so near, how could she think about a smell, even a smell that reminded her of . . .

"Dead, Ki! Sven's dead! Will you call a Harpy by his name! By the Hawk, Ki, it's a Harpy!"

Vandien was back, staggering wildly, belaboring Sven and

the children with the buckle end of a harness strap. He was weeping and shrieking in his horror. The buckle caught Sven in the mouth, but still he smiled. On the temple, and still he smiled and reached out his strong, rounded arms to take Ki into them, to draw her close to his high blue chest and gaping turtle beak that would snip off the top of her skull.

Ki screamed. She dropped to her knees and scrambled away from them. "Mama, Mama!" called Rissa, but the voice was too high, too sugary in its betrayal, and that blue shirt of Lars's had been a mangle of red rag wrapped about bloody meat when Ki had buried it beside the road; and Sven had never, never smelled like that, like carrion and old bones, tatters of meat on yellow bones. Haftor had said they would never give up and here it was again, a battered blue Harpy that staggered after her, his wings frozen half-outstretched by scar tissue, blind on one side of his face, the tissue on his chest and legs burned away like roasted meat in a hot fire shriveled to tendons, standing frozen against the high bird chest. The little arms clawed at Ki as the knife came to her hand, catching in her hair. She struggled free, her hair ripping out of the widow's knots. "Sven!" she roared, and for one second more she saw him, and it was hot agony to plunge that blade into his bare chest, so wide and fair before her. But then it was shriveled and blue, and Vandien was flailing the monstrous bird head like a thing gone mad, yelling wordlessly as he used the buckle to fling bright bits of blue flesh and chunks of pale bone and blood, red as a Human's, spattering across the snow. The Harpy sank like a burning ship going down into white seas, its bird skull shattered. And still Vandien yelled, until suddenly he had to stop. The buckle fell lifeless to the snow. He stared at the bloody buckle as if it were a snake, his eyes wide with dismay. His body heaved as he panted in short, hard breaths of the cold air. The movement of his body dashed the blood from his face in spatters.

Ki stepped back and away from it all. The Harpy did not move. But Vandien did. He shook and wept and staggered about in the snow. Blood streamed from his face. The Harpy's talons had opened a slash that began between his eyes and ran down across the bridge of his nose, to trail off down his cheek into his beard and off the corner of his jaw. His face was ruined.

"Ki," called a voice, and she looked to where Haftor lay dying in the snow. His black eyes were wide with madness; she dared not approach, no matter how his arms reached for her beseechingly. Haftor wavered, and Ki's mind twisted as her ears buzzed louder. She saw she had been mistaken. It was Rissa, battered and scratched, but alive and reaching for her. Somehow she had survived it all, had never been dead. "Rissa!" Ki whispered. She fell on her knees by the child.

"You've killed me, Mama," Rissa whimpered pathetically.

"No," moaned Ki. She reached to touch the soft little cheek. But before she could stroke the pale skin, the child faded to blue. The Harpy's golden eye gave a final, mocking swirl and stopped. Its little blue hands fell to its chest, empty.

The great taloned legs of the Harpy gave a sudden jerk. Abruptly, the buzzing in Ki's ears stopped. She saw, as if for the first time, the huge blue body sprawled dead on the snow, the horses spooked far up the trail, and Vandien sinking to his knees, eyes blind with pain and horror.

Eight

SHE rose and went to Vandien, steadied his head against her body as she gently pushed his face back together. The cut was ragged. It would not close smoothly. She took his hand in hers, forced his fingers to open to hold the torn flesh in place. She left him sitting in the snow, staring at the body. She made her way back to the mounds of snow that marked their buried supplies. She found the brown tunic he had brought along for her, tore it into strips. It made coarse bandages. But it was not the type of wound that could be bandaged tightly shut. Ki had to be content with trying to stop the bleeding. When she was finished, one of his eyes was covered by the makeshift bandage, and he could barely open his jaws to speak. It did not matter. There was nothing to say.

Ki's familiar whistles and curses brought the horses back. Sigmund was steady as Ki loaded Vandien haphazardly onto his back. Vandien pulled himself up into a slump. His hands tangled in the thick mane. Ki did not bother to reload the supplies on the horses. They would pick them up with the wagon when they brought it this way.

She went to take a final look at the Harpy. She let the crumpled blue image burn itself into her mind. There were no more Harpies stalking Ki now. And no more Sven, and no more children, a small voice in her mind whispered. Ki ignored it.

A glint of silver caught her eyes. She squatted down by the body. She leaned forward, sucking her breath in harshly.

It was loose on the Harpy's skinny forearm. A twisted bolt of lightning. Ki freed it gently from the hard blue flesh. The cunningly worked silver was smooth and cold in her hands. She knew with a sick feeling that the good folk of Harper's Ford had found their scapegoat. The silver caught the sun as it whirled out over the deep valley, sparkled once more as it tumbled endlessly down, its flight lost in the shining white of the snow below it. She let Haftor go with it. She trudged dispiritedly over to where Vandien slumped on the horse, oblivious.

"We are going back to the wagon," she told him gently. "There are things in the wagon I can use to make a better bandage for you."

Vandien gave the barest nod. "I've never killed a sentient being before," he explained. Ki nodded.

Ki mounted Sigurd, and Sigmund fell in behind her. The grip of the cold was cracking the land. Ki felt the membranes of her nose stick together with the cold, felt the skin of her face stiffen with it. It leaked into her body where the Harpy had ripped her cloak. Ki felt oddly untouched by it. Cold was, after all, only cold. It could kill you, but that was all. And there were times when dying or living did not seem to be all that different from one another.

Last night's winds had swept away the horses' tracks, but it was easy enough to keep them on the ridge of ice. It ran down the center of the trail. Ki tried to think of it only as an easier way to get back to her wagon. She would think of it as an obstacle to her wagon when she had to face it. For now, she had Vandien to worry about. She reined her mind away from the Harpy images of the morning. They were dead, a long time dead, she reminded herself. Even Haftor—ugly, crazy Haftor. She could not change it. She forced her eyes to Vandien. Blood had reddened the bandages and was beginning to drip sluggishly from the side of his jaw. The tunic strips were saturated with it. His color was ghastly, his eyes too deep. Damn the man! Why had he chosen her to steal horses from?

The light burdens of Ki and Vandien did not trouble the horses. They trudged willingly through the snow. Ki's head still gave her a jab of pain whenever she moved too suddenly. She kept the grays to a walk, for Vandien's sake as much as her own. They made good time. Vandien had been right about that. A person on horseback would have had little trouble with his pass. Ki smiled bitterly.

A bend in the trail brought her wagon into view. Ki had never approached it from such a distance. The blue panes of the cuddy were sparkling with a layer of hoarfrost. The winds of the night had swept a light layer of snow over and around it. It looked as if it had been abandoned for centuries. As they drew nearer, she saw that the snow close to the wagon had been dis-

turbed, and recently. A dim foreboding overshadowing her,
she tried to think of ways to approach the wagon cautiously.
But there was no shelter to take cover behind, no way to hide
from the Sisters that loomed above them, or from whatever
might be inside the wagon. A glance at Vandien made her
want to hurry. He swayed visibly at every stride Sigmund
made. Ki reined in her impatience. To hurry the horses now
would only make it worse for him.

He seemed to feel her eyes on him. He gave her a one-eyed
glance. "It is only the pain, and the horror," he explained.
"The wound itself is not that grievous."

Ki looked long at the red stain that began at Sigmund's with-
ers and crept partway down his dappled shoulder. Another
slow drip fell, to deepen the color and enlarge the patch.

A short distance from the wagon Ki halted and slid from Sigurd's back. "Wait here," she commanded him needlessly.
"I want to check the wagon first."

"It had stood long in the shadow of the Sisters," Vandien
replied gravely.

"I don't think they made the tracks around it," Ki snorted
and set off through the snow. The wind seemed more chill
away from the moving warmth of the horse. She was awakened to how the huge body had warmed her legs and thighs, of
how she had profited from his rising body heat. It was as if she
had shed another cloak. She pulled her own cloak closer together where it had torn.

The wagon was dead. The frost was thick on its panels.
Swept snow had covered the singletree and heavy harness
straps that were stretched out before it. The tops of the tall
wheels were frosted with snow. Lines of snow clung to the
wagon wherever it had found the tiniest purchase. Nothing
alive waited in that wagon, Ki felt sure. She stopped by the
first impressions in the snow and felt relief at her own foolishness. The Harpy had called here first, only to find his prey had
fled. With a pang, Ki realized that but for the team's presence,
the Harpy might easily have passed them by where they slept
under the snow. She smiled hopelessly at the thought. It
made as much sense to her as any other reaction.

The cuddy door was frozen shut. Ki hammered it loose with
repeated blows of her fist, until suddenly it slid a small distance, and then scraped all the way open. She whistled to the
team, and the horses came on at their usual methodical pace,

bringing Vandien only incidentally.

She was rummaging within her cupboard for supplies when she felt the wagon give. Vandien's bandaged face appeared at the cuddy door.

"I didn't think you could manage that alone," she greeted him.

"It couldn't be as bad as it looks," he replied. She took his arm as he climbed in, and he sat down on the straw mattress gratefully.

He watched her tear a finely woven green gown into strips. "You may as well rest here for a few moments," she suggested, moving to the door. "I'm going to make a fire and melt some water. I have no salve or unguents to treat such a cut, but at least we can wash it out. A Harpy's talons usually carry all sorts of filth. Those who survive the wound often die of an infection." Her hand went to the side of her own face as she remembered gratefully Rifa's soothing oils and gentle hands. But her wounds had been scratches compared to Vandien's slash. And Rifa and her healing powers were a dream and a memory away.

Ki frowned at the dimming light as she emerged from the cuddy. The sky had remained clear, but somehow the snowy pass seemed darker to her now. A trick, perhaps, of the dark shiny rock looming over the wagon in startling contrast to the snow—or of eyes that had grown accustomed to the cuddy's dim interior and now faced snow again.

The fire was easily kindled. The snow seemed to melt and quench it every time Ki thought she had it started. The wood itself seemed impregnated with ice crystals and loath to take the flame. But at last the orange flames blossomed freely, and Ki set her blackened kettle packed full of snow to heat.

Vandien lay still as a dropped doll. Ki stood over the mattress, looking down on him. His face was small and lopsided under the red and brown bandage. "I'll have to take this one off so we can do a better job."

He nodded. His eye was distant but clear. Her awkward knots had caked with moisture and blood. They were frozen. The damp bandage was a stiff mush of ice-blood on his jaw. Vandien twitched as Ki slid the blade of her knife carefully beneath the layers and sawed through the cloth. It parted raggedly before the sharp blade. Ki laid the parted bandages back gently from his face. The blood had smeared around the wound. The flesh had slipped, and the cut hung open. Ki set her teeth at the thought of touching it. She felt an echo of the anguish she had felt when she stood over the bodies of Sven and the children. The closer she was to their pain, the hotter burned her own. Blood had leaked around the eye closest to the wound, to congeal there. The eye was caked shut with it. Vandien read her face as if it were a mirror, and went pale. He closed his other eye.

The little fire burned valiantly. The kettle water was not boiling but was hot to Ki's wary fingertip. She lifted it from the fire, to carry it cautiously to the wagon. The shadow of the Sisters loomed over her, darkening the trail. Ki noted with annoyance that the team had moved off and were farther from the wagon than she liked them to stray. It was no matter. A shake of grain upon the snow and a whistle would bring them back. But not just now. She had Vandien to tend to first, and she was weary. Every step she took seemed an effort. Her feet were weights at the ends of her legs. She thought longingly of sleep. Vandien would have to rest for a while after she had finished with him. She tried to tempt herself with the thought of hot tea and a kettle of soup. But it seemed a pallid attraction next to the sweet forgetfulness of sleep.

One green rag she soaked in the warm water to gently sponge the blood away. His eye was revealed, closed but still sound in its socket. Washing the blood from his face did not make the slash look any less angry. Steeling herself to the necessity, Ki held the cut open as she trickled a little of the warm water into it. It seemed that as much blood as water washed out of it for her efforts. Vandien scowled and tried to lift his head from the wet bedding. He opened his eyes to look at the red puddle and promptly closed them again.

"More water than blood," Ki assured him, hoping he would believe her. She wasn't really certain of it. "And a free-bleeding wound cleanses itself. So the Romni teach."

"And the moon keeps track of our sins. They teach that, too," Vandien replied grumpily.

Ki held the cut delicately closed, the skin lined up in its original place. The thinner cloth of the gown was a better bandage, easier to wrap firmly and tie in tighter knots.

"The Romni would have shaved around the wound, too, but I have no tools for that."

"Don't fret about it. I have no courage to let you try."

Vandien started to sit up, but fell back heavily. "My head feels so heavy. All of me feels heavy."

"Loss of blood makes you weak. And killing another thinking being makes the soul sick inside you. I know. You may as well rest. I'll make some hot food."

She left him, sliding the cuddy door shut behind her. The shadow of the Sisters overcast them deeply now. The glitter was lost from the snow. Ki looked up at the blackness that loomed over them and longed suddenly for their beauty to reach her as it once had. But all she sensed was their watching.

The fire had gone out in a puddle of black water. Ki moved on leaden feet to the back of the wagon to get the last of the wood. They would miss it tonight, but she felt she must have some hot food to put some strength back into them, to give her the energy to attack the problem of the ice ridge. The last sack of grain lay in the back of the wagon beside the pitiful pile of wood. She might as well do that, too. It was an effort to pull the heavy sack to her, to tug it open and spill a feed of grain upon the snow. She looked up, whistling for the team. They were nowhere in sight. Their passage through the snow was plain. They had headed back toward the campsite and the dead Harpy. Ki cursed their sudden whim and set out to retrieve them. They would never hear her pathetic little whistle now that they were around the bend of the mountain. And once they reached the two sacks of grain at the camp site, they would have no inclination to return.

She forced her leaden feet to jog trot through the broken snow. They moved slowly, but their strides were long. Ki panted as she tried to catch up. The thud of her own feet echoed painfully in the side of her head, and the cold poked at her through the rent in her cloak. Damn the man and the horses and the snow and the Harpy! And damn Rhesus for his crazy scheme to get his jewels safely to his home. And damn her heavy head that wanted to nod off her neck, and her heavy feet that seemed to gather snow and weight at every step. And Damn the Sisters, who could cloud the daylight with their shadows.

By the time Ki had reached the bend in the mountain, she had catalogued and damned every adverse condition in her life. It was a small satisfaction, but it seemed to warm her a little. And the grays, looking almost a dappled black in contrast to the snow, had on another whim stopped just around the bend of the trail. They set their ears back at her language, and disapproved when she tried to drive them back toward the wagon. Sigurd remained impassive to her halter-tuggings and slappings of his immense rump. It was only by mounting the more placid Sigmund and taking Sigurd in tow that she was able to get them moving back toward the wagon. Sigurd came sulkily, dragging his heavy hooves through the snow and snorting disdainfully at the bovine spirit of his larger and stronger partner.

But round the bend of the hill, Sigmund, too, came to a halt. His ears pitched forward with interest, but he would not take another step. Ki was a jigging monkey on his back, for all the good it did her. Tears of rage stung her eyes and froze on her lashes. She stared longingly at her wagon, thinking of the firewood that rested inside its shadowed box.

Her eyes caught on the wagon. Its box was shadowed deeply, blackly shadowed, as if the snow had turned to congealed blood. The snow about it was as black and deep as the rock of the Sisters that overshadowed it. Ki glanced again at the clear sky. The sun struck her eyes. The shadows of the Sisters lay on the wagon by their own will, not by the sun's casting.

Ki joggled her heels against the barrel-body she straddled. Sigmund shook his head. She slid from him and went ahead on foot.

There was a dividing line, a place where white snow gave way to deep black shadow. And the shadow was deep, seemed to tell Ki's eyes that it was a tall, standing liquid in which she must wade. She glanced up again at the sun, shaking her head in consternation. She stepped into the blackness.

Eerie. She stood, one foot atop a flat black lake of shining, eternal depth that did not reflect her. As Ki watched, her foot sank slowly into its surface. The black stuff pressed heavily about it, squeezing it tightly, like no mud that she had ever struggled through. In dismay, she tried to snatch her foot back. It came slowly and only with great effort. But her foot came out clean, undamped, no trace of clinging black. Ki stood again on hard ice beneath snow.

She looked to her wagon. The black sea had engulfed most of the tall wheels, lapped motionlessly about the bottom of the box. It had buried and quenched her fire, had covered the harness that lay before the wagon. And still the level rose.

"Vandien!" She roared the name with all the power in her

lungs. The black stuff swallowed up the sound, reduced her shout to a whimper. Ki's breath came raggedly. She heard motion behind her, saw the horses wisely retreating around the corner of the mountain trail. She wondered what they knew, and how.

"Vandien!"

Her scream was a whisper in the night. She imagined him asleep, his head heavy on the mattress, his body drained of blood and strength. He would die in the shadows of the Sisters, crushed as the legends had warned. She could not save him. She could not save anybody, not Sven or her children, or even ugly Haftor, and not Vandien. To venture out on that black stuff was foolish heroics. Her death would be an empty gesture, like bandaging a corpse. No one would expect it of her, not even Vandien. She watched the blackness lap higher. It would be like putting socks on a frozen foot, as insane as . . . as fighting a Harpy with a piece of harness.

She wanted to run, but could not. Each time her foot touched down, the black stuff caught at it. Her whole body was heavy to her, her hands were weights that swung at the ends of her arms; her head, too heavy, wobbled on her neck. Even the air she tried to suck into her lungs seemed thicker, rancid somehow. There was no stir of wind. The black stuff made no sucking noises as it grudgingly released her feet. No noise existed on its black plane. And it was rising, visibly rising. Even as she watched, another spoke of the tall wheel was swallowed. It lapped, it climbed. And her feet dragged in it, threatened to spill her face-first into it. She grew heavier with every step, her arms dragged down from her shoulders; her chin kept dropping to her chest. Crawl, crawl, pleaded her body, but Ki saw herself horizontal on that blackness, never rising again.

At last her hands clutched the sides of the wagon. She clung to its wood like a drowning swimmer working her way along a steep bank.

"Vandien!" she gasped, the words falling heavily to the blackness, scarcely reaching even her own ears. There was no reply.

She fell on her knees onto the wagon seat, scrambled to open the cuddy door. Impossibly, the blackness was rising up inside the wagon as well. There was not enough space to clamber into the cuddy and stand. The black stuff was nearly level with the bottom of the cuddy door and rising as Ki watched. Soon it would reach the sleeping platform. "Vandien!" she screamed. He stirred faintly and failed to raise his bandaged head.

"Tired," he mumbled complainingly. "Feel weak." He closed his dark eye again. Ki's hand sank deep in the muck, her fingers disappearing in it immediately. The black gripped her, squeezed her hand like a well-met friend. With a half-sob, she snatched her hand back. It came out clean, with a shoulder wrenching effort. Her breath jerked in and out of her body. She would scuttle across the top of it, swiftly, not give herself a chance to sink. She would do it now. She would do it this instant. The black rose a little higher, crept over the edge of the seat plank. Ki's cry strangled in her throat.

She would have done as well trying to scuttle across the top of a lake. Under her full body weight, her hands sank wrist-deep, to be pulled out ponderously. There was no purchase to drag her knees and legs out of the stuff. With a wail of hopelessness, she launched herself forward, her full body length. Her hands fell on the edge of the mattress, gripped its straw-stuffed cloth. She could not drag herself to it. She could not pull it toward her. Everything was sinking, was held in the blackness.

The light in the cuddy went dimmer. Ki glanced in alarm at the tiny window, then back at the cuddy door. The seat was covered. Every moment the space between the top of the door and the blackness grew narrower. The blackness was rising up around her legs, holding them as tightly as leather boots as it lapped against her thighs.

"Vandien!" she screamed the name, and the sound seemed to reach him. His eyes opened a little. The strain on her back was terrific. She wanted to drop belly-first in the blackness. The weight of her body seemed to increase every moment. "The shadows of the Sisters, Vandien. We have to get out of here! You aren't weak, it's the shadows. Come on, man, damn you!"

The mention of the Sisters seemed to prick him. The dark eye came alive, looked about him. Panic ignited there.

"We have to get out of here!" he exclaimed. The words barely brushed Ki's ears. A hysterical giggle burst out of her at the inadequacy of his statement.

He rolled onto his belly as if it took all his strength simply to shift his body. He stared at the narrow hatch that remained of the cuddy door. Ki knew that her legs were nearly completely encased in the stuff. His dark eye widened in terror.

"Forgive me, Ki," he said, or so his soft words seemed to be. He reared his body up on his knees and fell forward on top of her. Her face plunged into the airless, lightless, sensationless blackness. Horror snapped her neck muscles, and her head jerked up. Vandien was slithering over the top of her, was using her body as a bridge to the buried plank seat of the wagon. One of his booted feet scraped across her back. With a heavy spring off her, he was free. He was kneeling on the plank, in the black stuff, but not sinking deeper.

She could not crane her neck to see him. She heard no more movement. Panic, anger, outrage at his treachery energized her. The black stuff had seized her belly, but her hands had kept their hold on the straw mattress. With the strength that comes only with death-terror, she pulled up. But even as her chest came free of the blackness, a strong jerk pulled her down into the muck again. Her hands snapped free of their precarious grip.

"Don't fight me!" The voice came from a world away. Then the grip on her ankles became the grip of hands, not blackness. She felt the solid, homey scuff of wood seat-plank beneath her toes. She tried to help, but her body was impossibly heavy. Thick as the black stuff seemed to be, she did not gain any when she pushed against it with her hands. She felt Vandien put his full body weight on her calves that now rested on the seat, and grab her hips and jerk upward. In reaction, her chin hit the black and was gripped by it. Her belly muscles convulsed in horror at its touch. The buck broke her chest and shoulders free, and then Vandien's arms were around her waist, helping her to draw her arms and hands out of it. The back of her head hit the top of the cuddy door as she was jerked through it.

There was no time for gasping, for rest, for thanks. Already the black lapped about their hips as they knelt on the hidden seat. Vandien's face was white with exertion beneath his stained bandage turban. Wordlessly, he staggered upright, to stand on the seat and drag himself up onto the roof of the cuddy. Ki had scrambled up to lie full-length beside him before he could offer help. Side by side, they panted like dogs, watching with dull eyes the black tide that rose around them. Ki desperately needed to rest, but there was no time.

The black stuff seemed to be rising faster. She heard the wood of the wagon groan ponderously in its grip. She gazed across the black sea to the far white of the snowy trail. She yearned, but she knew they would never make it. They would sink, smother and drown in the blackness. Crushed by the shadows of the Sisters. She turned her eyes up to the immensity above them. Vandien's gaze followed hers. They had no further capacity for awe, they could not marvel at the beauty of the revealed silver faces. They looked on what few had ever seen: the features of the Sisters, stern, uncompromising, watching their black veils drop upon the trail. Their faces were too pure to be Human, unsullied by the emotions of lesser beings. Vandien stretched appealing hands forth to them. If the wide silver eyes saw his plea, they made no sign. The black rose higher. Impossibly far away, the white snow shone invitingly. The Sisters lingered in their kiss, their eyes impassive, their hair streaming silver.

"To die, while looking on such beauty," breathed Ki.

Vandien picked up her hand to gain her attention. His eye flitted to the cliff edge, or where it had been. Ki understood. Better quickly than slowly. The edge was close enough that conceivably they might make it. And if they smothered along the way—did it matter where one died, on top of a wagon or crawling toward suicide?

Ki tried to struggle to her feet, but Vandien dragged her flat again. He slithered off the wagon top and into the blackness. It was now only a hand below the level of the wagon top. She watched him go, expecting to see him founder in the stuff. But he kept his hands and legs constantly in motion, his body twitching back and forth as if he were in a fit. Like a swimming snake, she thought, and then the better image of a water-skating insect came to her mind. His constant twitchings and jerkings kept him on the surface, scuttling along, giving the black no time to grip him. She wished she could manage it. But her body was too tired, her muscles screaming, her head pounding. Vandien twitched and writhed along, moving slowly toward the edge of the trail. Ki watched him go, felt a weary gladness for him. The wagon creaked alarmingly beneath her. It slowly began to lurch. Ki longed for the will and strength to follow Vandien. He did not look back. The black rose toward her, touched her foot with soft hands.

Ki scuttled. Terror, not strength, and the whip of panic moved her body. The top of the wagon disappeared even before she had her body completely off it. She did not look down at the stuff beneath her, but jerked and flopped along like a fish drowning in air. The black seized and released her, seized and released her, and each time it gave back the foot, the knee, the hand with greater reluctance. The air was too heavy to breathe. Ki could not get enough air into her lungs. Any trace of sound in the air was squeezed out of her ears, pushed away from her. The edge of the cliff was incredibly distant, and Vandien nearly as far. Blackness was closing in from the sides of her vision. Logic told her that her body was protesting its abuse, was retreating into unconsciousness. But a subliminal horror rose in her, told her that the blackness at the sides of her vision was the same blackness that tried to suck her down. Ki willed her body to greater effort.

Vandien slipped over the edge. He reached it, and without a pause scuttled headfirst over the drop-off. She heard no scream as he went. The beginning of his fall was slow, for the black stuff held him, dragging him back so that it took forever for his body to tip over the edge. His legs were going down. Ki mindlessly made a final effort to catch up with him, to join him in his fall.

His boots vanished. Ki wallowed on, alone in the black, not fighting to survive but only to choose her own method of dying. If her body must be crushed, let it be smashed on rocks and eaten by birds, not engulfed in a mindless black ooze. Her legs were slowing, refusing her frantic commands to crawl faster. She seemed to sink deeper with every move, to make no forward progress at all. She could not see the edge. Her head was too heavy, she could not hold it high enough. She had to look down on the shining black that granted her no reflection but tried to pull her down. Her nose began to bleed; she had to gulp air through her mouth. The blood from her nose fell in thick drops on the black surface, to be swallowed by it. Ki angrily snorted the blood from her nostrils and crawled on.

The edge! Ki stared down a sheer wall of blackness that suddenly became a wall of stone and snow. Ki gave a yelp and flung her head and shoulders over the edge. She pulled her hands free, and her arms, and dangled them down to the snow, so far beyond her reach. The white valley floor, with its dark dots of brush, was as far away as the sky. The black sucked at her belly, took her feet and ankles. One more flop, one more surge, one more belly-wrench of muscle.

She was over! She dangled, head down, but the black would not release her body. It was a controlled fall as she slid, belly against the black, feet nearly straight in the air, down the face of the sheer black wall. She looked down at the valley floor, white-mantled and horridly far away. She oozed slowly toward it. The blood from her nose choked her, and she retched as her body fought for air.

Her wrist was gripped. She turned startled eyes to Vandien's snow-white face. His dark eye seized her as hard as his hand. He had been shouting, but the black had eaten the sound.

"Turn your body!" he screamed in her ear, and she made out his words. "Turn your body while the stuff still grips you. Force your feet to come down first."

He was clear of the black, clinging—she knew not how—to the snow and rock that sheared off the trail. Her muscles screamed as she wrenched her too-heavy body about, forced it to bend and obey. Vandien braced her hand against the tiny ledge he had found in the cliff edge. Ki wished for her gloves as she gripped the freezing rock. The black stuff had long ago sucked them from her hands.

Gradually her body weight came down, and her shoulder and arms twisted unnaturally as she tried to fold her body sideways. With a silent sucking, her feet came clear of the black. Ki found her body sliding in an arc. The whip of her released body cracked, and she nearly lost her precarious grip. Then she was clinging, toes and fingers, body spread, beside Vandien. She pressed her face into the cold snow and the solid rock. She licked the dampness of melting snow flavored with her blood. The cold, thin air flowed into her lungs delightfully. For a long time, it was enough to cling and breathe and wet her mouth with snow.

"Ki!" It was a shout by intention, but a whisper by effect. She turned her face to Vandien wearily. Whatever it was, she wished he would keep it to himself. She did not want to speak or think or struggle anymore. Let her cling here until her strength gave out. After that, at least it would be quick.

"Watch me!" She did, with weary eyes that only widened a little as she saw him risk his hold by trying to scramble upward. He thrust his free hand back into the vertical black wall just

above the snow and rock. It gripped him. He hung by its sucking grip as he raised his other hand and thrust it in beside the
first one. He braced his feet lightly against the cliff face. Ki was
only mildly intrigued by his performance until he drew out one
bare hand and stuck it in as far away as his outstretched arm
would reach. Then he drew out his second hand, plunging it in
close to the first one. His body scraped against snow and rock
as he dragged it after his hands.

"Come on!" She read from his lips the words his mouth
roared. Then he was doing it again—draw out a hand, stretch
the arm, thrust in the hand, follow with the second hand,
scrape the body along. He did not look back.

Ki watched her hand idly as it clawed up the rock and snow
and crept into the dark grip of the black stuff. She shivered as
she felt her hand taken in its fingerless grasp. She swung for an
instant, trusting to that black suction. Her shoulder cracked
ominously as she thrust her second hand into the black wall.
Her toes scrabbled against rock.

Pull out the first hand. Dangle and reach for another hold.
Her second hand was beginning to slip free as she thrust in the
first one again. It was a more precarious way of moving than
it had appeared. The effort of scraping her body across the
rock face dragged at her hands, trying to pull them free of her
gripless black hold. Pull, thrust, dangle; pull, thrust, scrape the
body along. No air to breathe with, her hands stretched high.
Shoulder joints threatened and warned. Ki remembered sickly
how the one shoulder had once pulled free of her body's command. Please, she begged her body. Pull, thrust, dangle; pull,
thrust, scrape the body along. Gradually the blackness became more solid. It held her hands more firmly, and for a few
moments that was a comfort, but then it became more difficult
to thrust the venturing hand in, harder to make the black relin-
quish the trailing hand. When her hands were in the black,
they were compressed tightly, emerging from it white, the
blood forced out of them. Ki folded her mouth tight and went
on stoically. Her hands were cold, colder than her body that
pressed and scraped across hard rock and snow. Her fingers
were numb, and the black was becoming so solid that she had
to batter her hand against it before it would sink in at all. The
trailing hand had to be jerked free with a snapping movement.
Ki felt tiny rippings in her shoulders, in the muscles of elbows

and wrist, tiny snappings and poppings. Puppet strings
breaking.

She jerked a hand free, reached, slammed it against the solid wall. She drew it back farther, smashed her fist against it.
It would not give. She dangled by one hand, and the hand
was beginning to send her sharp messages of pain as the black
crushed it. Ki squeezed her eyes shut, made a final driving
blow against the wall.

"It doesn't work with rock." Vandien seized her knotted
fist, heaved at it. She heard his body scrape and slide over
snow. She could hear suddenly, she could breathe, and when
she opened her eyes and looked, she saw that she had reached
the end of the black wall and had, indeed, been trying to force
her fist into solid rock. She jerked her screaming hand free of
the black wall, entrusting her weight unthinkingly to
Vandien's grip on her wrist and forearm. He grunted as he
took her weight, then, with a heave, she found the edge of the
world was under her armpits. She scrambled frantically, her
boots treading air, and with another heave she was up. Panic
sent her body scooting further along the flat trail top. She
didn't even try to rise but slithered along. Vandien didn't
mock her. He was too busy copying her.

They stopped to lie close together in the snow, bodies
touching at shoulders and hips, heads cushioned on their arms.
Ki listened to Vandien pant. Or was it her own hoarse breathing? The air came easily, the snow was cold to rest in; she was
tired, and she did not wish to lift her head, but she knew she
could if she tried. She was alive. She raised her head enough to
gulp in a mouthful of snow. Her teeth hurt as it melted in her
mouth, but she took another. She rolled her head over to one
side to look into Vandien's face.

She studied the face so close to her own. He watched her
from under half-closed lashes. What she could see of his face
was drained of blood and lined with weariness. A large part of
his bandage was red and wet. The snow closest to his face was
melting with the red.

"You look like an actor painted for a play," she panted.
"White face, black beard, green and red bandage. You could
be the corpse in the scene."

"Not this scene," Vandien grunted. They turned together
to look at the solid black wall that reared up from the trail only

a few steps away. Ki felt a pressure against her leg. She jerked away from it, and Sigmund, offended, snorted. Behind him, Sigurd was leisurely scratching the side of his nose against his black foreleg. They seemed mildly curious about Ki and Vandien in the snow, but not greatly interested.

"My loyal beasts!" Ki scoffed.

"Smarter than you were," Vandien rejoined.

They remained prostrate in the snow, breathing and resting. Ki's body ached all over, her head throbbed, and she felt marvelous. The cool of the snow began to make itself noticed. Her hands were bare of protection, her gloves lost in that blackness. The cold pushed at her through her rent cloak. She smiled weakly at the thought of it. The Harpy of the morning seemed a lifetime away now, and of small import. She reached up wearily to pull her hood up over her head. She would have to get up soon and do something. She lay still, wondering what something she would do.

"Ki!"

She opened her eyes grudgingly. She wondered when she had closed them. The sun was far down the sky. One side of her body was cold. She pulled the covers over her more tightly and her eyes started to slide shut again. Then she realized that the covers were her own cloak and Vandien's that he had spread to cover them both. The side of her body that shared his warmth was comfortable enough, but her feet were tingling. Time to move. She shifted.

"Be still!" Vandien hissed.

Ki froze. His eye was dark and intent, staring from beneath his bandage that now showed a pale layer of frost over the red. His expression brooked no questions. She moved her eyes to see what he saw.

The silver Sisters had gone gray. The black was rising, was writhing back up to them in whirling drifts and eddies, in every shade from palest gray to black. It flowed up like layers of silken webbing, veiling their beauty once more from lesser eyes. Ki took one final drink of their heartless majesty before the rising black made them again impassive stone.

"They were guardians, once," Ki breathed.

"Sssh!" Vandien nodded slowly.

"How could I fall asleep so close beside them?"

The black on the Sisters grew darker every instant. On the trail where it had lain the wall of it was becoming lower, sinking as the black mist that formed it wafted back up to the Sisters.

"We were out of their shadows," Vandien murmured, becoming bold enough to speak. "They are monstrously fair about it. Only in that one spot do they hold sway. That is why the trail, coming and going, avoids the look of their eyes, stays hidden for as long as it can. They are slow to react, I suppose. Perhaps they guarded against creatures more ponderous than we know, or perhaps they were instructed to barricade and block, not destroy. How can we know? Or maybe they did a thing that we can never comprehend at all, and the danger they present to travelers these days is coincidental. We are young on this old world, Ki."

"My wagon!" Ki replied. She drew herself together, rose, leaving Vandien to scramble after her. The last drifts and snatches of mist were rising, flowing back into place. Ki walked unhesitating into the area they had just vacated. She had to step down off the layer of snow and ice where she and Vandien had napped to tread the bare rock of the trail, exposed flat and smooth where the black had been.

Ki had once seen a Romni wagon that had slid and rolled off a mountain path made treacherous by spring runoff. She had marveled at the clean snapping of the heavy wood, great horses thrown about like puppies, at the litter of small debris strewn down the side of the cliff like bits of bright paper. But never had she seen wood crushed, the fibers compressed together so tightly that they crumbled away from one another afterwards. Her wagon had been crushed and smeared across the stone like a bright insect smashed on a window pane.

Here and there her eyes picked out the details her mind did not want to know: the woeful head of a wooden horse, intact, but its body crumbled away; a rag of bright curtain; flat, crumpled copper that had been a kettle; straw crumbled to chaff; a single bright flower painted on a board that had survived.

She did not scream; she did not speak. Vandien's boots scuffed on the rock as he strode up to her. He took her upper arm to lead her away, but she shrugged him off. Only her eyes were alive as they flickered and danced over the wreckage. She began to tremble. It started as a shivering and increased in tempo until Vandien wondered if she would convulse in a fit. She prowled shaking among the wreckage of her life.

Vandien observed her. She moved slowly, stooping to pick

up a treasured fragment. She cradled it against her body for a few steps, then dropped it to pick up some other remnant. She seemed to choose them at random: a scrap of leather, the handle of a mug, a rag of bright fabric. She clutched and discarded each in turn. She moved aimlessly through the rubble, keeping nothing of what she gathered, impervious to the cold that made her hands white and red. Finally, she let a little fur boot tumble from her hand. She watched it fall. Her trembling passed.

"It will be night soon. We have no more time to waste here." Her tone almost implied that Vandien had kept her standing about. With a purposeful stride, she crossed the rocky trail to climb up the packed snow and ice. "It will be dark soon," she called back to Vandien. Her trembling had ceased. She made a grab for Sigurd's head, and he swung it willfully away from her. She slapped him sharply on the shoulder and made a second, more successful grab. She was looking up the hill of his rolling, dappled shoulder when Vandien came up behind her.

"Boost?"

"Then, how will you get up on Sigmund? You look like you feel worse than I do."

"I wouldn't claim that distinction. Ki, I am sorry for the things that have come to pass."

"Are you? I wish I could be. I wish I could feel anything about them."

He caught her leg, threw her up on Sigurd's back. She rode over to Sigmund, snagged him, and led the more docile animal back to stand on the snow beside the ice ridge. Vandien launched himself at the broad back, nearly overshot onto his face, then scrambled into position. They headed the horses around the curve of the mountain and back down the trail. The wind blew stinging ice crystals into their faces. Ki rode with her hands tucked under her thighs for warmth, letting Sigurd follow his nose.

They would have passed their supplies in the darkness but for the body of the Harpy. It stuck up, too large and angular a shape to be completely covered by the blowing snow. Ki reined in beside it, looking down without pity on the scarred features, the ruined body. For the first time, she realized how much damage the fire had done to him. Thick scar tissue stretched on his chest, and she saw that the fingers of his small forearms were curled permanently into fists.

"What kept him going?" she wondered to herself.

"Hate." Vandien spoke from the darkness beside her. "What will keep you going now that he's dead?"

Ki was silent for long moments. She listened to the silence of a night broken only by stirring wind, a shifting horse, Vandien's breathing. What was left to her? She had no man or children to cherish; she had no Harpy to fear and hate; no wagon to shelter and preserve her grief in; no friends to return to. She felt peculiarly emptied. The debris of her life once more sifted through her hands. She raised her hand to a bulge that still nestled inside her shirt.

"I have my freight to deliver."

Vandien laughed low and unpleasantly. "I wondered when it would dawn on you. It will be a surprised client that receives it! Need I recommend to you that you go armed?"

Ki gave him a peculiar look. "Armed?"

Vandien shook his head at her. "Still she trusts. Do you believe that it was fate that decided to give that Harpy another chance at you? Was it fate that sent you through this particular remote pass on a fool's errand, with a handful of trinket gems as cargo?"

Ki's eyes caught what little light there was. Vandien recoiled from that look. "Be careful how you speak of Rhesus!" she warned. "I have dealt with him for many years. I know him."

"Perhaps. But I know gems," Vandien returned coldly. "I have handled some in my time, enough to know fine from poor. And what you have in that pouch would do more credit to a tinker's tray than to a lady's wrist. Two are flawed, one is badly cut, and the other two of little value—not enough to be worth sending someone through this pass in a wagon."

"He gave me a good advance against their delivery," Ki replied stoutly.

"No doubt he could afford it if someone else was footing the bill. And would the advance seem so large if he never expected to have to pay the rest of it?"

A small doubt uncurled inside Ki. Swiftly she catalogued her dealings with Rhesus, finding a resentment here, a bitterness there. To her, their dealings had always seemed fair, the agreed-upon price had always been paid. Now she saw that, to Rhesus, that would mean that he had never made a shrewd bargain such as he liked to strike, that he had never been able to force from Ki more than he had paid for. Such a thought might rankle with a man like that. Ki's shoulders slumped another notch. Was there any direction that treachery could not come from?

They ate salt meat in darkness, then huddled close and impersonal on the shagdeer cover, the cloaks thrown over them. Ki closed her eyes, feigning sleep. Vandien was not deceived.

"There is a fine wainwright in Firbanks."

"I don't go that way. I have freight to deliver in Diblun."

Vandien sighed. "I feared you would insist. Ki, will you take the chance for that petty vengeance, and make it a framework for your life? And then what? After the merchant, will you find who bribed him and take another revenge? Take my advice. Don't go to Diblun at all. Let it go, and be free of it. You owe him nothing, and the right person could sell those gems for you and get you something out of this mess."

"I promised to deliver them. Regardless of how he has broken faith with me, I shall not break mine. And I do have questions for him. I doubt it was a Harpy, burnt and blue, that came to him and asked him to arrange my little journey. Harpies are lacking in such subtlety. To me, it smells like a Human."

"To track down and be avenged on." Ki did not reply. "And when that quest is settled?" Vandien left her no time to reply. "Ki, have you never considered living?"

She was quiet beside him. He knew she did not sleep. He gave it up. "My face throbs like this—beat . . . beat . . . beat . . . beat . . . beat . . . ." Vandien counted out his pain. He began to reach a hand to his bandaged face, then stopped himself. "We have no more clean bandage material, do we?"

"I'll see what I can find in the morning. Vandien, I have never chosen death."

"Then you run remarkably close company with it, for entertainment, I suppose. Falling Harpies and bogged-down wagons put a certain edge on life. I have not been bored riding with you. But what of yourself? Shall you never take joy in anything again?"

"I don't know." They listened to the ponderous sounds of Sigmund folding his body down to the ground for the night. "Maybe. I don't think I really want to. How could I?"

"I saw a child at a fair once who bought a little cake at one of the stalls. In the jostle of the crowd, all the sugar tumbled from its top. 'It's all ruined now!' he cried, and dashed the little cake into the dirt to be trampled by the crowd."

"A man and two children!" Ki's voice trembled in outrage. "Not sugar on a damned sweetcake, Vandien!"

"So, by all means, dash the rest of your life into the dirt!" His anger matched her own.

"And what do you suggest?"

Ki had the last word. Vandien had no answer. They settled deeper into the coverings, huddling closer to one another. The wind did not scatter snow over them tonight. It seemed to have changed directions. There was only the cold night full of icy stars that pressed down on them, keeping their bodies curled for warmth. Ki closed her eyes.

"I could make you an offer," Vandien ventured cautiously, almost as if he did not wish Ki to hear him. The night held its breath, listening. "I could offer to never give you anything that I didn't give freely, with no thought of repayment, without even a thought of the giving."

Ki was silent, sleeping perhaps. Or she had not heard him. Or she did not care to answer. Or she would not.

"And what would you ask in return, Vandien, you scrawny bit of road baggage?" he asked himself in a strained falsetto.

"Why, exactly the same from you, Ki," he resumed in his normal voice.

Silence. The stars pressed down on the earth, and Sigurd slowly followed his teammate's example. He placed his large body close to Sigmund's, sharing warmth.

"Since you put it so attractively, Vandien," the falsetto replied, "I'll have to leap at the chance. Why don't I travel with you to Thesus? We could horrify all your relatives, and they would probably give you twice as much money as usual to make yourself scarce."

"Wonderful, Ki," Vandien resumed. "I dreaded the thought of walking that far alone. We'll leave for Thesus first thing in the morning."

"Go to sleep, fool," Ki growled.

"Now, there's a thing we both agree on," Vandien mumbled.

NINE

SALT meat and cold measured their days. The grays grew thin, Sigurd becoming more snappish, Sigmund more docile with privation. Ki rebandaged Vandien's face at intervals with the remaining scraps of tunic. The slash was red across his olive skin, but it stayed closed and did not ooze or swell. The grain bags became empty too fast, but the team traveled much farther in one day than they would have pulling the wagon in two. By days, Vandien sat upon Sigmund's wide back and wove stories for Ki on his story string. Sometimes she remembered to smile at the amusing parts, and sometimes he told them for the benefit of Sigmund's flicking ears. At those times, Ki was busy weaving stories for herself. A dozen times she imagined her confrontation with Rhesus. She would deflate that pompous little man, and then he would admit to her who had hired him for his dirty little bit of deception. And Nils. For she was sure it had been Nils. From Nils she would demand her accounting, not only for this attempt on her own life, but also payment for Haftor's. But there Ki's thought soon eddied and swirled pointlessly. What could she demand of the old man as fit atonement? Was there anything she could take from him that would assuage that gnawing feeling of injustice within her? Another Ki would have been wolfish for his life. But that Ki would also have burned with a white-hot anger. The Ki that rode in front of Vandien only felt a sense of a task left incomplete. She felt a compulsion to tie up the loose ends, to put a final stamp on this series of injuries and revenges. To be done with it all.

The trail on this side of the mountains was more direct in its route. They came down through wooded country that let them kindle a fire, even though they had nothing to cook over it. Game seemed plentiful on this side, but Ki would allow Vandien no time to pursue it. She pushed on toward her goal relentlessly, counting still the days before her freight would be overdue.

There came a morning when Vandien glimpsed the rising smoke of a chimney far down their day's path. He gave a whoop that startled both horses. Ki glared at him.

"An inn, a Human inn! It's called Three Pheasants. Ah, tonight, Ki, we shall have a fire, and hot food, and cold beer, and beds under a roof. And what a tale I shall have to tell Micket, who runs the inn."

Ki pulled in Sigurd slightly, to sit looking down the slope of the mountain over the tops of the snow-frosted trees. She could make out the clear white of an opening in the trees, a cleared path of ground surrounding the inn. The smoke from the inn's chimney was a grayish haze against the pale blue sky. She nudged Sigurd on again. "We shall reach the inn after noon, but before nightfall," she pointed out.

"With time to order up a hot tub of water and soak before we go to the common room to tell tales and eat fresh meat and drink. And these beasts will have the clean straw and fragrant hay they so richly deserve."

Ki made a sour face at Vandien's sybaritic tone. "I'm not in the habit of sleeping at inns, and the pass cost me more time than I had reckoned on. I have to keep on my way, Vandien."

He heaved a sigh of resignation. "Well, at least we shall be able to take on some fresh supplies and get a kettle. Must we press on to Diblun so fast, Ki? I tell you, the man will not be glad to see you."

"*I* must." Ki accented the pronoun, glanced across at Vandien. "And you know, as I do, that our trails part soon. I will be going to Diblun. Your road to Firbanks would be in the opposite direction, if I am not mistaken. I have never been there."

"I have no pressing business that commands me to be there by a certain day." Vandien forced joviality into his voice. "We can settle your business first."

"No."

Vandien looped up his story string, put it into his pocket. Ki tried to see his face, but he turned it from her.

"You have never rebuked me," Ki struggled, picking words. She felt the nails of her fingers digging into her palms. "You have never talked of what I owe you, never cast it up to me that your face . . . that there will be a scar always. . . ."

He did not turn to her. "Part of my offer, remember? To never give you anything that I could not give freely."

"Damn you!" Ki hissed. "Vandien, cannot you see it? It would be empty between us. I am not ready to take a man. Desire is dead in me. I cannot pretend. I would not."

"I don't recall offering myself to you in that capacity." Vandien spoke quietly. "The offer was made as a friend. Nothing more." He looked straight ahead as he rode. A rush of blood dyed Ki's cheeks, and she was torn between anger and embarrassment.

"It was a natural assumption for me to make!" she blazed at him.

"Only if it was in your mind before I made my offer," Vandien countered loftily.

The truth of his words silenced Ki. Damn the man! Must he always voice the words that brought her the most discomfort? His eyes were still fixed far down the trail. She was glad she did not have to meet his eyes. He raised a pale hand to his mouth to cover a cough. Ki stared fixedly between Sigurd's ears until the noises of his choking fit could not be ignored. Then she turned stern eyes on him, to find that he was barely able to keep his seat and cover his laughter.

"Damn you!" she cried in fury, and swung at him so violently that she found herself sliding down Sigurd's broad shoulder. Vandien's hand under her arm, hoisting her back to her seat, was no comfort.

Ki jogged her heels against Sigurd, and he moved out ahead of Sigmund. Her back was arrow-straight as she rode on before Vandien. Her hood covered her still reddened ears.

"In case you have forgotten," he called to her in a totally unrepentant voice, "my offer specified that I would never give you anything with any thought of repayment, or debt invoked. And that was what I asked of you in return. That you would never give me anything that you did not want to give."

"Until you gave me a big belly, and I gave you a child, and we could each accuse the other of violating our agreement!" Ki did not look back as she spoke.

Vandien clucked his tongue. "Are you still thinking of me in that capacity? Don't give it another thought, Ki. If I had the ability to do that to any woman, I would not be roaming the roads now. I would have inherited my parents' lands, instead of them going to my cousin. And if I chose to roam, when I returned I would not be an embarrassment to my uncle."

Ki shrank from the edged affability of his tone. She slowed Sigurd until his pace matched Sigmund's and the two were abreast. She tried to meet Vandien's eyes, but he kept them away from her face. The slender story string came out of his pocket as if by magic.

"And now," he orated minstrel-style, "I shall tell to thee the tale of the son of the Vandet and Dienli."

The string leaped and settled on his fingers, and he held it up for her, a sign on each of his hands. "Thus was he named, for Van the first son, and Dien also." Ki's unwilling eyes were drawn to the string, captured in its mesh.

"They were proud at the birth of their son," Vandien went on, holding up the complicated star that, for his people, signified birth. "He was marked with the sign of the Hawk from his birth, and they judged it a sign of good fortune." The string flipped and settled. But for his graven face and stony eyes, Ki could have believed that he was telling her stories with the string, showing her the remembrance keys as he went along, as he had now for days. "Vandet and Dienli celebrated their adulthood, their joining, and his birth for many days. But Dienli was to die when the child was too young to even remember the color of her eyes. (But they tell me, Ki, they were as dark as my own.) And Vandet was to fall from his horse in a hunt before the boy was tall enough to pull back the string of a bow. The care of the boy passed to his uncle until the boy was old enough to prove himself a man.

"Now I digress to tell you the customs of my wondrous people: A boy becomes a man when he sires a child. A girl is a woman when she bears. And until a child is produced, the act of mating is the healthy play of normal children. No binding may occur until a child acknowledged by both is born. No child may inherit until he has supplied the next heir for the property. Now, as the lands to be inherited were large and the boy was the sole inheritor, there was much anxiety that the boy's hands should be on the reins as soon as possible. An easy matter, to make a baby grow in a woman's womb. But the boy's uncle would take no chances. He would permit no young girls who might be too young to bear, or woman who had not prov-

en her ability to reproduce. He selected instead for the boy
suitable women, older women, widows whose men had died,
women who had proved themselves fertile, some with children
nearly as old as the boy. And he was put to them like an
unproven bull put to a series of cows. At first it was done with
dignity. The boy would first meet the woman, speak to her,
know her a few days before it was demanded of him. He found
it an awkward thing, to be bedded with women that reminded
him of a mother he had never known and to know that the first
to conceive by him would become his life's partner. It made
the boy's task . . . difficult. As months passed, and women
passed, the pace became more frantic, the uncle constantly re-
minding the boy of the shame he risked if his failures became
known. The boy had a long string of names to pass on—it was
a matter of honoring his forebears. The boy became unsure.
The women the uncle could find became less tolerant, and
more mocking. Until at last a woman went to the uncle and
told him that she would waste no more time waiting to be
studded by a young gelding."

"Enough," said Ki quietly. Vandien turned a cool, empty
eye on her above his smiling mouth.

"Do not interrupt the story, Ki. Did you like the last sign I
showed you? It means gelding. Like the horse you bestride.
Now, attend while I finish.

"Word spread, of course. To keep as much of the name intact as possible it was necessary that the boy's cousin inherit.
He had produced a fine, fat baby a year before by a sweet and
wild little girl in a nearby village. (It seemed to give neither of
them any problem.) The inconvenient boy left quietly, and
when he infrequently returns, he is given enough money to let
him disappear again. One does not encourage family disgraces
to hang about the doorstep. And so the story has a happy
ending."

Vandien snapped the string flat between his hands. It
snaked back into his pocket.

"Vandien, I am sorry. . . ."

"That I am a gelding? But I am not, of course. It was
only a surfeit of overripe sweets. I tell you the story just to
show you that I would not ask of you anything you would not
give willingly. I would not ask such an act of anyone."

"Enough, man!" Ki snapped. Then she went on more gently. "To say I am sorry is not enough. It is the greatest cruel-

ty I have ever heard done to a child. But my pity . . ."

"Keep your pity. That isn't what I asked for."

"I will not take anyone into my life. I have no room for it. I will not offer that which I cannot deliver. The tasks I have before me are for me alone. I have no life to share."

"Choose life, Ki. Choose it one more time."

The inn yard came into view. A light snow lay on the frozen ground. Wheel tracks and hoofmarks scarred the open yard, and a very young stable boy swung on a gate. It was a battered, homey place, more welcoming than the Dene inn had been. The stable boy stared at them as they pulled in their huge mounts. Ki slid down Sigurd's shoulder. Vandien attempted a dignified dismount, only to have to drop the last part of it.

"Shall we go in?"

"No. I have unfinished business to attend to." She stepped forward, embracing Vandien quickly, awkwardly. She stepped back to Sigurd quickly. "You will be able to reach your home?" Her words seemed to care more than her voice.

Vandien stared at her. He did not offer her a leg up, but forced her to clutch Sigurd's mane and scramble up him in a most undignified manner.

"Of course." Vandien dropped his words softly in the snow. "There are folk enough hereabouts that know my name, if not my face anymore. I shall be fine."

"I am glad of that. Fare well." She did not look back. Vandien stood in the frozen inn yard, watching after her. Sigmund trailed obediently behind Sigurd without need of a lead rope. A small smile came to Vandien's lips. He knew Ki better than she knew herself. Any moment now, she would rein the horses in, would pause, and then would turn back for him. He would be waiting. A knowing smile flickered over his face. He hastily wiped it away. The grays were growing smaller in the distance. Ki's words had had a fine ring to them, but he knew what was in her heart. Ki sat straight and ridiculously small on the immense beast. The stubby tails of the grays, docked for their pulling, switched as they walked.

Vandien watched the empty trail, waiting for them to come back from around the bend. The cold began to nibble at him. He pulled his hood up tighter, thrust his hands deep into the cloak pockets. He drew one hand out slowly in disbelief. He looked at the three silver minteds on his palm and remem-

bered the awkwardness of Ki's hug. He turned eyes of pain
and anger to the empty road. He raised his hand high to dash
the coins into the snow. But instead, his fist sank slowly in de-
feat. He tossed the coins instead to the amazed stable boy. His
shoulders slumped as he wandered to the door of the inn. Unfinished business, indeed.

Rhesus's man stared at the unkempt woman on the door's
threshold. Two gaunt, gray horses wandered free in the street
before the door. The woman's cloak was rent as badly as any
street beggar's. Her long brown hair was a tangled mass that
straggled out on both sides of her neck beneath her hood. Her
face was pinched and drawn. Her green eyes burned.

"He did not bid me to watch for anyone coming to deliver
merchandise," the man told her suspiciously. Slowly the tall
wooden door began to swing on its greased hinges. "Wait
here. Let me ask him if he expects you."

"Exactly what I wish to ask him myself," Ki objected. The
man recoiled from contact with her dusty clothes as she
squirmed past him under his arm. She prowled up the tiled hall
like a hunting cat, peering in first one narrow doorway and
then another. She gave the waiting man a glare. She had no patience left for civilized behavior. She had not paused since she
left the inn, but had forced the grays on, making them subsist
on what small pasturage they could find in the snow-sprinkled
meadows. She had blotted out thinking by constant action.
She had not even taken time to make herself clean. She had
pushed on to this confrontation, and would not be cheated of
it.

"Rhesus!" she bellowed. Her voice echoed strangely. The
man behind her scurried away down a side corridor, as if he
did not wish to be present when his master found a madwoman
loose in the house. Ki padded down the hallway. She heard a
sudden rustle of clothing and a woman's voice raised in a whisper of alarm. She stepped to the doorway of that room, but
Rhesus himself suddenly filled it. His pudgy hands danced
nervously up the front of his loosened shirt. His fat spider
body jounced upon his skinny legs.

"Ki!"

All the answers rattled across his graying face. It sagged
flabbier as she smiled at it. From inside her shirt she drew the
small leather pouch, tumbled the gems out onto her hand. Her

eyes did not leave his face as she held them out for his inspection. "All there, Rhesus. And no doubt fully as lovely and priceless as when I left Vermintown with them."

"No doubt," he agreed nervously. But he reached no anxious hand to seize them. Ki shifted her hand, let the stones tumble about in her palm.

"I shall not bore you with the perils I encountered on my way here. You know I have never raised my price because I found a road more difficult than I had bargained it to be. That is the business of a teamster—to know the roads well enough to strike the bargain beforehand. And it is the merchant's business to know what he can afford to pay for such a job."

"Of course, of course." He glanced back nervously at the room he had just left, then stepped forward suddenly to indicate another door. Ki watched him quickly gather up the reins of control, saw his face tighten as he convinced himself that she suspected nothing. Already he was regaining his aplomb, taking control of the situation. "Would you care for food, Ki, a little wine perhaps? I have ripe fruit from . . . ."

"No," Ki cut in. "Money, and a little talk. That would satisfy me best, Rhesus."

He nodded quickly, his nervousness baring itself again in the tremble of his jowls. He trotted a few steps down the hall toward the doorway he had indicated. Ki did not budge. She did not care if it troubled him to have her so near his nest. She casually held up one of the gems between a thumb and finger, looked at it critically. "I know very little of gems, Rhesus. Of that I am sure you are aware. Where would a person of my background find the opportunity to become a judge of such things? But I have an eye for beauty. Look at it, Rhesus. Blue as the sky. No, bluer than that—blue as a diving Harpy. How shall we value a gem such as this? Worth a woman's life, or shall we say a man's blood?"

Rhesus saw it all sliding away from him. His thin legs were trembling under his bulk, threatening to collapse. His pale face went green, in contrast to his gaudy clothing. Ki met his eyes calmly, her face as untroubled as a spring day, her mouth smiling sweetly. She watched his plump face ripple with emotion. But he would retain his bluff to the last coin.

"This way, Ki. Let us settle our accounts." There was a tremble to his trot as he hurried her down the hallway. He led her into a plain room that understated the wealth of the house.

The floor was tiled a deep, rich brown. Tapestries of feasts and huntings draped the walls. No window admitted natural light or spying glances. A tall cupboard stood in one corner, its shining dark wood matching the table in the center of the room. The table was littered with scrolls and counters, while several slender brushes rested in an upright stand beside pots of variously colored inks. There was a single, ornately carved chair at the table and a bare, low bench set a distance before it. Ki had played this scene before with Rhesus. Always he sat in the tall chair, protected by the table, and played with counters and talked of increasing expenses, while Ki sat silent on the low bench before him, her legs stretched uncomfortably in front of her until her silence extracted from him the previously agreed-upon price.

But today, when Rhesus let her precede him as guest, Ki crossed the room with a sure stride, pulled out the chair, and sat in it. She watched the last hopeful doubt drip away from Rhesus's face. His body caved in on the low bench. Sweat broke out in tiny, shining beads on his upper lip.

"I am, as you say, a merchant," he began.

"I did not know you trafficked in blood," Ki interrupted his apologetic tones. "Or my prices would have been higher. But seeing that you do, we shall make our settlement now. First, the remainder of what you owe me for these 'priceless gems.' "

Ki boldly took up a stack of counters, measured out what was due her in a stack on the table. "That is correct, is it not?"

Rhesus scarcely glanced at the pile. "It appears to be," he mumbled.

"Certainly it does. But appearances can be deceiving, Rhesus. Let us consider a philosophical question. Goods can be paid for with money. But how shall blood be bought?"

The plump jowls trembled a moment, became suddenly firmer. Rhesus drew himself up straight on the low bench. Watching, Ki was reminded of a toad puffing himself up to croak. But she would have trusted a toad's yellow eyes more than the round, piggish eyes that fixed on her now.

"Do you threaten me, Ki? With what? Kill me by your own hand, and you shall not escape the justice of this town. They value me here, for the trade I generate. Shall you bring charges against me? Who listens to a wandering Romni? What evidence do you have? You have not been killed. I see no mark of wounds upon you." He folded his fat hands on his knees and met her eyes as if he had made a point.

"An interesting philosophy." Ki slid down deeper in her chair. Her dust-stained boots rose to rest on the corner of the shining table. She gave a slight kick to get more comfortable, and Rhesus flinched as her heels scored the wood's luster. "Surely if you are dead, Rhesus, it will make small difference to you if I am punished for your murder or not. But it might inconvenience you in a small way if a certain Romni driver and his family stopped smuggling perfume jewels into Coritro for you. Although they are illegal there, I have heard they still bring you a good price. It might be an even larger problem for you if all the Romni stopped doing carting for you. But I am not threatening you, Rhesus. I am only showing you that I know how to threaten you. I do not want your blood. I do not consider it of equal value to the blood that was shed. Nor do I want your money, other than what you owe me for the delivery."

Ki watched with narrow eyes as the plump little man shifted about on the bench. His fat fingers were squeezed by narrow rings, making them look like sausages. The sausages met and tangled together. His little round eyes rolled about the room, looking everywhere but into Ki's. Ki continued to stare at him silently. His mouth worked in and out.

"So what do you want of me? Here, I will pay you your money for the delivery, and then you will go."

He rose and bustled across the room to the cabinet. He fished in his pocket for a small key and unlocked one of the drawers. Ki heard the chink of coin and the shutting of the drawer. He hurried back, to stack before her the silver minteds he owed. No more and no less. Ki nodded and scooped them toward her. She let the gems fall from her hand onto the table with a rattle like gravel.

"And now you will go," he said. His eyes glistened as he watched Ki leisurely transfer the stacks of minteds from the table into her own personal pouch. His lower lip jutted out plump and wet as he considered the scatter of trinket gems he was receiving for it.

"You needn't look so bitter," Ki said softly. "I doubt that you are taking a loss."

"That's my business," Rhesus snapped.

"Exactly. The business of a merchant who traffics in

blood. I have no experience of how such a fee is set. Tell me, Rhesus, how much was my life bought for? And by whom?"

He moved briskly to the bench before the table, sitting as alertly as a begging dog. A pink slug of tongue wet his lips. "Is that what you would have from me, Ki? It will cost you." He settled himself with a wiggle of satisfaction at finally taking control.

Ki could not find the anger she needed to deal with him. Only a weary disgust filled her. She let him rant on.

"You might like to know, Ki, that at no time was your life, or death, mentioned. I accepted a . . . a fee, shall we call it? Only to see that you took your wagon through a certain pass. No time limit was set upon me, only my word that at some time I would see that you passed that way. And that was all. How was I to know it would be dangerous to you? So, be not angry with me. We may still do business together, you and I." He paused to nibble speculatively at his thumb nail. "I think, to be just, that my price for the information will be equal to the minteds that I just . . ."

Ki did not wait to hear. She felt no anger as she slowly lowered her worn boots from the table. She felt nothing as she swept to the floor the pens, the counters, and a flurry of scrolls. Rhesus screamed high, but Ki's eyes were cold as she upset the table upon the tiled floor, with a crash that sent splinters of polished wood flying. The carved chair rose lightly in her weathered hands, to arc across the room and cave in the front of the shining cabinet. Rhesus fled from the room, squeaking. Ki followed him with her panther's stride. He fled without grace or logic, looking back fearfully as he huffed up the hall. Silent and relentless came Ki. She heard a girl's voice raised in a question as Rhesus darted into the room Ki had first seen him emerge from.

It was a room of whites and yellows, of creamy floors and soft white rugs, of tapestries of flowered fields. A huge divan dominated the center of it, surrounded by filigreed tables bearing an overwhelming assortment of sweetmeats and fruits. A girl started up from the divan as they entered, Rhesus quivering and staggering as he fled. She gasped at the sight of his pursuer, Ki, ragged, dusty, and wooden-faced.

Ki halted at the sight of her. It was not her extreme youth that shocked Ki, though the image of that child in Rhesus's embrace was a blasphemy against beauty. Nor did the girl's nudity and carefully erotic body paintings surprise Ki—it was the necklace of circling silver Harpies that adorned the slender throat, and the azure and cobalt Harpies that swung from each pink ear. Ki stopped.

"From her forge and anvil come the best metal workings the family has ever seen." Haftor had said that. He had been right. Once a person had beheld the work of Marna's hands, ever she would know it. Ki did not realize that she had advanced on the girl until she felt the cold silver of the necklace in her hands. The girl fled, her bare feet pattering across the cream floor, her white neck marred by the burn of metal rudely jerked from it.

Ki could not focus her mind on Rhesus's shrill cries as he frantically jerked on a summoning bell's rope. She tried to remember Marna's face. It would not come to her. She could find only Haftor, battling his madness, his eyes intense with a vengeance he would never satisfy. Haftor had learned to hate too well. Would Ki school Marna to it also? Ki flung the Harpy necklace from her violently. It rattled and slid across the floor to wrap around Rhesus's foot. He ceased his yammering long enough to stoop and seize his treasure.

"Give her this," Ki said suddenly into the jolt of silence. "Tell her she succeeded. Tell her it came from my body. Tell her to be at peace, for it is all over."

Ki groped in her belt pouch, and the silver hair-comb came readily to her hand. She drew her fist back to fling it at him, but found she could not do it. She strode across to where Rhesus cowered to press it into his wet hands. A twinge of regret at parting with it surprised Ki. She froze the emotion. She spun on her heel and strode out the door, to pass between two bewildered serving men as they hastened to answer Rhesus's summons. She let herself out.

TEN

FIRBANKS was a dusty, cold little town huddled between two forested mountains. It possessed a single inn, run by a Human and a Tcheria in partnership. To Ki's regret, the Tcheria managed the food area. There were no tables and benches, only squat-legged trays full of sand raked smooth. Tcheria preferred it so. Guests were expected to crouch on straw mats beside the trays while they ate. Ki found the trays too tall if she sat on the floor, and too uncomfortable to hunker beside. She had brought one of her blankets up from the wainwright's and, in defiance of local custom, folded it for a cushion. A young Tcheria of the third gender had raked her sand table smooth and brought her hot food and a yellow wine. Ki's nose told her that the bread was freshly baked. She picked more cautiously at the grayish hunks of meat and green sprouts that swam in her bowl of greasy broth. She frowned at the thought of the two copper dru that had paid for it.

The wainwright had demanded nearly all the money she had as an advance before he would begin work on the wagon. She and her team were making a small wage, pulling logs down from the mountainside. It would be enough to pay for the wagon's completion. Ki stifled the impatience that rose in her at the thought of the days of work and waiting before her. She had, she reminded herself, no fixed goal. No matter how often the idea came to her, she would not push on to Thesus. Bad enough that she had stopped at the Inn of the Three Pheasants to ask after a man with a bandaged face. Micket, the innkeeper, had been surprised at her queries. She had not enjoyed the speculative look in his eyes. And worse, that she had sought out in Firbanks a wainwright that recognized Vandien's name. To go any further would be to admit to more than concern for his safe journey. She sipped the yellow wine, frowning at its curious flavor.

Besides, no doubt Vandien was long gone from Thesus by now. And if he wasn't, he would be before the damn wagon was finished.

The wagon. She sipped more wine, as if to drown the thought. No matter how many times she explained it all to the sweating wainwright in his shop, no matter how often she measured out the spaces with her hands, it would not be the same wagon. This wainwright of Vandien's had his own ideas. He wished to set the wheels differently so they could be exchanged for skids in deep snow. He wanted to make the cuddy larger and put a second door that went out the side of the wagon. He insisted that she needed more and larger windows, and a wider bed. Every day Ki told him exactly how the wagon was to be. And every day, when he spoke of how his work went, it had been done as he had suggested. Today Ki had threatened not to pay. He had said,"So, build it yourself if you are so particular." The man was impossible. She didn't know why she dealt with him. He was as impossible as Vandien himself.

She took another sip of the wine. She was becoming accustomed to the flavor. It was all the inn offered.

A patron nudged her shoulder in passing. Ki turned to glare at the knees behind her. Boots of soft leather were fastened right below them. Ki's eyes traveled up. She could not speak.

His eyes she recognized. He had scraped away all his beard except for a moustache above his unsmiling mouth. His hair had been trimmed back off his shoulders. The scar was a pale track across his weathered face. It pulled one eye askew. His face and body had fleshed out, much to his advantage. The soft linen shirt that opened at his throat was clean, the saddle pack slung over his shoulder was supple new leather. He wore a curious vest with a strange blue pattern worked into it. On one hand was a plain ring with a single stone set into it. A slender rapier in a battered sheath dangled at his side. He did not smile as he gazed down on her.

The saddle pack dropped to the floor on the other side of the sand table. He sat on it, pushing his rapier's hilt to swing the weapon out of his way. He set an empty glass on the table and put a spherical bottle of the yellow wine beside it. He nested it down into the sand with an expert's touch. He placed both elbows in the sand and leaned his chin in them.

"All Tcheria utensils have round bottoms. Now you know why they use a tray full of sand. Nothing tips over."

"Oh." His solemnity daunted her.

"You finished up all your business in Diblun?"

"Yes." Damn his grim face. "I delivered my freight."

He nodded sagely as she spoke, pouring wine for himself. He took a long sip of it, waiting. Ki looked down at her bowl, her long hair spilling forward to hide her chastened face. A heaviness of a chance lost grew inside her.

"I saved Sven's things for you. I knew you would want them."

"I don't. Get rid of them, Van."

His face went white and taut. He stood up, nearly knocking over the sand table, wine and all. The black hurt in his eyes was unmistakable now. Humans and Tcheria turned to watch. Vandien stooped to snatch up his saddle pack, growling as he did. "There was no call for that, Ki. Just tell me to leave. I only meant well."

Her knees bumped the low table as she rose in awkward bewilderment. She spread the fingers of one hand, forced it to settle on his shoulder. She tugged him back to face her. His lips were tight, his scar a whiter seam across a pale face. Under her hand, rage coursed through his body.

"And I only meant well," she explained. "Why do you take offense?"

He looked down at her hand on his shoulder. Gradually his breathing slowed and his shoulders lowered. He glared around at the folk who stared at them, searing them with his eyes. Humans and Tcheria suddenly resumed conversations, picked up glasses again. Vandien dropped his saddle pack beside Ki's folded blanket. Ki sat hesitantly, and Vandien settled cautiously beside her.

"Among my people . . ." Regret tinged his voice, and he began again. "Among those with whom I have had to deal these past days, to shorten a man's name is insult most vile. It shortens the man. It implies he is a disgrace to the unnamed parent, or unclaimed by one."

"Among my people, it is a sign of affection. And the Romni do not cherish the possessions of their dead."

"I did not know you were Romni."

"Neither did I. But it is so."

Vandien refilled both their glasses. "We do not get many of them on this side of the mountains." He smiled speculatively. "They are a life-loving people, so I have heard."

"So we are."

Vandien looked at her steadily. "Your hair is longer than I supposed it, unbound like that." He touched it gently with the back of his hand. Ki smelled the fern-sweetness of his skin. She smiled.

Fantasy from Ace
fanciful and fantastic!